Our Cousin Rosanna

By the same author

The Spirit of Millie Mae

Our Cousin Rosanna

Sheila Newberry

ROBERT HALE · LONDON

© Sheila Newberry 2004
First published in Great Britain 2004

ISBN 0 7090 7531 6

Robert Hale Limited
Clerkenwell House
Clerkenwell Green
London EC1R 0HT

2 4 6 8 10 9 7 5 3 1

Typeset in 10/12½ pt Palatino by
Derek Doyle & Associates, Liverpool.
Printed in Great Britain by
St Edmundsbury Press, Bury St Edmunds, Suffolk.
Bound by Woolnough Bookbinding Ltd.

For: Judith Murdoch, in warm appreciation of her belief in, and encouragement of my writing.

Acknowledgements

I wish to express my warm thanks for the help given by the following:

My mother, my aunt and cousin Pauline for memories of Mepal, on the Fens, where I stayed as a young child, and where I, too, saw a floating moon ... And remembering Pauline's brothers and their kitchen puppet shows. John for aiding me with the research, as always.

Janet Beck (for memories of the *Muck Works* at Lynn) and her friends Margaret and Mary from Pentney, for their wartime recollections. Hilda Bond and Sheila and John Simpson from Gayton for local lore. Joy Reynolds, who also enjoyed exploring Lynn.

St Margaret's Church, Lynn. (The eloquence and enthusiasm of the guide lingers long)

King's Lynn Museums

True's Yard

The Town House, Lynn

and,

the evocative streets and dwellings of old Lynn, the docks, the great river and the fishing boats; the statues, including George Vancouver, who sailed off into the unknown and made his mark in Canada; and those local people who gave me a 'glimpse in passing', a few words to whet my curiosity further.

Bibliography

East Anglia & The Fens, Rob Talbot and Robin Whiteman, Weidenfeld & Nicolson.

The Northenders, Patricia W. Midgley. (A real salty taste of Lynn as it was, in the past.)

The Faces of Lynn, (Video)
'The faces' pictured were excellent with the local history imparted by local folk.

Prologue

1968

They parked the hump-backed van 'nose to peg' on the river bank. The scrubby, triangular field bore a number of rectangular yellow patches and the tracks of many wheels. This quiet afternoon in late June the pitch was deserted, so Rosanna and Sim had the prized site.

Rosanna descended barefooted, via the rickety orange-box, from the high cab. Her flowing, flimsy skirt caught in the door as she slammed it.

'Hang on, stay still, or you'll tear it,' Sim told her calmly, as she cried out. Being so tall, he didn't need the step: he simply reached out, freed her carefully. Then he lifted her down and whirled her round to face the sun-dazzling water, where someone had heaved a large, flat stone to the edge. 'See, somewhere to sit and watch the boats go by, Rosanna.'

She grimaced ruefully, gesturing at the converted ice-cream van, the previous owner's name painted over with multicoloured flowers. Sim's brushstrokes were more careless than inspired. The sides of the van were still embellished with unlikely chocolate flakes stuck into rippled snowballs in danger of toppling golden cones, and frozen, fruity orange-bars on sticks. 'Not even a *wafer* Sim. We didn't stop to shop, going round Cambridge . . .'

'Had to keep going: didn't like the sound of the gears,' he pointed out. 'I'll go to the farm, and see what I can scrounge. We need water from the standpipe in the yard, we can't dip our bottles in the river, not nowadays.'

He had a smiling, tanned face, black, wiry hair hanging way past his shoulders, a glinting ring in his earlobe: he was nothing like Derry, as she remembered him. She flung her arms impulsively around Sim, hugged him tight. Her shell beads made their mark, for his shirt was

11

unbuttoned.

'Hey!' he said in mock protest, 'what's that about?'

'About coming back,' her voice was muffled, 'after all these years . . .'

He freed himself, put his hands on her shoulders, gazed thoughtfully into her upturned face with its pale-painted lips, hazel eyes outlined with kohl. She was not as young as she seemed – perhaps ten years his senior, but she'd not said. The attraction had been mutual, when they met a few weeks ago. Maybe it was not love as she once knew it, but that had led to despair, to her present unconventional life.

Her long, light hair and loose clothing suited her; it was hard to imagine her in the pert mini-dresses, white tights and high boots of the city girls who thus proclaimed their liberation. That new world she had discarded, along with her family: Wendy and Baz, her parents; Russ, her brother and Marcy, her little sister; her aunt Janet and her husband Jim; Grandma Birdie, only she and Jim were long gone; and, perhaps most of all, her cousin Merle, and Derry, who wasn't really a cousin at all.

'You've been here before?' he asked. He knew nothing of her past, whereas he'd confided to her what she'd already guessed regarding his: drop-out from university; disapproving family; joining the endless trail. In search of . . . what?

'I was born a few miles upriver. It's tidal, the Great Ouse. I sailed along it once to the Wash . . .' Her husky voice trailed off. With Derry, she thought, and with Merle. . . .

The sudden splash of fish in the water startled the stillness.

'Tell me later. Better get on,' he added laconically.

When he returned with a plastic container of water in one hand, and a box under the other arm, she was sitting on the stone, her legs tucked under her skirt, combing out her hair. No pile of sticks, no fire, no spitting kettle. Just her banjo, on the grass beside her.

He said merely: 'You look like a mermaid, Rosanna.'

'I was dreaming of a floating moon . . .'

He showed no surprise. 'Maybe tonight, you never know.'

PART ONE

Chapter One

1938

'Rosy, wake up!' Merle hissed in her ear. 'There's something you *must* see, but don't make a sound. . . .'

It was a summer's night, with moonlight flooding the surrounding fens; the time when Rosanna Bloomfield was four and her cousin Merle Bird seven years old.

They crept past Grandma Birdie's room, which she shared temporarily with Rosanna's mother Wendy; past Merle's parents' bedroom. They hesitated briefly by the little flight of stairs which led to Derry's attic where he'd pinned a paper on the door: ENTER AT YOUR PERIL! which Merle ruefully said meant *them*. Then they went stealthily down the main staircase, through the big kitchen to the unlocked back door.

'I haven't got my slippers on,' Rosanna whispered. Mummy would be cross if she knew. She shivered in her pyjamas because she wasn't wearing her dressing-gown either. The temperature had dropped sharply from the heat of the day. She wanted only to dive back into bed under the covers, but where Merle led, she must follow, as Merle followed Derry.

'Don't be a baby ,' Merle whispered back. 'Nor have I.' But once outside, she gripped Rosanna's hand tightly.

Across the way, the pumping station was brightly illuminated. There was the insistent throb of the engines as the pistons worked smoothly away, for the water-levels were constantly monitored. Last spring, after anxious weeks of heavy rain, with the army standing by awaiting orders from the Catchment Board, and evacuation of the farming families a distinct possibility, the Ouse had finally overflowed and flooded the fens, a disaster from which the fenlanders were still

15

recovering. The house smelled still of river water, Merle's mother Janet said, even though it had dried out.

The odour of oil and grease threatened, as usual, an upheaval in Rosanna's tummy. She willed herself not to retch. Through a window, they glimpsed Merle's father Jim in his dark boiler suit, rubbing his hands on a rag. His balding head glistened with sweat. He was talking to Nipper, his assistant. The children didn't stop, as they usually did, to see which of them could hang upside down and turn over the most times on the cold metal bar that provided a handhold up the slope to the door. Rosanna had chinked her teeth on the metal yesterday and she seemed to have the taste of it still in her mouth.

They scurried along the plank bridge over the river, disregarding the danger of splinters in bare feet. The river narrowed at this point, a hundred yards from the isolated house. When they reached the middle of the bridge Merle commanded Rosanna to look down.

'I-I can't. I might fall in.' The wooden rail was decidedly shaky.

' 'Course you won't. I've got a hold on your trousers, lean over as much as you like! See it? A floating moon! Dad says it's lucky, so you and me can make a wish . . .'

Rosanna's terrified scream echoed around them; she was aware not only of the wavering reflection of the full moon, but of a mass of wriggling black shapes highlighted in the water.

Instantly, Merle clapped her hand over Rosanna's mouth.

'*Snakes!*' Rosanna choked, as Derry glided alongside and leapt from Jim's rowing-boat to the bank. He tied up before turning his attention to the little girls, transfixed on the bridge.

'Didn't expect to find *you* here, giving the game away with that racket,' he scolded. 'They're elvers, Rosy, baby eels. This was once the Island of Eels, after all – how Ely got its name, before they drained the fens. I've been *miles* up river,' he boasted. 'Caught a fish with the old meat-hook, and I was looking forward to a fry-up. But here's Uncle Jim with the dog.'

Jim took in the situation at a glance. He scooped Rosanna up on his shoulders, saying mildly:

'Just look at you in your jimjams. I don't know what your mother will think!' He put on a gruff voice for Merle and said *she* was old enough to know better. He gave Derry a look, but allowed him to bring up the rear as they walked to the house, with Topper the Jack Russell leaping up and nosing at Derry's haversack, which held the fish.

'He didn't tell me off, not then,' Derry said ruefully next morning at breakfast. 'He bagged my catch and said if I was keen to work at nights, I could clean up an oil spill. *Your* fault, Rosy, startling Nipper when you yelled. I wanted to get to bed, as the feast was off, but no such luck . . .' He didn't look bleary-eyed; at almost thirteen he seemed to have boundless energy and, as Janet remarked, he appeared to grow taller by the day.

'He didn't whop you?' Merle asked. Not that her easy-going father had ever laid a hand on her, his only child. She was well-named, with those blackbird-wings of hair framing her freckled face and bright, dark eyes.

'Not his way, you know that. I've to chop a load of wood this morning for the stove. I thought I was on holiday while my parents are abroad!'

'No such luck,' Merle mimicked him saucily.

Janet turned from the kitchen stove where she was cooking eggs and bacon for Jim, who was washing and changing after his night's stint.

'No such luck for you either, Merle. You can help with washing-up. Fancy taking Rosy outside at that time of night – and scaring her, too . . . If you've finished your boiled egg, ask Grandma and Aunt Wendy what they fancy for breakfast – hint that it's time to rise and shine. The sun's been high this past hour or so . . .'

'Can I go, too?' Rosanna asked quickly. She wiped the egg yolk off her mouth with her serviette, bunching it clumsily through the Donald Duck ring, kept for her exclusive use. Aunt Jan knew how to make you feel special.

'All right. But no jumping on Mummy, mind, she can do without that, at the moment. Put your dishes in the sink. A bit more bacon, Derry?' Janet winked at him, to show she wasn't cross. He was Jim's nephew, one of the Bird clan, but she was as fond of him as if he was her own flesh and blood, like Rosanna. She'd have loved a big family, but was nudging forty now. Looking at her, you could imagine what Merle would be like later on.

'Right ho, Aunt Jan, thanks,' Derry agreed readily. He patted his lean torso. 'Wonder why I'm so thin, when I eat so much?'

'*Worms!*' Merle called back, as she scuttled up the stairs with Rosanna at her heels. 'There's nasty medicine for that . . .'

'That's not nice,' Rosanna reproved her.

'You're shooting up,' Janet told Derry. 'You'll fill out later; be broad like your dad and your Uncle Jim, I reckon.'

Grandma Birdie was still snoozing. Time had ceased to matter to her. Sometimes she went to bed in the early evening, even before

Rosanna at seven o'clock; sometimes she was still pottering about at midnight, making messy fish-paste sandwiches which she shared with the mewing cats, and cocoa. Cups set down carelessly left white rings on the table. Janet's way was to allow her to do as she liked; her mother-in-law had been kind to her when she first married Jim, left King's Lynn, and had to learn fen ways.

Wendy sighed, came to reluctantly. 'What's the time?' she yawned. Rossanna resembled her mother. Both had biscuit-coloured hair, hazel eyes, snub noses and fair skin. Although Wendy had long since outgrown her sickly childhood, Janet cosseted and protected her younger sister still.

Wendy was expecting her second child at any moment. Her husband Basil hoped to return from sales trips round the agricultural merchants of East Anglia in time for the birth. He'd taken the precaution of leaving his wife here for the last month of her pregnancy, though at home in King's Lynn medical facilities were more easily accessible. Janet had cared for Wendy when Rosanna was born; she'd do the same for the new baby. It was a family tradition.

'You know I can't tell the time yet,' Rosanna reproached her mother now. Daddy had decreed, with a nudge from his wife, no wrist-watch until she had learned to do so. He was the more easy-going of her parents and Rosanna missed him when he was away.

Merle regarded the Roman numerals on her watch. She herself had only recently fathomed the numbers out. 'Thirty-five minutes past – no, twenty-five to eight! Mum says what d'you fancy for breakfast?'

'Nothing,' Wendy said faintly, just as Grandma Birdie decided:

'A nice poached egg, lovey. Make sure the white ain't watery, mind.' She put one sticklike leg out of bed, then the other, with a pink bedsock hanging off her toes, pausing to get her breath back, before the rest of her emerged.

'Get up and get washed, then,' Merle told them cheekily. 'Nothing won't take long to cook!'

How could it take any time at all? Rosanna puzzled.

Then Wendy was gulping and saying:

'Get Jan – right away, girls—'

'Do as she says,' Grandma Birdie advised, suddenly galvanized into action, reaching for her flannel gown hanging from the bedknob, and her slippers, under the hang of the bedspread. There wasn't time to ferret out the missing bedsock. 'Better get me teeth in, I suppose,' she added.

Why did Grandma Birdie need her false teeth, when she usually didn't bother? Rosanna wondered.

*

The girls were dispatched to watch Derry splitting logs on the splinter-covered patch of ground outside the woodshed. Nipper whizzed past on his bike, his long legs pumping like the greased pistons he had handed over to the relief engineer. He was heading towards the road.

'Gotta fetch the doc, Jan says keep the gals out here, Derry – s'long as it do take . . .'

Rosanna's face puckered. Derry put a comforting hand on her shoulder.

'Mummy—' she began uncertainly. She'd been told about the baby of course, even where it was growing, Aunt Janet had insisted on that, but no one said how it would escape from Mummy's tummy. Would it burst, like a balloon? She shuddered. Derry gave her shoulder a squeeze.

'Your mum's all right – nothing for you to worry about. Babies get born every minute all over the world. You can see her as soon as it's all over. When I've finished up here, we three might go for a walk.'

'Can't we go out in the boat?' Merle wheedled.

'Maybe.'

'I'd rather watch your puppets, Derry,' Rosanna said, thinking fearfully of what she'd seen in the water last night. Whatever the others said, she *knew* they were snakes . . .

'Good idea,' Derry approved. 'They'll have to let us in sooner or later. Treat for this evening, though, eh?'

Doc Baxter bumped his car along the rough track, veered to the cinder drive to the house, tyres squealing, waving at them through the door flap.

'Shouldn't be long now,' Derry assured Rosanna.

'*You* don't know,' Merle reminded him. 'You haven't got any brothers or sisters.'

Derry chopped into a large log, making them jump as wood-shavings flew.

'Feels as if I have, with you two tagging along all the time. . . .'

They were having a 'scratch lunch' on the river bank. Jim sat with them for five minutes while they ate cheese rolls and Grandma Birdie's rock-of-ages jam tarts.

Merle poked Rosanna on the back.

'Uncle Jim,' Rosy began reluctantly.

'Yes, Rosy?'

'Can Derry take us out in the boat?'

'Don't see why not,' he agreed unexpectedly. 'Just to the bend, mind, not to Ely. It's easy to imagine it's not as far as it is, when you can see the cathedral: it's an illusion, you see . . '

'Like the floating moon?' Merle asked.

Just what was an illusion? Rosanna wondered.

'It's all that sky, the water-level above the land. Bewitching, that's what your mum said when I first brought her here. Sometimes I get the feeling I'm still at sea.'

Rosanna found that puzzling. What did he mean? She looked up. In the vast sky a cloud or two billowed like ships' sails.

'Might have good news, when you get back. Listen for my whistle.'

Rosanna took off her sandals, following Merle's example, because there was the usual puddle in the well of the boat. Derry steadied it, with one foot on the bank, settling her beside Merle, opposite the rowlocks.

'Only fish today,' he whispered. But she daren't look at the water; she watched Derry at the oars. Droplets showered them; pleasant in the heat. She noticed the scab on one knee, which he'd scraped a day or two back when he'd slithered down the rough bark of the big tree where he was building a hide. There weren't too many trees on the marshes, he'd said, so you had to make the most of 'em. There was plenty of wild life to watch.

The scab was inflamed at the edges, with gathering yellow pus spots; she recalled a recent throbbing graze on her elbow. She rubbed the place surreptitiously. Uncle Jim said the soil round here was grand for growing vegetables, but good at growing germs too, like lockjaw, which sounded alarming, if you didn't watch out. Derry didn't make a fuss about that sort of thing, he'd insisted it was nothing when Janet tried to examine it yesterday. He was so much older and braver than she was, though he was visibly wincing now as he flexed his legs with the effort of rowing.

'One day,' Derry told them, his floppy fair hair lifting off his fore-head in a sudden, welcome river breeze, 'I'm going to circumnavigate the world; I'm going to sail across the great oceans and round the Cape of Good Hope.' His clear blue eyes looked beyond them, as if out to sea. He came from a family of sailors, after all: his forebears from Lynn had trawled the icy waters round Greenland in the last century.

'And I'm coming with you!' Merle asserted confidently.

Rosanna wanted to echo that, but she knew they wouldn't believe her. She was a cry-baby, as Merle said. Derry was much kinder. That's why

Merle was jealous: Aunt Janet sometimes reproved her for that.

They duly turned at the bend; they swished through the water and were soon back at their mooring. They heard Uncle Jim's whistle as they stepped out on to dry land, and it was echoed by the exuberant honking of Doc Baxter's horn as he left the house. The baby had arrived!

Chapter Two

Wendy, propped up in bed, cradled a little white flannel-wrapped bundle in her arms. Rosanna glimpsed a red, wrinkled neck, black hair; this gave her a funny feeling inside, she didn't know why.

'Not now, Merle,' Janet restrained her, as Rosanna went through the door. 'I'll be back in a few minutes,' she called out to her sister. 'Jim's phoning Basil's office, to see if they can contact him. Perhaps they'll let him come straight here when they hear what a rough time of it you've had.'

'You've got a baby brother, Rosy, are you pleased?' Wendy asked. Her voice sounded funny, faint. 'Would you like to sit by me, and hold him?'

Rosanna shook her head, but she said what she thought her mother wanted to hear.

'He's nice, Mummy. What's his name?'

'Russell, we thought, Daddy and me, because that was my maiden name. Russ for short, goes with Rosy, doesn't it.'

Rosanna wasn't sure, but nodded dutifully. 'Have you got to stay in bed?' she asked. Was Mummy ill?

'For a few days. You need rest when you've had a baby, you see . . .'

Janet reappeared. 'Isn't he lovely? What a whopper! Nearly ten pounds. Rosanna, you're a very lucky girl; downstairs now, it's teatime. I have to see to Mummy.'

See to what? Rosanna wondered. And why was she lucky? If she hadn't seen the snakes last night, she would have wished on the floating moon for a baby sister because no brother could ever live up to Derry.

Merle set the chairs out in a semicircle in the kitchen. Rosanna, on her father's lap, leaned possessively against his hairy tweed jacket, sniffing the reassuring odours of pipe and brilliantine. She fiddled with his tie

22

while Captain Codswallop, that spiky old fisherman, with red cheeks and nose, white beard and fierce eyebrows, berated his wife as usual. The puppets' heads were rough-hewn by Derry, he'd improvised the script, and his hands manipulated them within their baggy clothes, courtesy of Janet's ragbag. The puppets wrangled on the shelf of the half-door to the pantry, where Derry crouched, unseen, on the stone-flagged floor.

Ma Codswallop disappeared under the counter, reappeared with a baby in her arms. She rocked it furiously, la-la'ing.

'What's this?' the captain cried. 'That ain't mine, I tell yer . . . I been away too long at sea!' He held up his hand, counted the fingers: 'One, two, three, *four* – years . . .'

His wife said in an aside: 'Not long enough, old feller . . .' Then, 'It's a wise child as knows its own father,' she insisted. She dodged the upraised stick he displayed threateningly, turning the bundle to face the audience. '*Look!*,' she cried, in triumph.

Derry had been busy with glue, cotton wool and Janet's only lipstick. The baby sported a beard and bulbous nose like the captain. Basil joined in the laughter.

'Are you trying to tell me something?' he joked to Derry. 'I didn't notice young Russ's moustache! Mind, I'd barely had time to tell Wendy how clever she was to produce a baby boy this time when Janet said Rosy wanted me to watch the show.'

'Off to bed now,' Grandma Birdie reminded the little girls. 'I'll be up shortly! I'm sleeping alongside you, tonight.'

'Are you sure you don't mind giving up your room, Grandma?' Basil asked. 'It'll be for a couple of weeks, I'm taking my holiday as from now.'

'My dear, it's no trouble.'

'Can someone give me a hand?' Derry called. 'My leg's stiffened up . . .'

'I knew I should've asked Doc Baxter to look at that, while he was here,' Janet worried.

'Stockholm tar, or a dab of iodine, that'll do it,' Jim advised.

'Not if I can help it,' Derry said, as his uncle hauled him up. His face was flushed.

'I'll pop in and say good-night,' Basil told Rosanna. 'Be good for Grandma Birdie, mind.'

'Can I go and see Mummy first? *Please*, Daddy.'

'Better not, darling, she's asleep, and so, I hope, is the baby. You can see them in the morning, but you must wait until after the nurse has been. No more jumping in our bed first thing . . .'

Rosanna's face puckered. 'I'm not a lucky girl,' she said loudly. 'I'm *not* . . .' Basil looked appealingly at Janet.

'Well, I think you are, Rosy, and you soon will, too,' she said, giving her niece a warm hug.

Jim and Basil raised a glass or two to the baby while Janet settled mother and baby for the night. She came downstairs just as Jim was about to go and check all was running smoothly under Nipper's care.

'Jim, get on the telephone over there. Tell Doc Baxter he's needed – this is an emergency, I reckon—'

'Not Wendy, is it?' Basil exclaimed.

'No, she's comfortable, apart from those wretched stitches. It's Derry, I looked in, and he's running a fever, babbling. He could have blood poisoning, from that scabby knee.'

'Bad enough to get the doc out again, is it?'

'I wouldn't say so if it wasn't.'

'All right, old girl. You get him ready. Shan't be long.'

'Want me to carry him down here, put him on the settle?' Basil asked.

'Good idea, Baz. Can you manage by yourself?'

'I'll shout if I need help '

'Oh, don't do that, we don't want the girls rushing to see what's up. . . .'

Rosanna, sandwiched between Merle and Grandma Birdie in bed, was still awake. She managed to free one hand, rub her tear-filled eyes. The stairs creaked. She strained her ears. There was Daddy's voice:

'Easy does it, put your arms round my neck . . .' and Aunt Janet: 'Careful, now . . .'

Then Merle shushed her, nipped out of bed and crossed to the window. It was still fairly light outside, the moon not yet shining, but there was a yellow dazzle from car headlights, visible through the gap in the curtains.

'Doc Baxter. Wonder why he's back?' Merle plumped back into bed, giving her cousin a push nearer their bedmate.

Mummy, Rosanna thought. Mummy's ill, though she'd said she wasn't.

'I need,' she said urgently, 'to go.'

'What, right now?'

'Yes, *now!*'

'You'll have to crawl over me, then, the potty's under my side . . .'

Rosanna made for the door instead, rushed out on the landing.

'Daddy, where are you?' she shouted. All the lights were on down-stairs. Her father hurried to the foot of the stairs.

'Get back to bed at once! Nothing for you to worry about! Don't let's hear another peep out of you, until morning . . .'

'Grow up,' Merle told her. 'You're not the baby of the family any more, Rosy Bloomfield.'

She feared more scolding in the morning, for only babies wet the bed.

But they let her sleep on, in her damp patch, and Rosanna only awoke when she heard Nurse Rayner's booming voice outside her door.

'Understand you had a disturbed night, Mr Bloomfield.' Daddy must be with her. 'Boy rushed to hospital – you could have done without that excitement, eh? What's the latest news?'

'My brother-in-law is ringing the hospital at ten. All well with my wife and the baby?'

'You've, ah, noticed something yourself, have you, Mr Bloomfield?'

'Well . . . I didn't want to alarm my wife . . .'

'Quite right. I'll ask Doctor to examine the baby thoroughly when he calls. Looks aren't everything, you know.'

They moved away, went downstairs, saying no more.

Rosanna put on yesterday's blue cotton shorts and sun-top. No socks, just Clark's criss-cross sandals. There was no one around to remind her to wash, or brush her hair. She felt suddenly hungry. But she'd look in at Mummy first, because hadn't Daddy said she could, once Nurse had been?

Her mother lay in bed, face turned to the pillow.

'Mummy,' she began uncertainly.

Wendy was crying. 'They think I don't know, but I *heard* them . . .'

'So did I, Mummy,' the words were tumbling out now. 'Derry's in hospital, he's prob'ly got lockjaw—'

'*Derry*? What *are* you talking about? Rosanna, come here, I need one of your hugs . . .'

But Rosanna, upset by Wendy's reaction, backed away, bumping into Aunt Janet as she came into the room.

'Now, now, what's all this?' Aunt Janet said soothingly.

Rosanna didn't understand. Everyone had been so happy when the baby was born yesterday, Derry had rowed them down the river; now *he* was very ill in hospital, and Uncle Jim was trying to get in touch with his parents, which was difficult because his brother, Derry's father, was a captain on a big liner and his mother had joined him for the Mediterranean cruise. Aunt Janet had comforted Mummy earlier and said they'd love the baby anyway, wouldn't they, *even if. . .* When she'd realized Rosanna was eavesdropping, she said:

'Why don't you go downstairs and find Merle, Rosy darling? There's nothing for you to worry about, nothing at all.' But, of course there was.

'Sandwich?' Grandma Birdie asked as Rosanna came in to the kitchen. She indicated jars of honey and marmite. The table wasn't laid properly and there was no sizzling bacon. Aunt Janet's floral pinny hung in folds on Grandma's spare frame. Merle sat at the table, licking her sticky fingers.

'Derry's at death's door,' she said dramatically.

Like Aunt Janet, Grandma Birdie tut-tutted and went: 'Now, now . . .'

Daddy and Uncle Jim appeared, enquiring:

'What's cooking, Grandma?' and Grandma smiled and replied:

'Wouldn't you like to know!'

So Uncle Jim stepped into the larder and came out with the cheese dish and said: 'Well, I *do* know: bread and scrape, always that, when there's a crisis in the house, isn't it.'

Then Doc Baxter, who looked as if he hadn't shaved this morning, put his head round the kitchen door and said:

'Anyone at home? Nurse said to make this my first call. . . .'

'I've to keep you occupied,' Merle told Rosanna later, sounding more like seventeen than seven. 'Uncle Baz asked me to. He wants to talk to Doc Baxter. Mum's catching the bus into town to the hospital, she's taking Derry a bag of things. Grandma Birdie's supposed to be in charge of us, while Dad is working, but she's mangling the washing, even though Mum said to leave it 'til she gets back. Fancy playing snakes – whoops! – and ladders? or ludo?'

'Dollies?' Rosanna ventured.

'Dolls are for babies, Rosy.' However, Merle opened the lid of the toy-box and rummaged around. 'Here's Ted, and here's Jazzy – her eyes have disappeared down her neck. Mum pulls 'em back with a crochet hook, they're on elastic, you see. Will she do?'

Poor Jasmine did indeed stare blankly, though she looked better when Rosanna covered her nakedness with crumpled clothes. She put her in the doll's pram and wheeled it round the kitchen floor.

Then Daddy came back; he grabbed hold of Rosanna and hugged her tight.

'I'm sorry I neglected you this morning, darling . . .'

Doc Baxter was right behind him; he cleared his throat noisily, and told Basil:

'I'm sorry, old man. They're the most lovable of all children . . . That's what he'll always be, a child. Make the most of him. You've got your lovely daughter. I'll call in again tomorrow. Goodbye, girls.' And he was gone.

'Put me down, Daddy,' Rosanna said, muffled against Daddy's chest.

Grandma Birdie was in the real world today. She plonked the linen-basket on the table and said encouragingly:

'A nice cup of tea, that's what we can all do with. . . .'

'I know you like grapes.' Janet handed the bag to Derry over the hump in the bedclothes where his leg rested in a cradle. 'Pips, mind, but don't spit 'em on the floor or the nurses'll be after you. Well, how's things today?'

'Not too bad. When can I come home, Aunt Jan?'

'Well, they're moving you to over by the door, they say. That's a good sign.'

A man in the next bed was racked by a bout of harsh coughing.

Janet pulled the curtains briskly round the bed.

'You should be in the children's ward. Poor chap can't help it, but think what you might catch . . .'

'I'm too long in the leg for the kiddies' beds, they say.' Derry picked off a sprig of grapes: 'Go on, you have some, too. How's the baby? Sorry I put a damper on the celebrations.'

Janet hesitated, then confided: 'The baby may be – well, not quite right. Wendy and Baz are very worried, as you can imagine. Doc Baxter's calling this morning to say one way or the other.'

'You shouldn't have come here, it doesn't matter about me,' Derry said, concerned.

' 'Course it does, Derry. Jim and me, well, we're responsible for you while your parents are away. You know, it's little Rosy I keep thinking about. She'll have to grow up fast, bless her. Wendy will have her work cut out, if what we suspect is true.'

'Merle looking after Rosy, is she?'

'She's promised to.'

'Tell them I'll be back shortly, to keep them in order.'
'I will.'

Rosanna didn't see Derry again because ten days later Daddy drove them home to Lynn. She heard him tell Mummy they would get a second opinion there, but Mummy wept and said what was the use? They both knew what was wrong with the baby and it couldn't be put right.

'Just love and accept him,' Janet said. 'He hardly ever cries.'

'Sometimes I wish he would.' Wendy sighed.

'When will Derry be back?' Rosanna asked, as they loaded up the car.

Janet gave her an affectionate squeeze.

'I'm not sure, lovey, but soon I hope. He's up and down, like a yo-yo, poor boy. But he's hobbling round the ward now, thank goodness. He wanted me to give you this.' She produced a carrier bag. 'Don't look inside 'til you're under way. His mother will be home shortly, and likely he'll be all right to go back to boarding-school in September, eh? Why don't you write him a letter, he'd appreciate that.'

'I can't write properly yet,' Rosanna reminded her.

'Well, draw him a nice picture; you can sign your name, can't you?'

'I'll write to him,' Merle decided. 'I can do real joined-up writing. Pictures are for babies.'

'Don't tease Rosy, Merle, you know how much you'll miss her.'

'All aboard!' Basil said, screwing on the radiator cap, having checked the water-level.

'See you at Christmas!' Jim called, ready to give a bump start if needed, but the little car moved smoothly away.

They all waved: Janet, rosy-cheeked from bending over the bubbling copper poking the linen; Grandma Birdie, hanging on to Merle so she wouldn't dash forward and get run over; Jim and Nipper smudged with oil.

In little more than a year's time, the war began. Jim, being in the Royal Naval Reserve, was called up; Basil joined the army, and Janet, Merle and Grandma Birdie left the pumping-station and moved to Lynn, to live with Wendy and her family in a terraced house near the Muck Works. As for Derry, evacuated with his school, Rosanna didn't see him for a long, long time. But she sat his puppets on top of her books on her bedroom shelf.

Chapter Three

1941

Topper leapt up at the letter box, barking, as the mail was discharged on to the mat. It was seven o'clock in the morning.

'Be quiet, dog!' Grandma Birdie admonished him. 'Leave the letters be: you know I can't bend down when I'm carrying the baby.'

The little dog licked Russ's outstretched hand. At two and a half, Russ was not talking properly or crawling yet, but his gaze was fixed on Topper and the smile that endeared him to all curled the corners of his mouth.

'Down!' Grandma Birdie reproved Topper. She shifted Russ on her bony hip. 'You get heavier every day. How about some breakfast, my lad?'

She carried him into the kitchen, strapped him into his highchair. He lolled, rather than sat, so she stuffed a cushion behind him. Topper took up position beside the chair. Now his master was away, he'd transferred his protective instincts to the baby. Anyway, he was in line for dropped bits.

Russ was still in his nightshirt and so was Grandma. She left his bathing and dressing to Janet, but she brought him downstairs most mornings. She hadn't realized it was Saturday, when Jan and Wendy looked forward to an extra half-hour in bed, before they pushed the pram to join the queues at the Saturday market. Mind you, the shop at True's yard was still the best bet for dried fruit and demerara sugar. No one could make a dark fruitcake to rival Janet's. When eggs were in short supply she made the boil-it-up-first-in-a-saucepan version, fruit, margarine, spices and sugar in a cupful of water, with a teaspoonful of bicarb to ensure the cake rose. It tasted good, but didn't keep so well. Grandma liked to sneak butter on her slice. Marge! Axle-grease, Jim

29

called it. They'd eaten dripping when she was young, mind; *that* had some guts to it.

She clearly recalled her early days in Lynn living in Half Moon Yard. Slum clearances a few years back had swept her old home away: that cramped cottage, where the front door opened off the courtyard into the living-room, starkly furnished with a table and three mismatched chairs, despite there being seven in the family, was gone. The one good chair with high back and arms had been reserved for her father to sit on when he eased off his seaman's boots and thick oiled socks, knitted by her mother, like his gansey, his intricately patterned sweater. Our Ellen, as she was known then, had never achieved the same skill with knitting-needles, and the pattern had been passed on to her younger sister. The unmistakable smell of boiling whelks in the big pot on the range, over hung by airing clothes, seemed to assail her nostrils, for her father and his kin had been fishermen, of course. Fish of all sorts had been their staple diet. There'd been no water on tap, a hard life, but good friends all around. They all watched out for and fiercely protected each other.

She left what was called the Northend, after her elder brothers had departed; left the bed she'd shared with three sisters in the one bedroom, up the steep stairs, next to the room where her parents slept; left that way of life at fourteen, when she went to work on a fenland farm, digging potatoes, pulling carrots from that friable black soil. Her back had troubled her ever since. That was where she'd met Jim's father; why she'd settled there.

She stood for a moment, head raised, as if scenting the air, smoothing her uncombed hair, then retied the girdle round her dressing-gown, focusing on the tasks ahead.

'Kettle,' she said aloud. 'First thing Jan will say is, "Where's the tea, Grandma?" ' She wasted three matches before she lit the gas.

'Now where have they put the teapot?' She took the cover off a dish on the marble slab in the tiny pantry. She sniffed. 'Strimps!' That was what Merle called the little crustaceans when she was, oh, about Russ's age. She'd been a bright one, well, she still was.

She carried the bowl of local brown shrimps to the table, sat down thankfully, and began to peel them. When she had a few on a plate, she abandoned the fiddly task, wiped her fingers absently on the table-cloth, and fed the morsels, held between finger and thumb one by one, to Russ. As his mouth opened, so did hers, in encouragement.

The kitchen was full of steam from the boiling kettle when Janet arrived, letters stuffed in her pocket, yawning widely. She turned off the gas, grasped the kettle with the holder Merle had made for her at school, and shook it gently to ascertain that there was enough water left to make the tea.

'Enjoying your breakfast you two?' she enquired. She yawned again. 'Seemed a short night,' she murmured. Thank goodness she didn't have to go to work this morning, or chivvy the children off to school.

There had been the great drama of Dunkirk last year, even though Basil came safely home across the channel, only to be sent overseas once more, after recuperating at home. All that worry saw Wendy on the brink of a breakdown. She no longer read the headlines in the papers or listened to the latest war news on the wireless. She seemed oblivious that it was her sister or Grandma Birdie who saw to the needs of her little son.

The Battle of Britain had followed; the bombing of London and the major cities, although, miraculously, Lynn had survived almost unscathed so far, and was therefore considered safe for evacuees. But with several aerodromes in the vicinity of the town, who knew what was to come, Janet wondered.

She took a sip of her tea, and sorted the letters.

'One from Jim, that's good; nothing from Basil, unfortunately, poor Wendy could do with a lift. Gas bill, I won't open that 'til I've got my strength up, eh? Oh, and this must be from Derry, so I'll leave that for Merle to open.'

Jim's letter made her blush: he put down on paper what he would never dream of saying. She missed him dreadfully; feared for his safety in the engine room of the *Shelduck*, if it should be mined; was anxious about the responsibilities he bore. It was the first time they had been parted in the fourteen years of their marriage. The last letters they'd exchanged had been written during their engagement – it was peace-time then, of course. She was proud of her petty officer, the way he'd risen rapidly up the ranks to become a skilled engineer, but she'd never wanted to be a naval wife. She tucked the letter in her pinny pocket.

'Jim sends his love to you, Grandma.'

'I should think so,' Grandma said. 'Bit of bread and butter, boy?' she asked Russ. She often forgot his name, called him Jim, Sam or Georgie, the names of her own boys, now in their forties. Her sons were named for her brothers, all lost in the Great War.

Merle tore the envelope open eagerly. She read the contents to herself first, ignoring Rosanna who was trying to see over her shoulder.

'If you've finished, let Rosy have the letter, Merle, it's addressed to all of us,' Janet reminded her daughter.

'Here you are then,' Merle said ungraciously to Rosanna.

Rosanna, going on seven, could read well now, although she still ran her finger along the lines, her lips moved silently as she absorbed each word.

Dear All,

Sorry I haven't written for some time, but we are slogging away for our mock matric. Next year will be the real thing, and I am hoping Mum and Dad will let me leave after the exams. Whether the war is still on or not, I intend to join the Navy. How are things in your part of the world? Maybe I can visit in the summer. Though Mum says it's safer inland here. I'm in the second eleven . . .

Rosanna was disappointed. The letter didn't sound like Derry; what was matric – and the second eleven? She wouldn't ask, or Merle would scoff as usual.

'Here you are Aunt Jan,' she said in turn, handing the letter over.

'What's for breakfast?' Merle asked, 'and can't anyone smell what I can . . ' She looked meaningfully at Russ.

'Well, you'll have to wait for sustenance then, while I see to it, won't you? Have a bowl of cereal in the meantime, you and Rosy, eh?'

'If Dad was here, you'd be cooking bacon and egg,' Merle complained, as she shook Force flakes into their bowls, and reached for the jug of milk, throwing off its beaded cover so that it rattled on the table.

'I wouldn't.'

'Why not?'

'You know why not. No chickens here, not enough garden, and bacon's a luxury nowadays. Come on, Russ, let's get you cleaned up.'

'Oi, where's *my* flakes?' Grandma Birdie asked.

Janet walked briskly along to the Muck Works. She was only able to work part-time because of the children but at least she was helping the war effort, she thought. The firm's end product was vital now that the country was growing almost all its own crops. The official name of the works was W. Norfolk Fertilisers, the original name being the W. Norfolk Farmers' Manure Company, hence the familiar expression. This was a farmers' co-operative formed in 1872 and the works had expanded greatly over the intervening years, providing welcome employment for Lynn. Nowadays, the latest machinery was both innovative and unique to the Muck Works. Despite the works being a vast concern, there was still a family atmosphere, with Dr Harry Brown, son of the founder, and his son Eric at the helm.

Women had been recruited in the early part of this year to help fill the gaps left by the men who had been drafted into the fighting forces. Janet was glad not to be involved on the chemical side, with all the hazards involved; she enjoyed treadling away at a sewing-machine, making up jackets and trousers from coarse sacking for the workers to wear to protect their own clothing. The suits were useful, but if they were splashed with sulphuric acid they and their wearers had to be immersed promptly in one of the baths full of cold water that always stood ready for an emergency. The unfortunate worker came up gasping and shivering in winter, but the method undoubtedly saved lives.

There was as much chatter as clatter at the sewing-machines. Janet was kept very busy, but it made a welcome break from the routine at home. She tried not to think of the muddle Grandma Birdie was likely making at this minute, or remember that she'd left Wendy in bed. She was thankful Merle was old enough to walk Rosanna to school, and that she could trust the girls to leave in good time.

She took up the big, sharp scissors, cut along the chalked lines. There's money in muck, she smiled to herself. And plenty of overtime here if only Wendy would stir herself and leave me free to get on with it.

' 'Bye, Mummy.' Rosanna touched her bare arm. Wendy stood in front of the long mirror, still in her silk nighty, the one Daddy had rolled up and somehow managed to bring home in his kitbag from France.

Mummy wouldn't wear it while he was at home: Rosanna had overheard her confiding to Aunt Jan that it might give him ideas and, well, supposing. . . . Then she'd wiped a tear from her eye and said fiercely:

'I *do* love my baby, I do!' And Aunt Jan hugged her and said:

'I know you do, dearie. Try to tell Baz how you feel, eh?'

'How can I Jan? The way *he* feels, right now . . .'

' 'Bye, darling,' she told Rosanna now. 'Have a nice day at school.'

Rosanna slid her arms round her mother's slim waist. She rested her cheek against the slippery silk. Her voice was muffled.

'Mummy . . .'

'Yes?'

'Oh, nothing.' She'd been about to tell tales, she thought. She mustn't worry Mummy about Merle's teasing. She still looked up to her cousin, strove to emulate her, but Merle was quite unkind some-times.

'Come on slowcoach!' Merle called.

Chapter Four

Grandma Birdie opened the door. 'Wendy! It's Mr Wish-Me-Dead.' She scuttled back into the kitchen, leaving the insurance man in the doorway.

'I'm sorry,' Wendy said, managing a nervous smile. She tweaked her skirt straight. She'd hurriedly stepped into it when she heard the double knock on the door. 'Come in,' she added. She didn't want the neighbours to know her business.

He propped his bicycle against the porch wall, bent to remove cycle clips, then followed her into the living-room. He sat in the chair she offered, and took his cash-box and notebook from his bag.

'Don't worry about the old lady,' he said, pencil poised. 'I get called worse than that. Comes of being Mr Whiston, I suppose.'

The insurance man looked as if he ought to be in the Forces, being not much more than thirty. 'Flat feet and bad eyesight, they turned me down,' he'd confided on his first visit some months ago, when he convinced Wendy of the benefits of insuring her nearest and dearest for a mere shilling per week. Janet disapproved, but Wendy daren't tempt fate.

'Here you are, Mr Whiston.' He dropped the coin in the tin box and turned the key.

'Ta very much, Mrs Bloomfield. I'm Charlie to my ladies, you know.'

'I prefer Mr Whiston,' she said primly.

'Well, I'd prefer to call you Wendy, nice name for a pretty girl.' His smile revealed excellent teeth, not stained with tobacco like Baz's. He was dapper in his pinstripe suit, and, Wendy noticed for the first time, good-looking, despite the thick-lensed spectacles. 'Any objections?' he added.

'I—'

'Oh come on! I know you're married, and so am I, well, sort of. My missus, we had no kids, she didn't want 'em, you see, left me six months after the wedding.'

'You don't know where she is?'

He shook his head. 'No. So we're both on our own . . ' He looked at her speculatively.

'I most certainly am not! I've got two children—'

'And family willing to look after 'em for an evening now and then, eh? Something tells me you could do with a change of scene, a bit of fun, no more than that, of course, to take your mind off your husband, fighting for his country, God bless 'im.' He rose, held out his free hand. 'Well, thank you, Wendy, think about what I said, and I'll be back next week for your answer. Unless . . .'

'Unless what?'

'You want to say yes, right now. How about tomorrow evening? Pictures? Or the pub?'

She was shocked. 'Oh, I've never set foot in a pub in my life . . .'

'You might be pleasantly surprised. Times is changing, Wendy.'

'I—'

'What time do the little 'uns get to bed?' he pressed.

'By seven-thirty . . .'

'I'll call for you then,' Charlie said firmly.

'Are you sure he's not the type to take advantage?' Janet asked bluntly. She could hardly believe her ears. Wendy going out for the evening? Whatever would Baz think? But maybe it was a sign that her sister was perking up, taking an interest in life again.

'I can look after myself.' Wendy actually giggled. 'Remember what you told me when I first met Baz, before we knew what a good chap he was? How to make him wince, and let go, if need be? I haven't forgotten.'

'Good! Ten o'clock curfew, lovey. I can't wait up for you, with work tomorrow, you know . . .'

'I know – thanks, Jan. You're a brick.'

The Eagle was packed with men in uniform and girls with piled-up curls in floral crêpe dresses and clumpy, ankle-strapped shoes. Their make-up was lavish and bold; bare legs were painted with gravy-browning. Wendy felt conspicuous in her beige costume, worn on her brief honeymoon and not much since, with gloves concealing her wedding ring. But Charlie acted the gentleman, settled her at a table for two, and fetched drinks on a tray.

'What is it?' she enquired nervously.

'Gin and it. Like it?'

She sipped apprehensively, made a face.

'Not sure? Keep trying, you will.'

'Tastes like castor oil . . .'

There was froth on his lip from his bitter.

'This is nice,' he said.

'The beer?'

'Well, yes, but being here with you. I don't care to drink on me own.'

'Charlie . . .'

'Yes?'

'I shouldn't – be here, you know. What would my husband say?'

Too late she became aware that the couple at the next table were listening in to their conversation with interest.

'Finished your drink? Maybe I shouldn't have asked you out, but I meant no harm, believe me. I get lonely in my flat. I came to these parts for *her*, you see. You can trust me, I promise. Want me to take you home?'

'No.' She made up her mind. 'My sister'd think the worst if I arrived back so soon. Can I have a cream soda this time, please?'

Charlie's flat was really a bedsit. He opened the door to the mewing of his cat.

'Waiting for your supper old feller?' He tickled behind the cat's ears. 'I've been out with someone I've had my eye on for ages, and if I play my cards right, she might be persuaded to come out with me again.'

'Just going to take Russ out for a walk,' Wendy said the next morning, after Janet and the children had departed. She busied herself buckling the pram harness. 'You all right for a bit, Grandma?'

Might have a snooze, Grandma Birdie thought. It was 10 a.m. but that didn't worry her.

'See you later, then.'

Wendy hadn't wheeled Russ out and about by herself for many months. She found herself walking towards the Saturday Marketplace, only of course it wasn't Saturday today. All those fine old buildings around the deserted place, brimful of history, with their oblong windows and small, sparkling panes. Dominating all was the beautiful priory church of St Margaret's, where she and Baz had been married, and where both Rosanna and Russ had been christened.

The interior was vast but serenely welcoming. Beyond the altar the daylight glowed through the stained glass and illuminated the lovely round window, where the saints surrounded Christ at the centre.

Russ lay contentedly in her arms as she surveyed the saints from a pew. She brushed his sparse hair with her lips.

'*You*'re a little saint, you are, Russell Bloomfield. It's taken me a long time to realize this, to get over my disappointment, but I'm going to make the most of having you, from now on. I wish I could have accepted you right away, like Baz, but better late than never, eh?'

Chapter Five

1942

Rosanna wasn't sure why she didn't like Mr Whiston. He walked into their house like one of the family, he said she and Merle could call him Uncle Charlie. But he *wasn't* their uncle. Merle told him so, adding: 'I'll call you Charlie, if you like!'

Merle was going up to the big school in September, and nowadays she had homework every weekend. Aunt Jan insisted she got on with it on Friday evening, while waiting for the copper to boil for their baths. This task was left to her if Wendy was going out: Rosanna and Merle overheard the sisters having a few words about that earlier this evening, which made Merle spread her books out on the dining-table without further quibbling. She quizzed Rosanna to see what she knew.

'Name two famous men of Lynn, connected with the sea, Rosy. Bet you can't!'

Rosanna went red because Mr Whiston was sitting in the armchair waiting for Mummy to finish powdering her nose upstairs, before they went out. Her mother would be laughing when she came home, and she'd hear Aunt Jan say:

'One too many, Wendy? Really, I don't know what your Baz would think . . .' Anyway, she'd ignore Mr Whiston's mouthing the answer.

'Nelson, and – George – George Vancouver!' she ended triumphantly.

'Ah, but what was George, er, George Vancouver's achievement?' Merle mimicked.

'He – he discovered Canada!' An old memory resurfaced, the day Russ was born, Derry rowing them up river and telling them he was going to . . . what was it? Circumnavigate the world. Something to do with a compass, she supposed.

'But?' Merle prompted, aware of Charlie's interest.

'Not the North-west Passage!' She wasn't at all sure what that was.

'And who found that, then?'

'Don't know!'

Nor did Merle, but she wasn't about to admit it.

'Poor you, when *you* have homework to do, Rosy.'

When Charlie rose as Wendy came into the living-room, she whispered to Rosanna:

'Nelson was a little man – *and* Napoleon – just like old Charlie!'

'Here you are, girls.' Charlie produced a packet of fruit gums from his pocket, which he tossed on to the table. 'Glue your teeth up with those, eh, and stop arguing.'

'Thank Uncle Charlie for the sweets, you two; he's naughty spending his ration on you.'

'Don't worry, Wendy, got allsorts to keep *you* quiet in the pics.'

'Don't forget to write to Daddy, Rosanna – I left a space on the air letter,' Wendy said. 'You can see yourself to bed after your bath, can't you? It would help Aunt Jan.'

'Shall I tell Daddy you've gone to the pictures?' Rosanna asked, more craftily than innocently, now she was eight.

Wendy flushed. 'I've told him all *my* news, you write yours.'

It was a balmy June evening. The white smoke from the Muck Works chimneys still billowed overhead as Wendy and Charlie walked arm-in-arm to their favourite pub. The smoke made the locals cough sometimes, but they didn't think too much about it; the works were so much a part of their lives.

Just a quick drink tonight, they decided, and maybe a bag of vinegary hot chips from the nearby fish and chip shop for Charlie to eat as they proceeded to the cinema. Wendy didn't really approve of that, but at least he didn't smoke, and now and then he popped a chip between her lips and she couldn't protest with her mouth full, she told herself. She guessed he didn't feed himself properly. When Baz comes home, she made her mind up, I'll have his dinner on the table soon as he opens the front door. . . .

They were familiar faces to her in the pub now. There was always a convivial atmosphere, and you could almost forget there was a war on.

It was dark in the cinema; they'd queued for their tickets and the big picture had already started. Wendy eased her feet out of her court shoes and pushed them under her seat. Before long, Charlie reached for her hand; it was the only liberty he took. When they got back Janet usually had the door open before she could fumble for her key, to preclude, she thought, any goodnight kisses. She didn't blame her sister for that, but she couldn't explain why these outings with Charlie were important to her. Jan would never look at another man. Was Baz tempted, being so far from home?

'Wendy.'

'Umm?'

'I want to tell you something . . .'

'Later, Charlie, I don't want to miss this bit . . .'

'It doesn't matter,' he said.

That Friday evening, pay-day, when the popular Eagle in Norfolk Street was full with servicemen enjoying their brief respite, an enemy plane droned overhead, off course, but intent on releasing its deadly cargo before making back to base. It passed over the brown, deep, chill waters of the great river, the docks. The explosion reverberated shockingly around the area as the Eagle received a direct hit. They heard the blast in the cinema and felt the tremor.

They ran all the way home. Wendy was sobbing, because they had glimpsed the devastation. The Eagle was no more. It was a great jagged pile of smoking rubble. Windows had been blown in in the vicinity; people had dashed for shelter. The emergency services were desperately working at the site, but the next day they would learn that the death toll had reached forty-two. Lynn was stunned by this catastrophe.

'I can't – go out with you any more,' she told Charlie. 'It could have been *us*, in the pub – what would have happened to my children? Please, it's – over; it should never have started . . .' She slammed the door in his face.

He headed automatically for his own place: climbed the stairs, spoke briefly to the cat.

'Out you go, old boy.'

I never told her, he thought, but perhaps it's just as well. I hoped – but what does it matter now?

He closed the window, pulled the curtains, locked the door. All his loose change went into the meter. He turned on the gas, opened the oven door. Best way. He didn't want to be a nuisance, an embarrassment. No note, no reproaches, no answers for those who would discover him. His bookwork was up to date for the company. No loose ends in that respect.

The hissing gas dulled his senses. Don't fight it. It shouldn't take long. . . .

There was good and bad news for Wendy and her family. Baz was wounded, seriously enough to be invalided out. The official communication stated he would be shipped home to hospital as soon as possible.

'Where will Daddy sleep?' asked Rosanna. Russ had graduated to her little bed, while she slept with her mother.

'I've been thinking,' Aunt Jan said, looking at her sister, sitting passively and pale-faced, clutching the letter. 'We ought to move out of town, after this scare. One of the girls at work told me there's a pair of farm cottages going on an estate, in return for working on the land, and cleaning and maybe a bit of cooking now and then, in the big house. It'd still be classified as war work, I reckon: we could manage the work between us. There's a local school, and a bus to town. It'd be a quiet place for Baz to rest up when he finally gets home, too.'

'Could we keep rabbits?' Rosanna asked eagerly. Mummy always said no, not here, it's not the place for pets.

'I don't see why not. Maybe a pig. They say you get half back if you let the local butcher have it. That'd certainly help out the meat ration . . .'

'Not the *rabbits!*' Rosanna cried in horror, as if they were a fact.

'You can't be sentimental in wartime,' Aunt Jan said briskly.

They arrived at the cottages on the edge of the common just as the summer storm broke. The girls and Grandma Birdie went in Wendy's house, chosen because the pump was outside the back door and she needed more water for washing than Janet, because of Russ.

'Hold on to Russ, mind,' Mummy warned Rosanna.

She didn't say they were not to go upstairs and explore, so they did just that. Through the grubby uncurtained front window, they gazed on an amazing sight. On the common there were giant mushrooms: tents from which men in battledress emerged, looking over at the van which had removed them from Lynn, courtesy of the Muck Works. Janet had learned to drive just before the war. Jim had insisted.

Two men, waterproofs over their heads, came hurrying over to the van where Janet and Wendy were sheltering while the heavens were zigzagged with lightning and thunder growled menacingly all around. The rain was pelting down. It was a spectacular performance by the elements.

'You all right, ma'am? Here, take these macs and get yourselves indoors. The men'll move your stuff in for you, when it eases up a bit. And we'll send over a billy of tea, and mugs . . .'

They drank their tea, watched gratefully as beds were carried into each cottage in turn, tables and chairs, and crocks in cardboard boxes. One of the men tuned the wireless so they had music to work by.

The stoves were lit, curtains threaded on poles, floors swept, mats put in place. As the sun came out, windows were cleaned, water was pumped, beds were made up. Then a meal was provided; stew with dumplings!

Their employer brought over the goat as promised, tethered it, and there was their milk supply.

At dusk, they said goodnight with fervent thanks to their working force, closed the doors and lit the oil-lamps.

Rosanna was glad Aunt Jan, Grandma and Merle were next door.

Wendy, Rosanna and Russ slept in Wendy's big bed that first night, with a nightlight on the landing shelf, and a potty under the bed, just like the old days on the fens, for the privy was down the garden path.

In the morning, just after dawn, Rosanna peeked out of the bedroom window. The tents had vanished. Some time during the night the soldiers had broken camp. It was as if they had never been there at all.

Later, they would discover that the troops had left not a scrap of rubbish behind. It would be some years hence before they learned that their friendly soldiers had been stopping off *en route* to North Africa, to join the Desert Rats.

Janet was awake early too. She kept to her side of the double bed as usual, leaving space for the absent Jim. Sometimes she put her hand out in the darkness of the night, touching his cold, smooth pillow. Then the silent tears would course down her face. With the men away she was the mainstay of the family. Had she done the right thing, moving them here, leaving her job, her workmates? It was almost the end of term, Merle was about to change schools anyway, but this might be more of a challenge to young Rosy. She was unused to country ways, apart from those pre-war holidays spent with them at the pumping station. Would Wendy be able to cope? Especially when Baz returned home. He had been wounded in the head, his memory was affected. His recovery would inevitably be slow and, it had to be faced, perhaps not complete.

She had another worry. Wendy didn't know about Charlie. Suspected gas leak, the *Lynn News* reported. Tragic death of young insurance man. It was believed he had no close relatives. Nice chap, said his landlady – could some kind person take on his cat? Popular with his clients, would be missed, his employers regretted. The inquest was still to come. In the flurry of the move, in the aftermath of the awful tragedy of The Eagle, Wendy hadn't yet surrendered her policy, as Janet suggested. After all, Baz was safe, if not the same man who had gone off to fight for his country.

Rosanna climbed back into bed. Her mother stirred.

'You all right, darling? Is Russ still asleep? Are you glad we're here?'

'Yes,' Rosanna answered to all three questions. It felt like home. . . .

Chapter Six

Out here in the sticks a warm, not unpleasant smell rose from fresh-splatted cowpats, raked hay turned pale gold in the sun, a distinctive whiff came from the bearded white goat that was staring at them inquisitively, jaws moving rhythmically, horns impressive but unthreatening.

The brown-and-white cows stared too, blinking their ridiculous cartoon eyelashes, and the horses clopped to the farm gate and swished the flies with their tails, snorted, startling the children, waiting for hanks of torn-up grass, or wrinkly last-season's apples which the girls, exploring yesterday, had discovered in the cellar, peppered with mouse dirts.

The cellar had been the original refuge when the siren wailed, warning of enemy planes overhead. The shelter in the field which superseded it was disguised by a roof-covering of turf, cropped indiscriminately by the cattle.

'You can be more startled by a cow, when you emerge at the all clear, than if it was an enemy airman waving a revolver at you,' Susie, the farmer's daughter observed, when pointing the shelter out to them. She'd popped over to ask Janet when she could start work. It was a busy time.

The horses' teeth were large and yellowy which made Rosanna feel nervous that first morning after breakfast when she hesitantly proffered an apple, but their breath blew soft and sweet on the palm of her hand as they gently mouthed the fruit. These two were working horses: deep-chested, muscular chestnuts, with great, fringed hoofs and tossing, noble heads. They were gentle giants, patient, plodding. There were also two ponies out to grass, which were more wary, as if expecting to be caught and saddled up, and an aged donkey, who bucked, kicked her heels up and brayed defiantly when the children tried to entice her to the gate.

Susie Peck appeared, bucket in hand. She was a matter-of-fact young woman in her late twenties, with dark-brown hair dangling like a bell rope with a tassel on the end. Her angular face was reddened from exposure to all weathers, with blue eyes that squinted against the brightness of the sun.

She offered the pail of feed to the goat.

'Mother named her Mrs Miniver, after the film, Min for short, you know, because no one can say she looks like Greer Garson. Didn't the brigadier say?' The brigadier was her father and they were already aware that everyone on the farm called him that, not sir, which you might have expected, as Janet remarked after his visit, him being a gentleman farmer. 'Don't yer know,' she added in a posh voice.

Now, Rosanna shook her head, saying shyly.

'That's my mummy's favourite picture, too. She saw it twice.' With Mr Whiston, she thought. She hoped *he* wouldn't call here, especially when Daddy came home.

'If you're interested,' Susie sized Rosanna up, 'I've a Shetland in the back paddock which you could ride if I can find time to teach you.'

'What about me?' Merle asked, before Rosanna could say: 'Oh, *please!*'

'How old are you – eleven? Maybe, if you're not too heavy, but you might be too long in the leg.'

'What about those ponies?' Merle persisted, pointing.

'The bay, Rum, is too old, her trotting days are over. I don't ride much now; I've outgrown the ponies. The roan, Strawberry – very original, eh? – isn't a novice ride. I started with the donkey when I was two years old, and then Grandpa gave me the Shetland. I've kept 'em all, even though the brigadier complains about the cost of feeding 'em sometimes. Anyway, the mothers and babies billeted in Roiston Hall enjoy the animals and that's a good excuse. We've moved to the home farm for the duration . . .'

'Not holding Miss Peck up, are you, girls?' Janet approached, ready for work in dungarees, head scarf and rubber boots.

'We're just chatting,' Susie told her. 'Our land girl, Vera, lives in, so she's already helped the cowman with the milking; she's earned her breakfast and five minutes' sit down. There's still the Tottenham pud to dole out to the hens, though: Mother's boiled up the little spuds and the peelings to mix in – they do like it sloppy.'

'What's Tottenham pudding?' Merle wanted to know.

'Household food waste. Haven't you seen the pig-bins in town? It ekes out the grain for poultry and pigs. The stuff gets cooked with molasses 'til it looks and smells rather like figgy pudding, but I don't intend to sample it, no fear! It's got what the brigadier calls blood and guts mixed up in it, too.

'We need you on the tractor shortly, Janet. We're hoping you'll give Vera some driving lessons. In return, she'll show you how to harness and work with the big boys.' Susie indicated the shires. 'Your sister'll be over at the house in an hour, will she? She's made arrangements for the children?'

'My mother-in-law will keep an eye on them, on the little boy mostly. Merle will look out for Rosy. Don't venture too far, girls, tell Grandma Birdie where you're going, and remember you mustn't leave gates open or go anywhere on the farm itself, without permission.'

'And keep your little dog on the lead; I've got a bitch in season, and can't be doing with pups,' Susie said sternly, but she smiled at Rosanna and Merle, adding: 'We'll see about the pony after work, eh, Rosanna?'

'Just because you're a little *squit*,' Merle used a word Janet and Wendy disapproved of, as they watched them go, '*You* get all the best things on a plate—'

'I do not!'

'Yes you do. *I* just get *Tottenham* pudding! Ugh, it sounds horrible! It's not my fault I'm tall, like both Mum and Dad, is it?'

'And it's not my fault I'm short like *my* mum!' Rosanna retorted, surprising herself. She turned towards her own front gate. It was a nice feeling, having their own home to themselves again, and despite Merle's bossy ways she was glad she and her family were just next door. She'd promised Wendy she would wash up then help get Russ ready to go to Grandma Birdie before Wendy went to work. She couldn't remember Mummy having a job before, Mummy said Daddy believed it was a man's place to provide for his family if he could, but she'd made a commitment, Wendy said, (whatever that was, Rosanna thought) because of the cottage.

The brigadier's wife immediately put Wendy at ease and told her to call her Mrs Peck, not madam.

'I went to a spartan boarding-school run by Anglican sisters. Susie followed in my footsteps, the girls were expected to make their own beds and keep their rooms tidy. We had to dust and polish and so on – wash up our tea things on a Sunday, the staff's afternoon off . . . Invaluable training. Which reminds me, I cater for the hall twice a week, would you mind helping me out with that?' Seeing Wendy's surprise, she added: 'In wartime: we all have to, as Vera puts it so succinctly, muck in.'

'Yes, of course I will.'

Mrs Peck was stooped, with a rounded back. She gave Wendy a wry smile when she caught her glance.

'I may have a dowager's hump my dear, be over sixty, but it doesn't stop me doing my bit.'

Vera, the land-army girl, was rinsing her plate and cup at the sink.

'Vera, this is Wendy Bloomfield. She's Janet Bird's sister. You're just off again, are you?'

'Yes, Mrs Peck.' Vera nodded at Wendy. She was a tiny girl, but as Janet would tell Wendy that evening, surprisingly strong, and a dab hand with a pitchfork and tossing the hay.

'See you at lunchtime, then. Ready for a tour of the house, Wendy? You'll find all the cleaning stuff in this cupboard, by the way . . .'

Wendy had never worked so hard in a morning before. The farmhouse rooms were big and lofty, there were cobwebs to disperse, a carpet sweeper which filled all too quickly and had to be emptied, dust which settled on surfaces just wiped, and the brick floor of the kitchen to be swept and mopped. She guessed it would be just as muddy again by the time she left.

Meanwhile, Mrs Peck chopped vegetables for a casserole, skinned and jointed a rabbit, refuelled the Kitchener stove, made a great bowl of junket, and a welcome cup of tea for the workers at eleven.

'You may bring your little boy along, you know, Wendy, if Janet's mother doesn't feel up to looking after him, any morning.' Mrs Peck sipped her scalding tea, made a face. 'I don't think I'll ever get used to not having sugar . . . How old is he?'

'He's four.' Wendy wondered if Mrs Peck knew about Russ. She decided to come straight out with it. 'He's what they call – a mongol, Mrs Peck.' With a sense of shock, she realized she'd never said that before.

'Not a nice name is it,' Mrs Peck put in briskly. 'Outward appearances shouldn't count. We, my husband and I had a little boy just the same, he died when he was fourteen, but we still miss him so much. We lost two other babies after him, before Susie was born, so he was very precious to us. We proved the experts wrong, he learned to read, if not to write, he could ride and swim, he loved to listen to the gramophone, he had many friends, and he enriched our lives. I *do* look forward to meeting your special son, Wendy.'

Wendy's back was giving her gyp, her hands were sore, but she was suddenly awash with happiness and relief. Like Rosanna, she instinctively felt at home here.

The silage was contained in a great wooden vat. Susie explained that the process began each spring, when the grass was first cut, then layered with molasses, which, as it fermented gave off that distinctive odour.

'The village children love to come and tread it down, because it's so squidgy and the smell is quite heady – you should just hear them giggling.'

'Merle and Rosy will volunteer, I'm sure,' Janet said.

'As the silage builds up, so do the sides of the vat. We bolt on further sections, see? Then, during the winter, these are removed when the contents go down. You'll be helping with all that. But next it's the harvest, of course, and then there's the sugar beet to lift. Now, hop on the tractor and show me what you can do, eh?'

'Ready, Rosanna?' Susie asked, adjusting the girth strap as the children stroked the stout little Shetland, and Russ emitted little cries of delight.

Rosanna looked at her brother. Her mother insisted that the girls bring him along to the paddock after tea.

'Susie once had a brother like Russ, she won't mind, I'm sure – *he* learnt to ride, Mrs Peck told me.'

Rosanna said generously: 'Let Russ have a go first, please, you can see how excited he is.'

While Susie led the pony, Rosanna and Merle walked alongside, supporting the little boy in the saddle. The expression on his face was enough, he had no need of words.

Susie lifted him down and gave him a brief hug.

'There, you're a natural, Russ. Now, stay put and watch your sister – and yes, Merle, you may have a turn, too.'

Chapter Seven

It was a summer holiday Rosanna would never forget. Like all the children round and about the farms, they were involved with the harvest. The nippy grey Ferguson tractor and the horses played an equal part. But it was the latter who supplied the ageless magic of harvest time. The girls perched precariously atop bales in the swaying cart, but when the midday sun was high they relaxed in the shade with the real workers, with bread and cheese, and bottles of cold tea. Their sunburned limbs were prickled; their heads protected by straw hats. Grandma Birdie brought Russ along at lunchtime, with some small treat, like sweet plums, or early Beauty of Bath apples.

'Hiya.' Russ beamed, plonking himself between Rosanna and Merle. When work resumed, he hugged them all, then toddled off, twig in hand, poking every cowpat on the way home. It was his favourite thing.

The ricks in these parts were boat-shaped. Celtic in origin, the brigadier surmised, rather than emanating from the Anglo Saxons who had dominated East Anglia for centuries, perpetuating their flaxen hair.

'What about *no* hair?' Merle whispered to Rosanna as they stared at his peeling bald head. The brigadier was keen to see what the working force were up to and to tell them what was what, but he didn't do much work himself. He issued orders, but Susie was in charge.

'Saxon or Celt?' Merle wondered impishly.

'Winston Churchill,' Rosanna whispered back, because the brigadier looked rather like him. Merle laughed out aloud. They were in tune that summer.

In the early morning, when the mist hung low, Rosanna, gazing through her window, fancied the golden boats in the distance drifted lazily on a sea of stubble. She didn't tell Merle, because when she'd asked: 'Remember the floating moon?' Merle had replied: 'It was an *illusion*, Rosy; a reflection.'

The excited farm terriers, including Topper, streaked after rats emerging from the threshed corn, and when Topper rolled over for her to tickle his tummy, Rosanna couldn't, knowing what he'd done.

'It's his nature, he can't help that,' Aunt Jan told her, but Rosanna shook her head.

'It's *cruel* . . . .'

The rabbits fleeing from the waiting youngsters armed with sticks sickened her too. She refused to eat rabbit pie for supper. Russ was feeding himself at last; he didn't mind what was on his plate.

'Oh, Rosanna,' Wendy sighed, 'What *am* I to do with you? Don't tell me you're going to be one of those vegetarians.'

'No, I don't like greens either,' Rosanna said dolefully.

'Your father won't be pleased at how finicky you are.' Wendy sighed.

'Can I go with you next time you visit him?' Rosanna asked hopefully.

'No, dearie, it's no place for you. Some are worse than him, it'd upset you.'

Rosanna wrote to Baz every week, though he was not up to writing back. She missed the blue air-letters with a message for her. Mummy folded the paper so her piece remained private. There was a sketch for Russ, as well. The last letter they received, before Baz was wounded, pictured a small boy building a sandcastle, but in wartime you couldn't go on the beaches, let alone dig in the sand, or dip a little tin pail in the sea, or scream in pretend fright when the waves rushed over your toes and splashed your knickers. However, Mummy and Aunt Jan said the drawing hinted at something else. Merle knew, of course. When Rosanna asked her she said:

'He's letting you know where he is. Simple eh?'

By the time the sugar beet was ready for lifting the girls were about to join their new schools. For Rosanna this meant a five-minute walk; for Merle, a cycle ride to town. The gap between them, in age and experience widened immediately.

Despite oozing confidence, Merle dreaded her first day. Susie found her old bike, and they cleaned it, rubbing rust from the bell, which to Russ's fascination worked, then Merle watched as Susie demonstrated how to maintain the machine.

Jan arranged for local children to include Merle among the pedallers to the secondary school. She wobbled behind them, but as Janet said, there wasn't much traffic these days, thank goodness.

That evening Merle ignored her aching calf muscles, the satchel full of homework, and when Rosy came round she impressed her with stories of how huge the school was.

'You'd never find your way round, Rosy, you're too dreamy,' she asserted airily. She exaggerated the perils of the gym, the vast sports field and flailing hockey sticks. She relayed the school nurse's obligatory talk, but not the sheer embarrassment of communal showers, discovering how well endowed some girls were. She imagined their amusement at her own lack.

That night, she choked back tears. She didn't want Grandma Birdie to say: 'What's up dearie? Shall I call your mum?' She didn't want sympathy. Never that. But maybe, when she got Mum on her own, she'd ask her to explain it all properly as the nurse suggested. She'd make friends, she jolly well would.

Rosanna didn't understand the growing-up bit. She broached the subject diffidently to Wendy, who assured her: 'You needn't worry about all that yet.'

When Rosanna was older, Wendy would tell her daughter: 'Ask Aunt Jan.'

At the village school alongside the church, Rosanna, to her relief, was casually accepted, knowing most of her classmates from harvest time. She didn't experience the barrier which still existed after three years between the local children and the remaining evacuees, the majority of whom had returned to London after the blitz. It was still 'them and us', although supposedly integrated, sharing the same classrooms and teachers. Confrontations flared up now and then.

That first morning, Rosanna took the only spare seat next to another relative newcomer named Rebekah. Her tentative smile as she set out her pencil-box and opened the *New Reader* slapped down by the monitor, was not returned.

Bekka, as the kindly teacher shortened her name, as she did immediately with Rosanna, calling her Rose, was excused the morning prayers because she was neither C of E nor Chapel. Instead, she perused a large dictionary. Occasionally, she copied a word into a notebook she had supplied herself, with unlined pages between shiny marble-patterned covers. A floppy white satin bow held flowing locks, gleaming chestnut in a shaft of sunlight. Bekka's fingers were long and slender, with tapering nails. Rosanna's own nails were bitten, a habit her mother sighed over: 'Why do you do it?' Now, she hoped that Bekka wouldn't notice.

She looks foreign, Rosanna thought, intrigued. It was break before Bekka said, with an unexpected London twang:

'Not bad here, eh? Coming outside?'

They sat on the grass. 'Don't drink from the fountain,' Bekka advised. 'It tastes of brass.' Children queued to jab the button, to slurp water.

'D'you come from London?' Rosanna asked.

'Yes. Is it obvious?'

Rosanna nodded.

'My father is half Italian, but his mother is a Cockney, so Dad has a British passport,' Bekka added proudly. 'We were in London during the bombing, then came to Norfolk because Dad is an interpreter at the Italian prisoner of war camp near here. Ket, my mum, works there part-time, too, in the laundry. So you see, we are not evacuees and—' she glared at the leapfrogging children, 'we're not the enemy, as they say, either!'

'That's a funny name, Ket . . .'

Bekka's dark eyes flashed. 'No, it isn't! It's Old Testament, like my name – Ketura was one of Abraham's wives – it's a family name, Ket's from the north.'

'I'm sorry, I didn't mean to be rude . . .'

'It's all right. Ket says I'm too quick to spit, like my father. Eyetie blood, she says. But not so my dad can hear! D'you want to be my best friend?' Rosanna didn't hesitate. Here was a younger, more serious version of Merle. She nodded.

'D'you like horses?' she asked. 'I'm learning to ride a pony on the farm. I'll ask if you can have a go, too, if you like.'

'Ket always says you should never say you can't do anything until you've tried,' Bekka said enigmatically. The handbell clanged. 'Time to go back to the grind. When can I come round to yours? This Saturday?'

'My mother will be out, visiting my father in hospital, but I don't think she'd mind because Aunt Jan will be there,' Rosanna said.

'Knock the dirt off!' The sugar beet was lifted, and now awaited cleaning and transporting away. It sounded easy enough, and Wendy was persuaded to earn a little extra in the afternoons, after her usual work and before Rosanna came home from school. Russ had a nap then, likewise Grandma Birdie.

'They can nod off together in my cottage,' Janet suggested. It didn't work out that way, though.

Three of the huge beets and the clods which clung obstinately to them were enough for Wendy. She wiped the perspiration off her fore-head, leaving dirty streaks and proclaimed: 'That's it!'

'You won't get paid for half an hour,' Janet admonished her.

'I don't care! It's the worst job in the world – I'm not tough enough for it!'

Susie, side-stepping the muddy globes from some rows away, where she was supervising the efforts of two youths who'd gladly seized the opportunity of work, however onerous, called out: 'Anything the matter?' in her carrying voice.

'Sorry, Susie, I'm giving up . . .'

'Don't apologize; we're not all Amazons! By the way, Mother was bemoaning I'd snaffled you when she wanted to ask if you could manage an extra hour or two baking. Some of the Americans from the new air base have accepted her invitation for tea, and are coming tomorrow.'

Janet said: 'You're on your way, aren't you, Wendy? Wash your hands first!'

'Plenty of eggs, Wendy, so we'll have a couple of nice sponges I think, don't you? Then you can sandwich 'em together with some raspberry jam – or did we give the last of that to the mothers and babies?' Mrs Peck asked.

Wendy went into the pantry to inspect the regiment of brightly coloured jars marching along the top shelves.

'Got one!' she called back in triumph.

'Good. No wooden pips in ours like there are in shop raspberry these days.'

'Scones? Rusks?' Wendy suggested, cracking six eggs into the largest mixing bowl. There were two smaller bowls to the set, which Mrs Peck cheerfully labelled: Adolph 1,2 and 3.

'Seedy-cake? We're not short of sugar. Got to show 'em how we eat, or rather, *used* to eat, over here, eh? Shall I let you into a secret, Wendy? We have friends in the West Indies, so the brigadier sends off a postal order every so often, and in return we receive a package of sugar. The Customs never say anything. D'you think that's awful? You look rather shocked, my dear.'

Wendy said quickly: 'No, Mrs Peck. After all, I suppose it all goes to a good cause – to help out the rations at the hall and that . . .'

'Make some buns while you're about it for yourself – you're seeing your husband tomorrow, aren't you? Otherwise, I'd have enlisted your help then.'

Wendy whipped with a will. Butterfly cakes, she thought, for Rosy to entertain her new friend. Artificial cream . . . She smiled to herself. Just a knob of marge needed, and no worries about the sugar.

Chapter Eight

The train was crowded as usual, but Wendy squeezed in by the window. She tilted the saucy bottle-green hat over her eyes to feign sleep because reading was difficult in such conditions. As the train rattled and jolted along, the passengers hanging precariously to the luggage racks swayed against one another, while the feet of the selected seated few were in danger of being trodden on.

There was a background buzz of conversation but Wendy had no intention of joining in. She used the tedium of the journey with its stopping and starting at every minor station to prepare herself for what lay ahead. She felt guilty that lately she'd been happy, despite not having Baz at home, and regressing to a simpler way of life with its lack of electricity, no water on tap, no bathroom, and cooking on an antique stove. The man she'd married after her brief working life in the seed merchants' office where they'd met, would have been upset, she knew, to see her cleaning another woman's house. Yet, cheerful Mrs Peck, with her genuine interest in the welfare of young Russ, had become a real friend.

She wore a neat costume which Mrs Peck had discreetly handed her when she finished work yesterday saying:

'The jacket doesn't fit me, I'm sorry to say, now I'm an awkward shape. It was cleaned before putting away, but be generous with the scent!' The old Basil would have been huffy over such a gift. The colour complemented her hat, being a paler shade of green. She looked elegant, but would Baz notice? She'd loosened her hair from the severe roll she'd adopted recently. Perhaps, subconsciously, she thought it made her look less attractive. After Charlie, that was a good thing. Baz preferred her hair curly: she'd dampened each strand last night, despite her weariness, before winding up in the steel curlers, with the crocodile *snap*!

Unexpectedly, Russ had clung to her when she took him to Janet earlier. 'Mud-Mud,' he implored in his gruff voice, which choked her. At his age, Rosanna had had an extensive vocabulary, and Merle had undoubtedly contributed to that.

The two of them were tussling over milking the goat. Wendy was pleased to see that her daughter stood her ground.

'You know it's my turn to squeeze! *You* hold the bucket! 'Bye, Mum,' she called out off-handedly. Rosy was giving up babyish things, like calling them Mummy and Daddy.

'Be good darling; I hope you and your friend enjoy what I've made for your tea,' she said. She wouldn't kiss Rosanna, not with her face against the goat's flank.

'I'd better be invited, too,' she heard Merle say, and she smiled ruefully. Well, there were six buns and a tinful of scones.

There was a scramble after alighting at the station, to catch the waiting bus, for there was an hour before the next one. Wendy was resigning herself to the delay, when the conductor hauled her aboard.

'Room for a little one!'

A plump woman shifted reluctantly, plonking her basket on her lap. Wendy was forced to leave her own basket in the aisle.

The hospital, a converted country house, was on the outskirts of the seaside resort. It was a ghost town nowadays, with its barricaded mined beach and pill-boxes; the once grand pier now in sections to prevent easy access to the town in the event of invasion.

They had enjoyed a lovely day here during their brief honeymoon. She and Baz had strolled along the length of the pier, leaned over the railings to watch the boats, chatted to the fishermen. They sat at the far end and ate cockles, followed by sticky peppermint rock, and put pennies in the machines in the amusement arcade. Wendy still had the little printed card from the fortune-teller's booth. When the machine was activated by her penny, a plumed pen held in a chipped plaster hand with blood-red nails and a glittering green gem ring appeared to write a message. When it ceased moving, a card would emerge from the slot with the words: YOU WILL HAVE A LONG AND HAPPY LIFE WITH THE MAN OF YOUR DREAMS, BUT BEWARE OF TEMPTATION WITH ANOTHER.

Could Charlie be classed as that? Not that we . . . But she couldn't be explicit, not even in her thoughts.

Most of the visitors hurried up the long drive to the hospital, Wendy bringing up the rear. The house was impressive, double-fronted and faced with knapped slate. She quickened her steps when she saw Baz sitting alone on the terrace outside. It was a sunny, blowy day, and instead of the usual pyjamas and dressing-gown he was dressed in the navy pinstriped suit she had brought last week, with a shirt and tie. Incongruously he wore slippers. She had forgotten to bring his shoes.

He looked at her with that little worried frown; she bent to kiss his cheek. Poor old Baz, she wondered if he knew her.

'How are you?' she asked.

After a while he said, fingering the livid scar behind his left ear: 'Very well, thank you.'

She couldn't get used to him without his moustache. The young orderly brought them cups of tea.

'Shall I help you with yours, old chap?' he asked. Baz still had trouble with co-ordination. Baz shook his head.

'She – Wendy – can manage, can't you?'

'See you later, then,' the orderly said.

'I might spill a drop or two down you, watch out,' Wendy joked, tucking his pocket handkerchief over his front. She tilted the cup carefully, allowing him to sip his tea slowly, just as she had done until recently with Russ. More likely the drops would be tears of relief, because Baz had at last remembered her name. 'I brought you a couple of little cakes, I made them specially,' she added softly.

Rosanna was now allowed to catch and saddle the pony herself. She'd learned quickly, Susie said. Merle and Bekka looked on enviously.

'Be back before dark,' Janet had cautioned.

'Ket's coming for me at six,' Bekka told her.

'Got your watch on, Merle?'

' 'Course I have. Why don't you come and watch us ride, Mum?'

'Because Russ is grizzly, that's why. He wants Wendy, but she won't be here for some time yet. And Grandma Birdie's already gone to bed . . .'

'What, this early?' Bekka could hardly believe it.

Now, she said to Merle: 'You've got *two* funny people in your family.'

'What d'you mean, funny?' Merle flashed.

'You know . . .'

'No, I don't. Grandma's worked hard all her life, now she's winding down, my mum says. Russ was born that way, but we all think the world of him.'

'Sorry!'

'So you should be! You're different, too, after all! And if you say anything like that again, I'll tell Rosy, and then she won't be your friend.'

'Oh, please don't . . .'

Rosy's the only friend she's got, Merle realized. She's quite nice really, but she's got to know that we Birds and Bloomfields stick together.

Mrs Peck spotted them through the kitchen window as she deposited the tea tray with its empty cups and crumby plates on to the big table. The visitors, she thought with satisfaction, had eaten the lot and compliments had been many.

'Susie,' she called through the hatch to the sitting-room: 'Rosy is going to ride – why not take our guests outside to watch, and I'll follow on.'

'Oh, Mother, you come too, leave the washing-up, I'll do it later,' Susie called back. Her father having monopolized the conversation with the Americans, now it was her chance, as he'd offered to see to the evening feeding of the stock.

At her mother's insistence, she'd discarded her jodhpurs in favour of a gingham dress with a Peter Pan collar, and powdered her nose. The frock was hopelessly out of date, but she cared so little about clothes, it didn't worry her.

There were four American officers on this occasion, three of them tall, broad-shouldered and good-looking, with ready smiles revealing strong, white teeth. The result of chewing all that gum, Susie wondered? They were in their mid-twenties, but their companion was shorter and older with less to say. Susie concentrated awkwardly on Johnny, so lofty he made her feel petite.

'The little girl reminds me of my younger daughter,' said a voice in her ear. Startled, she turned, her gaze level with the older American. 'What's her name?' he asked.

'Rosanna – her family call her Rosy . . .'

'She handles the pony well. You teach her?'

'Yes.' Susie was aware that Johnny had moved away to chat to her mother.

'My daughters ride. It comes natural, being brought up in Texas.' He had a very pleasant voice.

'Excuse me, but you are. . . ?' she asked.

'J.P. Burlson, known to all as Burl, ma'am.'

'And I'm Susie, not ma'am,' she told him. 'Do you farm back in Texas?'

'My family do. As the younger brother, I got the chance to join the USAF.'

'Don't you miss your family?'

'Sure do. My two girls are looked after by my folks. My wife, in case you're wondering, left me when the littlest one was less than a year old.'

'I'm sorry . . .'

'No need. It was quite a while ago now. You still single, Susie?'

'I-I'm needed here, especially since the war . . .' she said.

Johnny gave the bell-rope of hair a playful tug.

'Wow! Anyone ever say you got beautiful hair, Susie?' Now there were *two* men vying for her attention!

Janet cuddled a fretful Russ.

'Now, now, darling, Mud-Mud'll soon be home . . .' However, it was an hour before Wendy's train was due, and then she had a long walk.

The little boy's breathing was laboured: were his lips tinged with blue? Janet made up her mind. She wrapped him round with her cardigan, made her way out of the house and hurried as fast as she could, across the field to the farm.

The Americans took in the situation immediately. While Mrs Peck ran indoors to telephone the hospital, Susie rounded up the children, swiftly unsaddled the pony, offered to take the children back home to await the arrival of Bekka's mother, then to supervise the others until their mothers returned.

Burl drove the Jeep to the hospital. The officers had come in two vehicles; his friends would return to base in the other one. He settled Janet in the seat beside him with Russ still clutched to her, and ten minutes after she had arrived at the farm, they were speeding along, with Burl promising to go from the hospital to the station to collect Wendy.

Russ was very ill; he was in an oxygen tent, Janet knew that much, but the medical team were reluctant to pass on any information, except to his mother. She sat outside the room, burying her head in her hands. Their own doctor said that children like Russ were very susceptible to chest infections, that his heart was weak. She could only pray. What would it do to Wendy, if. . . ? She shuddered.

The American had been very kind, told her to be strong, in his soft voice.

'How shall I recognize your sister?' he asked.

'She's wearing a green costume; she's small and fair-haired,' she floundered. 'Here . . .' She'd snatched up her bag at the last minute before making her dash; she found an envelope, a pencil, and scribbled: *Wendy. Russ in hospital. This gentleman kindly offered to bring you here. Love, Janet.*

'Mrs Wendy Bloomfield?'

Startled, Wendy nodded. She read the note. The next thing she knew she was almost fainting in his arms, and he was supporting her.

'You OK?' He sounded far away. 'Hold on to me, that's the way. I have transport over here, we'll be there before you know it, Wendy.'

Chapter Nine

Janet hurried along the echoing corridor to meet her sister. Wendy appeared to be in a daze, stumbling along with Burl's arm firmly round her shoulders, and her hat awry. A nurse who passed them with a squeaking trolley laden with medicines, glanced back at the couple, then held up a hand to halt Janet in her flight.

'Don't worry. Sister Jones says he'll be all right. Are these his parents? Please reassure them, then send them straight along to Sister's office – no one is allowed in to see the little boy without her say-so . . .' She pushed open the adjacent ward doors and disappeared within, with her portable dispensary.

'Take a deep breath,' Burl advised Wendy. 'Your sister's smiling, see? It can't be that bad. You talk to her, and I'll wait over there on that bench.' He gently detached himself, gave her a little push towards Janet.

Wendy didn't hear a word he said. She allowed Janet to take over, to lead her on to the door of Russ's room.

'Sit down,' Jan said, indicating the chairs outside. 'Now, Wendy, you're in a tizzy, and that's understandable, but Russ is out of danger though you can't see him yet. When you've got your breath back, we'll see the ward sister.'

'I . . . had a funny feeling this morning, when he didn't want me to go . . .'

'Perhaps he didn't feel well then, but it's hard to say with him, isn't it. Don't blame yourself, dearie. It all happened in a rush. How was Baz?'

'He actually knew me today, Jan, he . . . seemed more like his old self . . .'

'There you are, then. One bit of good news, and you're bound to have another. Sister's office is at the end of the corridor.'

Sister Jones, with her frilly cap and bow tied under her chin, was brisk but reassuring.

'His heart beat is not so erratic; he is breathing more easily, but he will need to stay here for a few days so that we can keep a constant eye on him.'

'Will he . . ' Wendy couldn't bring herself to say it.

'Will he recover? We have every reason to think he will, my dear. However, you have to face the facts: it is very possible that your child may be prone to further attacks – any infection could trigger one off.' She paused. Then: 'Make the most of him, while you have him. He's a dear little chap . . .'

'When can I see him?'

'How about now?' Sister Jones rose, came round her desk. 'Then I suggest you go home, try to get a good night's sleep, and contact the hospital after eight in the morning. Visiting hours on this leaflet, no young visitors, I'm afraid, but if you are discreet, *you* may visit any time and we will turn a blind eye, eh?'

'May my sister come in with me now?' Wendy asked.

Sister Jones hesitated briefly. 'Again, discretion is the key word. Ten minutes – and it's best if you don't wake him if he is asleep, just look, don't speak . . .'

Russ lay motionless in the cot, but was breathing unaided, with the sheet and blanket tucked neatly round him, apart from one arm to which was attached a drip. Looking at that round little face with its blunt features, so unlike his sister's, but just as dear to her, Wendy mouthed: 'Darling. I love you.'

Back in the corridor, Burl asked with concern: 'How is he? Want me to take you home now?'

Wendy's face crumpled. She fished for her hanky. It had been a long day.

Janet answered for her: 'Russ is out of danger, thank God. Yes, please, we ought to go – the family must be worried sick. Oh, and I hadn't thought – shouldn't you be back at the air base? I do hope you won't get into trouble.'

'Weekend leave, first since we arrived, though we are not yet fully operational; non-stop since Pearl Harbor, when the US joined the Allies,' he reassured her. 'Nope. The other guys will cover for me; sure been glad to help.'

Susie was feeling rather harassed. Fortunately, Bekka's mother had arrived on time to collect her daughter, but there were explanations to make and Ket was chatty. Susie learned something interesting: there was talk of some Italian prisoners of war being allowed to help out local farms, under supervision, and Ket suggested that Susie write to the camp authorities and tell them of their need for extra labour.

'Have a nice time, apart from all the excitement?' Ket asked her daughter.

Bekka nodded. 'Mrs Bloomfield makes smashing cakes. But I didn't get a ride on the pony, after all . . .' She'd got on well with Merle, they were similarly self-possessed and articulate. Rosanna, worrying about Russ, had retreated from the spirited arguments over the board-games. She was no match for Merle even at draughts. Bekka, like Merle, was determined to win.

After Bekka and her mother eventually departed, Susie had to cope with Grandma Birdie, who came drifting downstairs, yawning, in her nightgown and half-mast bedsocks.

'Is it morning? Why are *you* here? Where's Janet?'

'It's night-time, Mrs Bird—'

'What's Rosy doing here then? Send her home to bed!'

'I can't – both Janet and Wendy are out.'

'They didn't tell *me*.' Grandma Birdie was aggrieved.

'Russ is ill, Grandma Birdie,' Merle put in, piling up the black and white pieces, with little clicking noises. 'They had to take him to the hospital.'

Grandma became agitated. Susie, flustered, signalled to Merle for help.

'Make her a strong cup of tea, that'll do the trick,' Merle said, just as they heard the Jeep arrive. It was dark outside, past blackout time.

'Good idea, especially now the others are back,' Susie said in some relief. She added: 'Don't rush out there, Merle, they'll be in directly . . .'

'I fancy a sandwich,' Grandma told her. 'There's a jar of Shippams open.'

'Mum said it was time we threw that out,' Merle warned.

'Never mind that. Have a sniff and you'll *know* all right,' Grandma said.

'Well, if I can't help any more here, I'd better go home – Mother will be wondering what on earth has happened,' Susie told them, after providing tea all round.

'I'll walk you back,' Burl offered immediately.

'There's really no need,' she insisted. 'Just across the meadow; I could find my way in the pitch-dark – which it isn't – without a torch . . .'

'Thanks for holding the fort,' Janet said warmly.

'Yes, thank you,' Wendy echoed.

'I'll tell Mother not to expect you for a few days, eh?'

'Please. And say I'm sorry . . .'

'My dear, you know my mother by now, her only concern will be for Russ, and for you. You'll be over as usual, I imagine, Janet, though?'

'I will,' Janet promised.

Burl went out with Susie to open and close the field gate behind her.

'I'll see you again, I expect,' she said in an offhand way.

'Sure,' he said easily. 'Tomorrow, maybe. I'm driving Wendy to the hospital. Not due on duty until the following morning.' Unexpectedly, he leaned forward, the gate between them, and kissed her cheek. 'Goodnight, Susie. Please tell your parents thanks for their hospitality, won't you? I surely appreciated it.'

As Susie walked away she thought wryly: the first man to show any interest in me since I left college and all that drama has to happen! Why aren't I small and vulnerable like Wendy? I do a man's work and I'm good at it, which maybe puts men off. Janet's strong too, but she's also – well, womanly and attractive . . .

'Try and get a sound night's sleep,' Janet told her sister. 'Are you sure you don't want to stay here tonight?'

Wendy hugged her. 'I'll be all right. Rosy, no more yawning, off to bed!'

'I'll leave you to it, then,' Burl put in. He retrieved his cap from the hook in the tiny hallway. 'Permission to escort you ladies to your door?' he asked.

He waited while Wendy lit the lamps downstairs. 'Well, if there's nothing more I can do? I'll call for you at nine-thirty, shall I?'

'Please.' On impulse, Wendy put a hand on his shoulder, moved closer and kissed him. 'Thank you for everything, for your support,' she said simply.

As he drove off, Burl gave himself a mental shake. You might be free, or sort of, because of the family back home, but she certainly isn't. She's got a sick husband, and two kids, one handicapped. Don't get too involved. Now, for a satisfying supper, the thin-cut sandwiches and cakes, which an English tea comprised, were tasty but couldn't compare with steak and fries and real coffee.

The American servicemen didn't yet realize that their ample rations, flown in from the US, bore no relation to what the British public now survived on. Here, in the Norfolk countryside, there seemed plenty to eat, and compared to what the population who lived in the cities could get, this was true. But the major proportion of home-produced food was strictly controlled; fair shares for all.

Wendy wore a plain blue dress, livened up with braid on the skirt, disguising the crease where she'd let the hem down because the fabric had shrunk in washing.

'You'll need a cardi,' Janet advised, so Rosy dashed upstairs and fetched a jacket in fluffy white wool knitted by Wendy in less hectic days.

She felt self-conscious as she settled in the Jeep beside Burl. As she waved to her family, she recalled sitting by Baz, with Russ in her arms and Rosy in the back of their own little car as they left the pumping station. They'd parted with the car when Baz went into the army, because she couldn't drive and anyway, petrol, they were told, would soon be restricted.

'Now, why the tears?' Burl asked, passing her his handkerchief. 'You heard the little boy had a reasonable night, didn't you?'

'It's not that.' She managed a smile. 'It's just, well, the fact that my husband isn't here, so I can't talk to *him* about it, he knew how to cheer me up . . .'

'And now?' They turned on to the main road.

'I suppose I'll have to be the strong one, especially when he comes home.'

'Any idea when that will be?'

'No. They say he's making slow progress, but I'm not sure . . .' She broke off.

'That things will be the same? You have to adapt. I had to, when my wife left.'

'I'm sorry, I didn't know.'

'I guess not. I have two daughters.'

'You must miss them.'

'Sure do. But I don't miss my ex-wife any more. The kids are looked after by my folks. She wasn't the maternal type. Well, here we are. Shall I wait in the car?'

'No, please – come in with me. That smell, it always gives me butter-flies . . .'

'Turns your stomach? OK. I'll try to look inconspicuous . . .'

Wendy looked at him. 'Hardly, in that uniform!' She actually giggled.

'Chin up, isn't that what you Brits say?'

'Mud-mud,' Russ greeted her. He was actually propped up in the cot.

The nurse smiled. 'Children are resilient, aren't they? Yes, he's rallied remarkably. He even ate a little arrowroot and drank some orange juice. He asked for something, we couldn't make it out; it sounded rather like *strimps* . . .'

'Oh, he really is getting better, then! He meant shrimps. Russ darling, you shall have your strimps when you come home.'

Chapter Ten

Burl's haversack bulged with surprises, including a hand of bananas, a fruit which Rosanna had not tasted for more than two years. Seeing her longing look, her mother whispered to her:

'For Russ: you don't mind do you, darling?'

But their new friend heard. 'They don't keep too long, so the children ought to share them – and don't forget young Merle next door.'

'I could make a banana custard for tomorrow, that will go further,' Wendy said. Pre-war, this had been a family favourite, although she rebuked Baz when he sprinkled sugar on his portion, for bananas were sweet enough without it.

'Mum . . .'

'Yes, Rosy?'

'Please can I take a *whole* banana to school tomorrow?'

'Isn't that a bit unfair to all the other children?'

'I guess you want to share with bosom buddies, right, Rosy?' Burl asked.

Rosanna blushed at 'bosom'. It had been featuring in whispers from Merle of late.

'I reckon you deserve your moment of glory.' Burl smiled.

Rosanna wondered, how many pieces can you cut one banana into?

'I thought you might squeeze the oranges.' Burl rolled them, one by one, across the table towards Rosanna. He knew what made children laugh.

'Russ likes to suck a sugar lump in an orange, keeps him busy,' Wendy said.

'He's busy now.' Rosanna watched her brother playing with his toy bricks. He'd climbed inside the cardboard box, after tipping them all out on the kitchen floor. Each time he leaned over to select a shape, the box tilted precariously; twice he rolled out, and doggedly got back in. He'd been home from the hospital for ten days now, and Wendy was considering returning to work.

'Take him with you, Mum,' Rosanna advised. 'Mrs Peck said you could.'

'I'm needed to help out with the mothers and babies, their regular cook is having an operation and will be off work for three months.'

'Russ'd have plenty of toys there to occupy him, especially that lovely rocking-horse that was Susie's.'

'*Spam!*' Wendy exclaimed, pleased, as Burl produced the last surprise.

'My favourite!' Rosanna picked up the tin. 'Can we open it for supper tonight?' She'd decided to eat meat again, as long as it wasn't rabbit.

'Only if Burl stays to share it,' Wendy told him.

'That's why I brought it.' He grinned.

Cubed, that tasty spam, when eased from its tin casing to wobble on a plate in its delicious jelly, with added diced vegetables and a quickly mixed and rolled piecrust over all, which, when baked, steamed appetizingly on their plates. Burl beamed at their compliments, but he said it was all down to Wendy's cooking.

Bekka came to see Rosanna and Merle on Saturday morning, when she was at a loose end, Ket being busy with their own laundry. Later, if the washing was dry enough after a morning blowing on the line, Ket'd be dashing away with the smoothing iron, just like the song they'd learned in their first year at school.

'Don't *your* mums complain that you get under their feet?' she asked plaintively.

'My mum's gone to see my dad,' Rosanna told her, 'so she can't moan at me today. And Russ is with Aunt Jan and Grandma Birdie. No one moans at *him*.'

'You'll have to help us with our jobs,' Merle told her in her forthright way. 'The quicker we finish, the sooner we can come out to play.'

Bekka had been wily enough to arrive after Min, the goat had been milked.

'She stinks,' she complained, as Min came up to her to the extent of her tether.

'What of?' Rosanna asked. They'd got used to country odours.

'Oh, goat, of course!'

Next job was helping Susie with her poultry. Then there were the stables to muck out, now that the horses were in need of shelter at nights; this chore was a fair return for riding the pony. Janet would sigh and say they too smelt far from sweet on their return.

She insisted that they put on their wellies, as the ground was squelchy and muddy underfoot. Rosanna and Merle were self-conscious in their new dungarees. This coupon-free remnant had been pounced on triumphantly earlier in the week, in the Lynn Tuesday market by Janet and run up with the expertise she'd gained at the Muck Works. Pity she hadn't used matching thread; the visible white stitching on the ugly tan material made the girls feel even more conspicuous.

'Dressed for work, I see,' Susie approved. So was she, in an old jersey of the brigadier's, and ancient army trousers, bunched at the ankle with baler twine.

'Except for me,' Bekka said. 'I'll watch from the outside.'

They collected the eggs first, lifting the hatch over the nest-boxes and feeling carefully in the straw. Rosanna picked up the broody hen and tucked her comfortably under her arm. She stroked the crown of the hen's head, crooning to her soothingly. 'Maybe Susie will let you sit on some eggs soon.'

'Nothing'll come of these.' Susie removed a feather or two from the basket.

'Why not?'

'Well, the old cock had a paroxysm, and snuffed it – we had him for lunch. The brigadier said we mustn't be sentimental and think, "poor old Lionel", but Mother says it's a relief not to hear that raucous crowing.' Seeing Rosanna's puzzlement, she added: 'The cock fertilizes the eggs, Rosy – that's his job. He has to earn his rations. Now, mind you give all the Tottenham pud to the hens.'

Rosanna had been alarmed when Merle pretended to taste it once, but now she smiled dutifully at Susie's joke, repeated every weekend.

Susie, strewing fresh straw, asked unexpectedly:

'Why haven't you done anything with your own gardens – dig for victory and all that?'

'Mum doesn't haven't much spare time,' Merle pointed out.

'And my mum's got Russ to look after.'

'Ah, but you've got time, haven't you? so why don't I give you half a dozen pullets and a spare coop then you can have your own eggs! You could feed that number on scraps and I could spare you a bit of corn.'

'You two are so lucky,' Bekka sighed enviously, when they had progressed to raking out Bonnie's stable. 'Ket says pets make too much mess. Did I tell you that she's changing her job? She's going to super-vise the laundry at the mothers and babies, which is good, because she'll be nearer home, and apparently I can have my tea there when I get out from school, as she'll be working longer hours.'

'Mum's working there for a while, so I'll get fed, too!' Rosanna hoped.

'Lucky beggars!' Merle told them.

'Hi!' called a now-familiar voice. 'Seen Susie, girls?'

'She took the eggs to the packing shed.' Merle pointed it out to Burl.

'OK. See you later.' He turned. 'Oh, I got a coupla Hershey bars for you – catch. Share with your friend, won't you?'

'Burl!' Susie was aware of her clothes, and the manure clinging to her boots.

'Need a hand?' he asked.

'D'you really want to?'

'Sure. Then we can brew some *real* coffee – I left a jar on the kitchen table – and you'll think about coming out for a spin, say, lunch and the flicks in town? I hear it's Bing Crosby, Bob Hope and Dottie Lamour in *The Road to Singapore.*'

'I thought you saw all the latest films in the camp cinema . . .'

'You reckon I'll worry about whether it's an old film, with you by my side?'

'You sound just like Johnny today, that's more his line, isn't it?'

'Well, it seems to work for him.'

'Just be yourself,' she reproved. Then the thought struck her. 'Did you hope to see Wendy this morning?' She tried to sound casual.

'I called there, but Janet came out from next door to say she'd gone to visit her husband. I said I had candy for the girls and she told me they were here.'

He watched the coffee bubbling, while she dashed upstairs to change.

She met her mother on the landing and informed her breathlessly that she was going out shortly.

'Is that all right, can you manage? The girls have just about finished the chores, and will be off home. I'll be back for the evening round.'

'Don't panic if you can't make it; the brigadier can muck in.'

'That's just it, he doesn't like to get his hands dirty,' Susie worried.

'Now, Susie, that's enough of that, just hurry up, and I'll entertain Johnny.'

'It's not Johnny, Mother, it's Burl!'

Mrs Peck advised: 'Don't get your hopes up too high, my dear.'

'Oh, Mother! I'm not throwing up the chance to go out! Anyway—'

'Anyway, he's looking in a direction he shouldn't be, eh?'

'If you mean Wendy, she's devoted to her husband . . .'

'I hope so. Susie – couldn't you let your hair down, for once?'

'Think that'll impress him?'

'You never know . . .'

'Home Guard this evening,' the brigadier reminded Susie. The threat of invasion might have diminished but the Guard still met regularly and were definitely on the defensive, The brigadier was proud of his local battalion, and kept them up to scratch. Poachers made crack shots, he told his wife, reformed or not.

'I'll be back by then, won't I?' Susie asked Burl. They were standing by the Jeep. Not a Hollywood limousine by any stretch of the imagination, being a drab olive-green and missing its canvas hood.

'Sure. I guess I'll be in time to meet Wendy off the train. OK, brigadier?'

The brigadier grunted. He took a sharp look at his daughter, in a smart check coat which she hadn't worn in years, with a fur collar which softened the angle of her jaw. Very thirties.

'Better tie that hair back,' he said. 'Or it'll blow all over the place and gum up the works . . .'

'Here,' Burl said gallantly, producing a white silk scarf.

Silently, Susie folded it and yanked her hair back. I can't change, she thought ruefully; when I attempt to, the chap I'm trying to impress doesn't even notice.

'Hi, Wendy, like a lift?' Burl asked, as she handed in her return ticket.

'Would I!' She climbed aboard gratefully. It had been a disappointing day. Baz appeared to have retreated into his own small world again.

'How'd it go?' he asked, as they cruised along, with muffled headlights.

'Not so good.' She shook her head sadly. 'The doctors say the same thing every time I ask: "He should be home soon." But it doesn't seem likely . . .'

'I'm sorry,' he said simply, taking one hand from the wheel for a moment, and pressing her own hands, clenched in her lap.

'Coming in for a while? Or have you got to get back?'

'Twenty-four hour pass – gotta make the most of those, because the base is about to receive a new intake. I'd better say no more, and leave it at that.'

Janet came out from her door, with Russ.

'Here's Mud-mud, dearie! He's ready for bed, as you can see.'

'You *are* good, Jan,' Wendy said gratefully. 'Where's Rosy?'

'Oh, I hope I did the right thing – she's staying the night at Bekka's. They went after lunch. I made them promise to be back in time for Sunday dinner.'

'Thanks, Jan. I don't suppose they'll get up to much mischief, do you?'

Burl swung Russ up in his arms. 'He's almost asleep on his feet! I'll carry him upstairs while you put the kettle on.'

'Tell me all the news in the morning, eh?' Jan remarked cheerfully. ' 'Night.'

'I'm not up to making you a meal, sorry,' Wendy said, when he came downstairs, having laid Russ carefully in bed in his small room, and covered him up. She had lit the oil-lamp on the table. It would soon be time for a fire in the evenings, she thought, but not tonight, I haven't got the energy for that, either.

'I had a real English tea out; Susie and I went to the flicks. I'll make the tea, though. You sit down and put your feet up.'

'I don't think I'll be good company, Burl. If you want to go, after the tea . . .'

'Nope. Cream in first, or after?'

'Whichever you like . . .' She couldn't help it, her own eyes were closing.

He slipped her shoes off, let her head rest against him. When she awoke she was vibrantly aware of their closeness. His uniform jacket was spread over her knees.

'Burl – what's the time? You ought to go!' she exclaimed.

'You really want me to?' He stroked her cheek, his gaze solemn and intense.

'I . . .' She made no attempt to move. His hands slipped to her shoulders, still caressing. Her breathing quickened in response.

'I'm lonely, too, you know,' he said softly. Then, inevitably, their lips met in a lingering, tender kiss. She recognized the longing in him. It had been there in Charlie, too, she suspected, but she had kept him at bay, not relaxing her guard. This was different. She'd known Burl such a short while, but that wasn't important. She was lonely, and aching for love.

'I don't have to leave until morning,' he said almost inaudibly.

*

I ought to feel guilty, she thought, as she slipped into the French night-dress, but I don't. It's so long since I felt like this; poor Baz isn't the man I married. Maybe I had the babies before I was ready to be a mother – not yet used to being a wife. I suppose I knew, and so did he, when Burl and I met, when Russ was ill, that there could be something between us, if we weren't careful.

He extinguished the candle.

'I looked in at Russ, he's sound. Wendy . . '

'Yes?'

'If you want to change your mind, don't be afraid to say. I know it sounds crazy, but I'm in love with you, and . . .'

She moved towards him, put her arms around him.

'Shush,' she whispered.

Janet lay awake next door. He hasn't left yet, she worried. Surely Wendy. . .? But it's none of my business. Jim will be home on leave soon, and I can't help thinking how that will be for us. Wendy hasn't got that anticipation, not with Baz as he is.

It was the most refreshing sleep Wendy could recall in ages. She felt both relaxed and positive; he slumbered on. She put out a hand, touched his arm. He stirred.

'Time to get up and go,' she murmured. She'd neglected to fix the blackout properly, so she could make out the time on the alarm-clock on the bedside table. That was set for six-thirty, and fortunately it hadn't yet shrilled and woken Russ.

He raised his head. 'Do I have to?'

'You know you do . . .'

He heaved a sigh, sat on the edge of the bed for a moment, in singlet and shorts, rubbing his eyes. He reached for his shirt. While he bent over the washstand, Wendy hastily dressed.

He turned.

'Don't tell me to forget what happened, will you? Because I can't.'

She shook her head. 'Nor can I. I . . . don't regret it, Burl – although I know I should – but it was only possible, you see, because Rosanna wasn't here – and Jan. I don't know what *her* reaction will be.'

'We'll find a way,' he asserted. He crossed the room, hugged her close.

'I don't see how. When Baz comes home, I can't let him down, Burl.'

'Let's leave it to fate,' he whispered back.

Chapter Eleven

There were eight mothers and babies at present, and another five young women expecting to give birth within the next few weeks. All came from the London area; only three were married, one recently widowed. Babies were put up for adoption within six weeks, and their mothers would have to try to put it all behind them.

Their comfortable surroundings: the shabby old mansion, kindly staff evacuated here at the height of the London inferno, the personal interest shown by the Pecks, was sometimes greeted with suspicion, but more often gratefully accepted. There was the odd moan about helping out in return for the privilege of being here, but as Matron pointed out, it was all good training for the future.

Rosanna and Bekka hurried up to the massive front door, and enjoyed a brief tussle over who should have the privilege of ringing the bell.

'Round the back,' a disembodied voice called from inside the house.

'Tradesmen's entrance,' Bekka said knowledgeably. 'Come on, then, Rosy.'

The lofty kitchen, with cupboards and shelves galore, and double Belfast sinks, was dominated by a substantial table, scrubbed white and scored by chopping knives. It was like a railway station, with endless comings and goings. Three expectant mothers were twisting onions from the dangling bunch, scraping mud from carrots and turnips, peeling potatoes and curls of great shiny green Bramley apples. Wendy kneaded a lump of elastic dough, rolling quarters of this to line pie-plates, seemingly absorbed in her task. Then she blinked at the girls.

'Like to help? I put some cake and biscuits out for you – see?'

'Can we eat first? I'm hungry,' Rosanna said.

'Didn't Grandma Birdie feed you properly at dinner time?'

'Mm. But that was *ages* ago. Where's Russ, Mum?'

'He's helping Ket fold the nappies in the laundry.' She indicated a door.

Bekka took a bite of seedy-cake. 'I'll see if I can do anything there, then . . .'

'Your friend,' Wendy observed, 'has been spoilt.'

'Bekka says, Ket says she's too cerebral for the common things of life.'

'Whatever's that?'

'Brainy, I think.'

'Crafty, more like. Here, I need this cheese grated, please.'

Rosanna perched on a stool and began the laborious task. When she thought Wendy wasn't looking, she pinched up a little cheese between finger and thumb and transferred it quickly to her mouth.

They didn't see Burl for a week or two, then he arrived unexpectedly one Friday evening, just after the children had been bathed in front of the Kitchener.

'Can I read Russ a story before we go up?' Rosanna asked. Russ climbed on her lap, clutching his favourite rag book.

'Well . . ' Then came the rapping on the front door. It wasn't Jan, or Merle, because they always walked in at the back door; family didn't need a 'Come in!'

Rosanna could see that her mother was flustered.

'I haven't emptied the bath water out yet,' she told Burl as he followed her into the kitchen.

'Came at the right time then, didn't I? Let me do it. Where do you tip it?'

'Down the drain outside. I usually bale it pail by pail . . .'

He put down his bag, then carried the tin tub by the handles, towards the back door.

'Open it for me, please, Wendy, then I won't slop over the sides.'

Wendy followed him. 'I'll show you where the soakaway is.' She closed the door behind her. 'Don't want to let the cold air in.'

'Chockit,' Russ said, pointing at the bag.

'You never know,' Rosanna told him. 'Want me to read from *Sunny Stories* tonight?' Reading to Russ was a good excuse to read from a magazine she was supposed to have outgrown. Bekka had scoffed when she innocently told her that Enid Blyton was one of her favourite authors. She'd wanted to protest: 'but that's how I learnt to read, because I felt I knew the children in the stories.'

She'd turned several pages before she wondered why Mum and

Burl were taking so long over emptying the bath. She couldn't hear them talking, either.

'Mum!' she called out anxiously.

They came in immediately.

'What's the matter?' Wendy asked.

'Oh nothing, I just wondered where you were.'

'Chockit,' Russ said hopefully again, in his gruff voice.

Burl opened the bag. 'Here. Know what this is, Rosy?'

'A guitar?' But she knew it wasn't the right shape.

'A banjo. Permission for an after-bath entertainment?' he asked Wendy.

She was folding the damp towels and hanging them on the clothes'-horse.

'Go on, then.' She actually sounded a bit short. 'I've got to get on,' she added.

'Come on, Wendy, join in.'

'What with?' But she sat down beside him on one of the kitchen chairs.

'O Rosanna, don't you cry for me,' he strummed and sang.

She knew better than that. 'It's not Rosanna, Burl, its Susannah!'

He wasn't deterred. '. . . with a banjo on my knee . . . you sing, too.'

> Oh give me a home where the buffalo roam,
> Where the deer and the antelope play,
> Where nothing is heard but the song of a bird,
> And the skies are not cloudy all day.
> Home, home on the range –
> Where the deer and the antelope play.
> Oh, give me a land where the bright diamond sand
> Goes leisurely down to the stream,
> And the graceful white swan goes gliding along,
> Like a maid in a heavenly dream.

Then Rosanna said: 'It's a bit like the fens, isn't it, Mum?'

'Just a bit,' Wendy agreed. She cleared her throat.

'Why are you crying?' Rosanna asked.

'Because – well, that seems like another world . . . Off to bed, yes, I mean it this time! Say goodnight to Burl, and thank you for the chocolate, and for singing to us, eh? You've got a nice voice,' she added, to him.

'Thank you. Glad you enjoyed it. Goodnight, kids.'

*

Rosanna couldn't get off to sleep. She crept out, sat on the top stair. Burl hadn't left yet. She was wondering if mum would be cross if she went downstairs and asked for a glass of milk, when she heard voices.

'The hospital want to try a new shock treatment, they want my permission.'

'They believe it'll work, do they?'

'They seem very hopeful.'

'Then you should say OK, honey.'

'If it works, then he'll be coming home . . .'

Rosanna felt a rush of excitement. Dad, here with them at long last!

The conversation appeared to be over. Burl must be going. Rosanna made her mind up. She'd go down and Mum must be so pleased about Dad, that surely she wouldn't be cross? Though if she woke Russ, Mum might not be so pleased after all, and would send her back to bed with a flea in her ear.

The living-room door was not closed to, so that mum could hear if Russ cried.

She peered round the door. At first she thought there was no one there. The settee had been pushed nearer the fire, and the high back was all she could see.

Then she realized that they *were* there, because of the throaty whisper: 'Rosy might hear . . .' and the soft, urgent response: '*Please*, honey . . .' There were sounds and little sighs she couldn't comprehend, but she knew instinctively that she mustn't alert them to her presence.

Back in bed, under the covers, she was still trembling. What she had overheard downstairs was to do with things that Merle hinted at. *You're too young to understand.*

Janet came out with it bluntly when they were walking across the field to work a few days later. The ridges were rimed with frost. Winter was almost here.

'What are you going to do about it, Wendy? Baz is having his treatment tomorrow, isn't he? He could be home within a month.'

Wendy didn't prevaricate. Jan knew her too well.

'I told him, I can't let Baz down, not after all he's been through.'

'Don't you consider you *have* let him down already, then?'

'Jan, I still love my husband. I—'

'Are you sure? You've changed, Wendy . . .'

'I've grown up at last. I'm not your little sister any more. Jan, I couldn't help myself. Oh, I know how good *you* are, how faithful to Jim – that you would never – but, Burl and me, I can't explain it, and – why should I?' She caught at her sister's arm. They were approaching the farm gates. 'I always felt it was like *that* for you and Jim – I envied you that. Burl'll do the decent thing: he'll stay away when the time comes. Until then, please don't judge us too badly . . .'

Janet looked at her. 'Wendy, I'm sorry, dearie, I really am. I've always been so lucky in that respect, as you've just reminded me. When Jim comes home, and that will be very soon now, there won't be any secrets between *us*.'

'Mum!' Rosanna said excitedly, one afternoon in the big kitchen. 'The school is going to put on a Christmas show, here, for the mothers and babies. The little ones are doing the Nativity, and, anyone who can play an instrument or sing will be welcome to join us. Could Burl bring his banjo?' She put to the back of her mind any unsettling thoughts. 'Will Dad – be back by then?'

Her mother shook her head. 'New Year, the doctors say.'

Bekka put in: 'Ket plays the piano by ear; Dad says she thumps too much, but she says it encourages people to sing to drown it. And, at my last school, my teacher said I was bound to be an actress, even though Mum says, no fear!'

'Russ will love all this,' Wendy said. 'He can't have enough music.'

Wendy begged a little treacle and white vinegar from the store cupboard. She didn't say what it was for, but Mrs Peck said of course she could have it. She gave her a keen look though.

'You're not looking so well, this morning, Wendy.'

'Just a bit off colour, that's all. Something disagreed with me.'

'How's Basil?'

'He's improving, every time I see him.'

'That's good. I must say it's very kind of Burl to meet you from the station as he does. I wouldn't like you walking that lonely road these dark nights.'

'He may not be able to do it much longer.'

'Action about to escalate?'

'I believe so. Thanks for this.' Wendy put the jar and bottle in her bag.

Wendy mixed the potion: six tablespoons of best treacle with half that amount of the vinegar, labelling it: CURE FOR SICKNESS. *1 Tablespoon in a tumbler of cold water, twice a day.* It had to be worth a try. She hadn't told Burl of her suspicions, but she'd have to confide in Janet, after Jim was home on leave.

Chapter Twelve

Jim came home with what he cheerfully called his swag-bag swung over one shoulder. 'Don't get too excited,' he told them, 'most of it's dirty washing!' He looked very smart in his best uniform, all shiny buttons and braided cap.

He was almost bowled over by Merle, rushing headlong down the path in order to be the first to welcome him home. He gave a rueful wave to Janet over his daughter's head. Then he called hello to Wendy, Rosanna and Russ, over the hedge.

'See you later!' they cho, and trooped back indoors.

Janet gave Grandma Birdie an encouraging nudge.

'Your turn, Grandma . . .'

Grandma looked her son up and down and said: 'I do believe you've grown, boy.'

Amid the laughter, Jim belatedly came up to Janet and said softly: 'You're as beautiful as ever, Jan,' and she knew her turn would come later.

There was a nip of rum for Grandma Birdie's tea from a bottle for her exclusive use; a pretty mirror, brush and comb set, backed with blue enamel, for Merle, and crystallized fruits for Janet which she generously offered round.

'You've lost a bit of weight, Jan,' he said, when he caught up with her in the kitchen, making tinned salmon sandwiches. His embrace nearly caused her to drop the plate.

'Careful!' She pretended to scold. 'Points for salmon don't grow on trees . . . D'you mind?'

'Mind what? Not chasing you upstairs right now?' he teased.

'Jim! I meant d'you mind me being thinner?'

'No: you still go in and out very nicely . . .' She had made her new jumper from wool donated to the mothers, who didn't knit, and the babies, who couldn't, in return for knitting for them. She put the plate down, turned to give him a real hug.

'Oh, you! But I'm warning you, I've got muscles these days!'

'Nice home you've made here, I wish I could stay for ever, not just for a week, but I'll be on patrol then in the Irish sea, so you needn't worry so much . . .'

'Grandma's muttering up at the table,' Merle said from the doorway, 'and I just had a sip of her tea and it's *horrible!*'

Janet brushed her hair, then rubbed glycerine and rosewater into her hands. They were rough to the touch, she thought ruefully. No silk nightie for *her*, but serviceable pyjamas, for as she said to Jim, sitting up in bed: 'It's cold in these here parts.' Anyway, buttons were soon undone. She blushed at herself.

'Mind if I read for a while, catch up on the local news?' he asked casually.

He's feeling unsure, she thought. It's been a year since we were together.

' 'Course not,' she said. She closed her eyes.

'Not going to sleep yet, are you?' He sounded anxious.

' 'Course not,' she repeated. Her thoughts were best kept to herself, for a bit. They were ones Jim might well not share. At thirty-nine, it could be her last chance to have another baby. Even if she became pregnant, which she acknowledged to herself was unlikely, recalling all the disappointments in the past, what would happen to their 'nice home' if she was unable to work on the farm?

She was actually drifting off when Jim turned the wick low in the bedside lamp. She waited for him to cuddle her close. Instead, she saw the flare of a match as Jim lit a cigarette. He had hardly smoked in the pumping-station days. His fingers were stained with nicotine now.

'Jan,' he began, 'there's something I've got to tell you.'

She was instantly alert. 'Yes, Jim?'

'I – I've let you down.'

'I don't understand, how could you?'

'How could I? I don't know – we were stuck so long in port for the ship's refitting after we'd made it back, goodness knows how, for we were battling with fires all over, after we'd been hit – and the chaps persuaded me to go out on the town, and I got talking to a young woman, who'd lost her husband at sea and – I'm *so* ashamed, Jan, I really am . . .' The cigarette wavered in his trembling hand. He stubbed it out in the saucer of his cocoa cup. 'Do I – do you need to know the rest? If it's any consolation, I can't remember any of it – just that I woke up—'

She pressed her hand tightly to his mouth.

'Shut up!' she said uncharacteristically. 'Shut up! I don't want to know!'

They still lay close, but rigidly apart. Her dream was dust and ashes.

'Can you forgive me?' he whispered at last.

'I don't know.' She turned away from him. 'I want to go to sleep now,' she said. They both knew that there would be little sleep for either of them that night.

In fact, she did succumb at last, exhausted, at the time she usually rose in the morning. Waking with a start, she put out her hand and there was the empty space, but this time hollowed out and still faintly warm.

The smell of cooking wafted upstairs, and she could hear voices. She forced herself to wash and dress, went downstairs. Jim was at the stove.

He turned and smiled at her; she could recognize the pleading in his eyes.

'Here you are at last, then, Jan. Breakfast is just about to be served!'

She looked at the heap of sausages on the top plate, warming on the side. Anger bubbled up inside her, spilled over.

'Why didn't you ask?' she raged. 'Those were for dinner! Wendy and the children are coming over.'

'*Mum!*' Merle was astounded. She'd never seen her mother like this before.

'I'm sorry,' Jim said miserably.

'No, you're not! Well, I don't want any, I've got to get off to work.'

'But I thought you were taking the week off, you said—'

'I've changed my mind.' She poured herself a strong cup of tea, aware of the shocked silence. She sat, hunched, at the table, her back to her family. Then she felt a grip on her shoulder.

'That's not the way to greet a hero, young Jan,' Grandma Birdie reproved her.

'Hero! You don't know . . .' Sudden, hot tears coursed down her cheeks, but she wouldn't turn and betray herself.

'Didn't he tell you, Mum?' Merle's voice was strident. 'Dad's getting a medal, for bravery under fire at sea – he *is* a hero. I'm going to tell them at assembly. Dad, can I have my breakfast now, or I'll be late for school?'

'I'm sorry, I didn't know,' she said. Grandma wiped her eyes with the corner of her apron.

When Grandma Birdie was upstairs, supposedly making her bed, and Merle had cycled off to school, Janet washed up the greasy plates and suddenly recalled it was her turn to milk Mrs Miniver. She and Jim hadn't exchanged another word.

He said at last: 'Are you really going to work?' as she put on her coat.

'No, they've got two Italian prisoners of war starting today, Susie'll be busy with them, but I have to milk the goat . . .' They were talking at least.

'Why the hat?' She'd bundled her hair up under it.

'So I don't mess my hair up, I washed it specially . . .' She was crying again.

He drew her, unresisting into the circle of his arms.

'Oh, Jim, why did you have to tell me?' she sobbed.

'We've always been truthful with each other.'

'Some things are best not said,' she said sadly.

'I know that now. D'you want me to go?'

'Go? Where?' she demanded.

'I don't know . . . I love you, Jan.'

'You told me enough times, in your letters . . .'

'But I'm *saying* it now, aren't I?'

'Come and help me with Min, and maybe, but I can't promise, we'll talk things through later.'

Rosanna had a secret letter to post. She'd taken a stamp from her mother's purse, but hadn't touched the coins. She'd never do that. Burl hadn't been over lately, and she wanted to ask him to play the banjo at the Christmas show, and help her to practise with the puppets. If only Derry was living near and could show her how to manipulate them. She walked to school by herself now, leaving the house after Mum and Russ. The post office was at the corner.

She saw Aunt Jan and Uncle Jim in the yard with the bucket at the ready and Mrs Miniver nosing at her feed. Poor thing, they'd kept her waiting this morning to be relieved.

Aunt Jan said: 'Better get going, Rosy, you don't want to be late.' Aunt Jan didn't look herself this morning, but nor had Mum. She hadn't got over her stomach upset; she'd rushed to the privy this morning, still in her nightie.

Rosanna had added a PS to her note:

Mum is taking me with her next Saturday to see Dad! I can't wait! Hope you can meet us from the train? Lots of love, Rosy XXX

Relief, followed by fear, was Wendy's reaction to the pain which doubled her up. She was cleaning the bedroom nearest the bathroom in the farmhouse, for they didn't need her over the way, when she was stricken.

She knew immediately what was happening. She crawled on her hands and knees to the bathroom door. Unfortunately, it was closed, and she couldn't stand up for the pain, to turn the handle. She tried to cry out, but she wasn't sure if Mrs Peck was still outside talking to the new workers.

Another agonizing wave gripped her, then she blacked out.

She came to, lying on Mrs Peck's bed, on top of the eiderdown, swathed round in towels, and her employer's hand steadying her head, while she tried to take brandy from a tooth-glass, despite her chattering teeth.

'Shock, my dear,' Mrs Peck said soothingly. 'Vera heard you call out, and came rushing up to see – she shouted to me from the window to ring the doctor. She's got Russ, so don't worry.' She paused delicately. 'We thought at first that you'd had an accident, but why didn't you tell me you were pregnant, Wendy?'

'I wasn't . . . sure,' Wendy managed, as the alcohol seared her throat.

'An early miscarriage, ah, I'll relay that to the doctor. You haven't – I'm so sorry my dear, but better to confide in me perhaps, and you can be sure I won't be judgemental – done anything to bring this on, have you?'

Wendy was patently shocked.

'Oh, no, Mrs Peck. I couldn't!'

'I'll ensure you're not asked that again. Ah, that must be the doctor's car . . .'

The Pecks insisted to Janet that they would keep Wendy with them for a few days.

'Doctor says she'll need boosting with iron tablets, but she's not in need of hospital treatment, thank goodness. You enjoy yourself with your husband home, and don't worry about Wendy. We can have Russ here, too, if you like.'

'It's very kind of you, but Jim's very good with him, he can stay with us. Grandma Birdie's his best friend, after all! And Rosy will be no trouble; Merle could sleep in with her, that will solve that. Thank you, Mrs Peck, for everything.'

Mrs Peck hesitated. They were by themselves in the farm kitchen.

'You know what the trouble was, I imagine, Janet? Any idea . . . who was responsible?'

'I can guess, but she hadn't told me anything.'

'I'm sure she would have done so, soon; you are very close.' Mrs Peck sighed. 'I do wish Susie could have had a sister.'

'I think that, about Merle.'

'Do you? Well, it isn't too late, my dear, you're still a young woman.'

I don't feel young today, I feel, oh, old and sad, Janet thought. I don't despise Wendy for what happened to her, so why should I reject Jim, for being honest with me? Because it hurts, that's why, it *hurts*.

'I can doss down here on the settee, now the girls have gone next door, and Grandma is keeping an eye on young Russ,' Jim said diffidently.

She didn't look at him.

'No, that's not necessary, Jim. I'm going up, now . . .'

It was quite a while before he followed her, He slipped quietly into bed. She touched his arm.

'Jim . . .'

He dared to edge closer to her. 'Yes?' he whispered.

'Let's – let's pretend it never happened. I love you, Jim, you know I do.'

Both of them were aware that they couldn't pretend anything of the sort. But surely time, and love, would ease the pain?

Burl waited for the train, but when it stopped, it was obvious that Wendy and Rosy were not aboard. This was the last train. Had they stayed overnight near the hospital? Wendy always said she couldn't do that, because of the children at home. He decided to drive over to the cottage.

He found the cottages in darkness. Both families must have gone early to bed, he thought. By the light of his torch, he pencilled a message on a brown-paper package, placed it under the front porch. Then he drove away.

'Oh, look, Merle,' Rosanna exclaimed, in the morning. 'The postman's been already – I didn't hear him knock.'

'You didn't hear him, silly, because *he* didn't leave the parcel. See, someone's written something on the front – shall I read it?'

Rosanna snatched the bulky odd-shaped parcel away.

'No! It's addressed to me, see?

Rosanna. I'd like you to have this, because I don't have much time for playing the banjo right now. I guess you came back on an earlier train.

Enclosed is a little book to learn by – I used it myself. Love to you all,
Burl.

'We'd better go and wake Mum and Dad,' Merle said, 'And tell them we had an unexpected visitor in the middle of the night.'

'Now you're being silly! We got sent to bed far too early, it was prob'ly only about nine o'clock.' Rosanna felt guilty that she hadn't let Burl know they wouldn't be on the train after all.

One night of love, Janet thought, while she and Merle waved frantically to Jim, who was leaning perilously from the open window of the carriage, before the billowing smoke obscured their view. That's all we managed, before Wendy's misfortune took precedence. But in a way it eased the strain; we didn't have to pretend that we were back to normal, because there was Russ to look after, and Wendy to visit and reassure all was well in her absence. She hasn't told me yet, and I somehow don't think she will, any more than I can confide about Jim and me. . . . But we know each other so well, we can comfort and sustain each other, without words.

Then she was aware that she was crying, and people were looking, and Merle was plucking anxiously at her sleeve and asking: 'Are you all right, Mum?'

And she heard herself saying: 'It's all been too much, Merle too much . . .' But she didn't know then that there was more to come.

The letter, despite the incomplete address, was delivered by the post-woman, with:

'I believe this might be for you – see, it says 'Mrs Bird,' then, 'The cottages, The Common, near King's Lynn' – in't no more like this near Lynn, is there?'

Janet had a funny feeling about that buff envelope. She waited until she was half-way across the field on her way to work before she stopped and opened it. She stood there, with the wind whipping, almost bowling her over, trying to prevent the two sheets of cheap, lined paper being torn from her grasp.

Dear Mrs Bird,
I am writing this, hoping it will reach you. Jim did not tell me exactly where you lived. Why should he, because he will want to forget what happened. But it's not as easy as that, I wish it was. He seems to be a decent sort. He said he would tell you, and I believed him.

In a strange way, I feel I know you, and can trust you, because he talked about you so much that short time we were together. You see, I need money, Mrs Bird, whatever I decide to do. I lost my Mum in the bombing. and there is nobody else I can ask. Please send what you can by return, because I will be moving on shortly, so you won't need to worry about me again. I don't want him worried about this.

Yours regretfully, N. Wallis.

Numb, from the cold and the words she had just read, Janet put the letter back in her pocket. Money! Jim had given her twenty pounds which he had saved, 'in case of an emergency'. Wasn't this just that – if it was true? It seemed to her it was, although she had no proof. She would buy a postal order at lunch-time.

Whatever I decide to do. . . . Those words would haunt her always.

Chapter Thirteen

There were freezing weather and dark days before Christmas, but Rosanna, her face half-concealed by her scarf, dampened by her breath, old sea-boot socks with the toes doubled under, and fingerless mitts knitted by Aunt Jan, was conscientious regarding her White Leghorn hens. They emerged from clucking querulously for breakfast before she'd a chance to eat her own, unlikely to include an egg for, as Merle said: 'Think about it, Rosy. Could *you* concentrate on laying an egg this blooming weather?' She had to break the ice on the water most mornings, which is hard when you lack muscle power, she sighed as she swung the pickaxe.

Next, she unlatched the shed door to see to Mrs Miniver. She didn't enjoy warm milk on her cornflakes, but they'd drained the milk-jug dry, because Min, too, was apparently practising a 'go slow' routine.

'Keep your side of the hedge!' she warned the whining Topper.

Merle, who was supposed to share these daily duties, as Wendy was still taking things easy, so Janet had more to do, was naturally nowhere to be seen.

'You get all languid, I think that's the word, at her age, Rosy,' Aunt Jan apologized for her daughter when Rosanna tapped on their door earlier. 'You cry over nothing, you have great spurts of energy, but you can't get up in the mornings. You'll be the same, in a few years' time. We all go through it.'

Thank goodness her mother was home again. Aunt Jan hadn't said what was wrong with her, and Rosanna didn't like to ask, in case it was really bad. To her joy, Rosanna was reunited with her dad last Saturday at the hospital. Mum explained why they had missed two visits with: 'Women's problems, *you* know, Baz,' and Dad, who was almost back to his old self mentally, if not yet physically, patted her arm and said: 'Never mind, old girl; now, don't you do too much, will you?' Then Mum blubbed again and told him she couldn't wait to have him back, and Rosanna butted in, feeling left out, and said nor could she.

Burl hadn't called, but Aunt Jan took her to one side and said not to ask Mum about *that*, because Dad wanted them all to himself when he had his feet under the table once more, whatever that meant.

'Anyway,' she added, 'I think Burl came because he missed his own children, but now he has more important things to do. After all, the Yanks are over here to help us win the war.'

It was a shame, Rosanna thought, that Uncle Jim was back at sea, the week he was home had gone all too quickly. Merle confided that Aunt Jan had done a bit of crying herself after he left when she thought no one was looking.

'When I asked her if anything was wrong, she said, "It's this darn war, Merle, it's going on far too long . . ." But I reckon she's at a funny age.'

Funny age? Rosanna thought. Isn't that what Aunt Jan had hinted, about Merle? I just wish everything was as it used to be; hope I never get to a funny age.

Now there was the Christmas concert to look forward to; it seemed there would be more players than audience, but that didn't worry the girls. They met in Rosanna's room after school. There was the pervasive smell of paraffin from the Valor stove. Ket wouldn't let Bekka out after dark. Maybe that was just as well, Rosanna thought ruefully, it was too small a space for two strong characters, arguing about what was what, and herself in the middle of it.

'I'll do the puppets, I can project my voice, and I'll write a new script as Mum thought that bit about a wise child knowing its own father, is tactless.'

Merle decided: 'You can play the banjo, Rosy, but not hit any bum notes.'

'That's *rude*.' Rosanna was shocked.

'It's old English, so it can't be! You can dress up like George Formby.'

'My teeth don't stick out,' Rosanna objected, but she knew it was no use. When Merle made up her mind, that was that. There had been a showing of *Let George Do It* at the village hall recently, an exciting wartime drama/comedy with George being mistaken for an intelligence man. Naturally, he got to sing and play the ukelele, but Rosanna hadn't liked that film as much as the one when George rode in the Isle of Man TT race. Legend had it that he really did all the stunts on the motorbike himself, but Merle said:

'They speeded the film up, Rosy, everyone knows that.' All right, she thought, it's an illusion, but it's still exciting.

Now she told Rosanna: 'Oh, shush! You can sing *When I'm Cleaning Windows*, or *A Little Stick of Blackpool Rock* – though Dad said that was a *double entendre*,' She was proud of her accent. Rosanna was suitably impressed.

'What's that?'

'That it means something else as well, I think: as I was trying to say, if you sing his songs, everyone will know who you are supposed to be.'

'Well . . .' Rosanna decided it wasn't worth telling Merle that George Formby actually played a ukelele, different from the banjo Burl had bequeathed her. Fortunately, she'd be in disguise, or sort of, as she was playing a part. 'Merle, please take great care of the puppets, as Derry gave them to *me*.'

'I expect he meant us to share them.' Merle jiggled them up and down, before Rosanna protested. 'Blimey, moth-holes; their clothes are falling to pieces.'

'Merle,' Rosanna hesitated.

'What is it now? Blimey's like bum, it's allowed.'

'How is it the mothers can have babies, when they haven't got husbands?'

'Oh, Rosy, you're daft, you are. You'll find out, one of these days!'

Janet was tinkering with the engine of the tractor when she became aware that the Italians were watching her. She straightened up quickly because hadn't Jim often told her ruefully that her rounded behind just asked for a sly pinch?

'I help you, Missis Bird?' the one called Gino asked. He had a long, smooth-skinned face with large, melancholy eyes. 'It won't start, yes?'

'Yes, I mean no . . .'

Both men were trusted to work with minimum supervision. On the back of their overalls was sewn a distinctive patch, to show they were prisoners of war.

She sensed that Gino admired her, but she was determined not to encourage him. Vera rather fancied the younger one, but Susie quietly advised her he had a wife and several *bambinos* at home in Italy. Not that Vera was missing out, now the GIs were here *en masse*. They seemed to be everywhere, in the uniforms so superior to British battle-dress. Some women resented their presence when their own men were fighting overseas, but on the whole the Yanks were popular, apart from the odd skirmishes in pubs and dance-halls, which were swiftly sorted out by the US military police, in their distinctive white helmets.

Apologies were always forthcoming, even when the Americans had not instigated the trouble, because they certainly gave as good as they got.

'You step aside, please,' Gino requested politely. Then he took the handle and cranked the engine. A few vigorous turns and the tractor throbbed into life. 'See, she need to warm up. Like all women,' he added to his friend in Italian.

'I tried that, but nothing happened,' Janet told him ruefully.

'So you, ah, tickle-ickle the wires?'

'Yes.' She couldn't help giggling, reminded of Russ and his excited cry of 'Ickle!' when they traced his palm, chanting 'Round and round the garden'.

Gino's smile widened. 'Now, you clear ditches – save us dig with spade?'

'Yes,' she said again. Then: 'You drove a tractor in Italy?'

'I work in my uncle's vineyard, we carry load on our back, but I learn to drive in Army. Bigger than this,' he added proudly. 'I drive tank.'

'Thank you for your help,' she said, as they drove off. Now I *have* encouraged them, she thought, but I mustn't let them become familiar. They're on the other side, after all. But the smile lingered on her lips.

Christmas Eve 1942

A large circle in the middle of the room was surrounded by easy-chairs for nursing mothers and Windsor chairs for adults. Children sat on a Persian rug at the front.

'It's a magic carpet,' Mrs Peck pretended, 'so mind you don't take off and send the ornaments flying.' The brigadier was acting as MC. Susie, a reluctant performer, offered to listen out for a seasonal surprise, hoping to be overlooked.

A gangway was left for the performers to come forward, following their introduction. Between times they grouped behind the piano, where Ket, resplendent in a gold-taffeta evening-gown worn years ago by their hostess at an officers' ball, played a medley of all the tunes to come.

The mothers and babies, outnumbered and wary of all this attention, whispered among themselves, and made the most of cuddling their offspring while they had the chance. Although asked, none had volunteered their baby for the Nativity, and Mrs Peck had had to hunt out a rubber doll, rather perished and with a poor complexion due to much scrubbing in the bath by the young Susie.

As tactfully requested, Ket made good use of the soft pedal as she played *Away in a Manger*. Joseph, as Josephs do, improved on his lines, prodding Mary with the words: 'Sit down, Mary,' adding in a loud whisper: 'You got to pretend it's a bale of straw . . .' The Inn Keeper bellowed his one line; 'No room at the Inn!' The little shepherds in their tea-towel head-coverings looked up to the star dangling from the beams, almost as cherubic as the golden-haired angels. The Wise Men were in fact girls, boys not trusted not to muck about and spoil it all.

Some serious singing was now required to bridge the comic acts to come. Gino's pleasing tenor voice saw the audience and performers hushed. He, too, stood beneath the guiding star, singing from the heart. The last quivering note, his expression said it all: Gino was transported home for that moment. It encapsulated the yearning for absent menfolk, for lost lovers, for an end to this awful war, which ironically, had brought them all much closer together.

The puppets popped up from behind the piano, where Merle sat on a stool, and argued on the piano top, while Ket provided the background effects.

Rosanna watched in trepidation, not for Merle, who was inspired and milking the laughs from the audience, but because she was on next. When one of the babies began to wail, Captain Codswallop chucked his own offspring in the air and cried: 'That's the way to make 'em chuckle!' And his wife put in quickly: 'But don't you lot try it!' to preclude the mothers following suit with the babies.

> It's Auntie Maggie's homemade remedy.
> Guaranteed never to fail,
> That's the stuff to do the trick,
> Sold at any chemist for one-and-a-kick.

sang Rosanna, rubbing her stomach as Merle had taught her, and worrying whether her trousers would hold up. She ended every chorus with strumming on the banjo, then: 'Turned out nice again, ain't it?' She didn't think she sounded anything like George, but to her embarrassment she heard thunderous applause.

'Encore!' Merle hissed, perched on top of the piano now. But Rosanna bowed, then fled to her mother and Russ who were sitting with Grandma Birdie.

'Zanna!' Russ greeted her, tweaking the strings of the banjo.

'Oi, boy,' Grandma Birdie reproved, yanking him back on her lap.

'You were jolly good, is that your lot, Rosy?' Wendy asked.

'I hope so . . .' she said fervently. 'It's Bekka next.'

'Miss Marie Lloyd, Queen of the Music Hall,' the brigadier declaimed.

> My Old Man said foller the van,
> And don't dilly dally on the way.

Bekka sang, wearing Grandma Birdie's old Northend shawl and a hat decorated with artificial cherries. She carried a cardboard cock linnet in a gilded cage and an empty bottle of Gordon's gin, provided by the brigadier and relabelled MOTHER'S RUIN. Bekka was ready to fulfil as many encores as demanded, having been well-tutored by Ket. However, she was not a natural like Merle, showing relief when the audience joined enthusiastically in the choruses.

It was rather an anticlimax when Susie appeared. She wore what looked like a flowing white nightgown and seemed statuesque this evening, rather than awkwardly tall. She sang *Silent Night*, simply and movingly in her high, true voice. Then, visibly relaxing, she led community singing, all the lovely old carols.

'Interval next,' Rosanna peered at the programme. 'Where's Aunt Jan?'

'Just about to bring on the refreshments, I should think,' Wendy told her.

'Bekka's dad is taking Gino back to camp now, but I hope the concert goes on to midnight,' Rosanna said, 'then we can walk home on Christmas morning.' I wish Burl was here, she thought, to see me play his banjo. I know Aunt Jan tried to explain it, but I wonder why he doesn't come round to see us any more.

'Ten o'clock finish, that's the aim,' her mother said firmly. 'Look, your brother's fallen in action already, and Grandma Birdie's nodding off.'

'I am not,' Grandma opened one eye. 'I ain't going to miss the grub!'

The Americans on the base were enjoying their own party, but it was they who'd provided the surprises: a basketful of delicious greasy, sugary ring doughnuts from the camp kitchen and assorted candies and oranges to share out. There were cards from those who were now old friends, including one which read: *Sorry can't be with you, Happy Christmas! Burl.*

When Jim had been home, he'd put an inner connecting door between the cottages. This was much in use tonight, when Wendy and Janet did the 'stocking' round, after they believed that the children, and

Grandma were asleep. Then they sat in Wendy's living-room toasting their toes by the embers, in the semi-darkness. Confidences were exchanged, except those that were too recent, raw, to bring into the open.

Wendy said suddenly: 'You know, I thought the day Russ was born was the lowest point of my life – but I'd never be without him now.'

'Of course you wouldn't, dearie. Wendy – are you, well, all right now?'

'Am I going to crack up like I did before, you mean, Jan? No, I'm not. You see, Baz was always the strong one, he spoiled me, you know that, protected me; now it's his turn, for the same treatment from me. He deserves that.'

'You're not going to see Burl again, are you?'

'No.'

'You won't – tell Baz about – you know, will you?'

'Oh, Jan, I'm too much of a coward for that. Anyway, what's the point? I – I got off lightly, didn't I?' She leaned against her sister's shoulder. 'I can't forget him, though, or what happened, and how I felt, and Jan – I don't want to . . .'

Janet's arm went round her. 'I've had my troubles lately, too.'

'I guessed that. You don't have to say. We're going to make this a happy Christmas, aren't we, for the children's sake?'

'Of course we are, we're lucky that they're still too young to realize about life's ups and downs; that you have to hang on in order to survive.'

Chapter Fourteen

New Year's Eve came, and Vera persuaded Susie to cycle with her into Lynn, for a supper dance and celebration put on by the Americans.

'You go, my dear, and enjoy yourself – we'll be with the mothers and babies, seeing the New Year in, with those who can keep awake; Wendy and Janet have promised to join us and maybe Grandma Birdie and Russ,' Mrs Peck told her.

'You do too much,' Susie said, seeing how weary she looked after making it a Christmas to remember for others as well as her own family.

'Your father will pour the drinks at midnight; apart from that we just plan to sit around and reminisce – isn't that what old folk are supposed to do?'

'You're not old!'

'Not as venerable as Grandma Birdie, certainly, but old enough to think it's time we had some grandchildren – that's maybe why I enjoy the babies so much.'

'I'm sorry I haven't lived up to expectations.' Susie smiled wryly.

'Oh Susie, you *have*! Go and put on your prettiest dancing dress . . .'

'Not hard to choose, I've only the one!'

The one and only dress, bunched out below her coat, made cycling somewhat hazardous. Along with muffled lamps and her skirts looped up round her middle, there was the distinct possibility of laddering her stockings on the bicycle chain.

It's a silly dress, and too flimsy for winter, she thought. Vera looks nicer in her red velvet; being petite, she can easily make a dress from a remnant, even though her stitching won't stand up to close scrutiny.

The hall was packed, the band warming up, and Vera's Yank, Chuck, seized her as soon as they emerged from the cloakroom, sweeping her on to the dance floor after a cheery 'Hi!' to Susie. Vera gave an apologetic little wave, and indicated a group of young men who were obviously looking for partners.

Susie made her way quickly to a corner seat close by the musicians. The music was loud but the beat of *In The Mood*, set her feet tapping. The dancers were jiving and furiously chewing gum. The staid dancing-lessons at school certainly hadn't prepared her for this, she thought. She'd always taken the man's part, being tall.

A familiar voice startled her. 'Didn't expect to see you here, Susie. Fancy a drink, and a dance later, if you can put up with two left feet?'

'Burl!' she exclaimed, showing her pleasure at meeting up with him again. 'I thought I was doomed to be a wallflower when Vera abandoned me. . . .'

'You haven't come with a partner, then?' he asked hopefully.

'No. Just Vera, for the bike-ride. What about you?'

'Nope. Not young or good-lookin' enough, I guess. Long or short?'

'Oh, cream soda, please, if they've got it.'

'Sure have. Back in a sec, as you Brits say.'

'I like your hair, it suits you,' he said a little later, as they sipped their drinks and shared a plate of sandwiches – oh that delicious soft, white American bread, she thought – I could wolf down a whole loaf of it without butter – so much more appetizing than the heavy, dry National loaf, which was their staple nowadays.

Vera had insisted on piling Susie's hair on top of her head with crinkly hair grips. It didn't feel too secure, and she'd shed a pin or two on the ride over. The stray tendrils actually softened the effect.

'It won't last, I suspect,' she said, looking speculatively at the last sandwich. 'It was Vera's idea, not mine.'

'Here, you have it.' he offered the sandwich. 'Plenty more to come. How are the folks on the farm?' he added casually.

She couldn't speak with her mouth full, so she nodded.

'Take that to mean OK?'

Susie swallowed, cleared her throat. 'You don't come over any more, Burl.'

'Guess you know why.'

She nodded again.

'I made a real fool of myself,' he said frankly. 'I just hope Wendy wasn't too hurt.'

'I – I'm not sure. She wouldn't confide in me, only Janet.' And my mother, she thought, a little jealous of Mrs Peck's interest in the family. Her mother had not enlightened her as to the cause of Wendy's sudden illness, but it did not take much guessing. It seemed obvious to her that Burl knew nothing of this, and that was the way Wendy wanted it, with

Basil due home in a few days' time.

'I should've stuck with my first attraction.'

'What d'you mean?'

'You, Susie, you. Is it too late to start over? I really admire you, see. We've got a lot in common – farming, horses – you like kids, I can tell, and we're both free and over twenty-one, as they say. Can't we be buddies, that's all I'm asking, because I sure can't handle another intense relationship. What d'you say?'

Susie didn't hesitate. 'Buddies, good pals. I'd really like that, Burl.'

Because they were of a height it was inevitable that they should dance cheek to cheek, which was apt, as that was the title of the music now playing. His hands loosely linked around her waist made it easy to slide her arms tentatively round his neck, like the other girls. There was little space for manoeuvering, it was only possible to sway back and forwards to the gentle, almost hypnotic beat.

There was almost a stampede when the band drummed in the New Year, with balloons released, streamers flying, and toasts proposed. When the embracing began, Burl looked at Susie and, emboldened by a couple of glasses of something stronger than cream soda, she closed her eyes in anticipation. Her hair had well and truly come down after all the dancing, and she thrilled at the intimacy implied as he twined his fingers in its mass. It was the brief brushing of lips which you expected from a buddy, she thought ruefully, but a perfect start to 1943.

Rosanna and Merle put up a WELCOME HOME banner for Baz, while they awaited the ambulance. Wendy had left first thing this morning, to accompany him home.

'I wish I didn't have to go back to school tomorrow,' Rosanna lamented.

'I don't suppose *they'll* mind that too much,' said forthright Merle. 'And I reckon Grandma Birdie will have Russ, so they can be on their own.'

'Maybe they don't want to.'

'Don't be silly, of course they do. Not that my mum and dad had much chance of that, what with Wendy being ill while *he* was home.'

'She couldn't help that! Anyway, Dad needs a lot of looking after still, and Mum says I've got to help all I can.' Rosanna blew up the final balloon.

'I suppose you've been banished from your mum's bed at last.' Merle always had to have the last word. 'You know why that is, don't you.'

Rosanna flushed. 'Oh, shut up!' She wasn't keen to share a room with Russ again. She was getting too big, so was Russ, but he was not aware of that.

'Naughty Rosy!'

'And don't call me Rosy, it's a baby's name.'

'You can't stop me. I've always called you that!'

They were saved from further argument, as the ambulance drew up outside.

'You're lucky, you are, ' was Merle's parting shot as Rosanna dashed to open the door. 'You've got your dad home for good, *mine*'s still in mortal danger.'

Baz went to bed soon after the children. He was white-faced and exhausted.

Wendy fastened the blackout.

'I'll try not to disturb you when I come up, eh?'

'Wendy.'

'Yes?' She smoothed the blankets, tucked him in much as she did Russ.

'May I have a couple of aspirin?'

'Have you got a headache?' She felt alarmed.

'Yes, but – not as bad as . . ' he paused, as if thinking what to say next. His memory was still patchy after the treatment he had undergone.

'As bad as before?' she guessed.

'That's it,' he said relieved. 'Tired, that's all – not quite sure . . '

'Where you are?'

He nodded slowly. She poured water, shook tablets from the bottle. He swallowed the pills.

'Thank you, Wendy. Please, can you stay with me?'

'Until you're asleep? Of course I will.'

'No, I want you to come to bed, now . . .'

Surely, she thought, he can't mean. . . ? But I can't upset him, not tonight.'

She slipped under the covers and lay beside him, her heart racing. Then she turned to kiss him goodnight.

'I love you, Baz; it's so good to have you home.'

There was no reply. He was already asleep. Gently, she placed her arm around him.

'I'll make it up to you,' she whispered. 'I really will.'

*

Janet and Vera were working with Gino today because his compatriot, Alberto, was confined to the camp with flu. They were sorting out the big barn. Wendy brought them a flask of hot soup, before she went home to see to Baz and Russ, spending time together under the watchful eye of Grandma Birdie.

They rinsed hands at the standpipe, then sat on the dwindling straw. It was Tuesday Market day; Susie had driven her parents to town. Time for tidying up on the farm.

'Just going to pop along to the shop,' Vera told them, brushing the crumbs from her green land-army jersey. 'Don't start 'til I get back, eh?'

She's going to ring her Chuck, Janet surmised. She winked at Vera.

'We're in no hurry, with the boss away. 'Bye.'

'Missis Bird – you have straw in your hair – see, here it is,' said Gino.

'Thank you,' Janet answered, 'So have you. Let me—'

She leaned forward, and before she knew it, she was looking into those expressive eyes, as he murmured softly:

'Yes?'

Janet jerked back immediately.

'Would you like an apple?'

'Don't take fright, Missis Bird, please. It's just – that I miss my woman.'

'Your wife? I didn't know you were married.'

'No. We had no time . . .' he shrugged expressively.

'Because of the war?' Why am I talking to him like this, she thought.

'*Si*. Soon, they say, it shall be ended for us. Then for sure, we go home.'

'And you will see *her* again, Gino, all being well.'

'But you see, I am *here*, it is hard. You are beautiful woman, Missis Bird.'

She laughed out loud, which made him smile uncertainly at first, then he joined in.

'No one ever told me that before.'

'But your man tell you . . .' he hesitated.

'He loves me? Naturally, he does. I'm well and truly spoken for, Gino.'

'What is that please?'

'It's – I think it's how you feel about your sweetheart. You wouldn't like to think that she had eyes for anyone else while you were away, would you?'

'You, and I, must be true?'

'*Now* you understand!' She stood up, looked round for the rake. I was almost tempted, she thought, to have a mild flirtation, but I know all too well what that can lead to. Feeling as Gino does, lonely, far from home, it would not take much encouragement from me. I've been thinking of myself, my own hurt, after Jim letting me down; I have to accept that he would give anything for it not to have taken place. And Wendy, poor girl, she lives with her guilt, too.

'Back to work, Gino. But if you want to talk about your girl, well, I'm listening, you know.'

Mrs Peck's hands were shaking as she buttoned her blouse. The doctor sat at his desk, seemingly absorbed in writing a prescription.

'Nothing will really help, will it,' she said deliberately.

He looked up. She saw the compassion in his expression. He was an elderly man, who had been semi-retired when war began, and the son who was born in his middle age, to his second wife, had been about to join the practice. Instead, with his father's blessing, he had become an army medic. Last year, the young doctor had been posted *missing, believed killed in action*. Somehow, the old man carried on. Hers was a familiar story: a lump, ignored, because she had no time to be ill.

'We all have a time to go,' she said slowly. 'It's just that I didn't think it was my time yet. I always thought, the brigadier being older than me, he would die first. I hoped Susie would marry one of these days, I don't want her to sacrifice any hopes she might have, to look after her father. How long do I have?'

'Difficult to say.' He blew his nose noisily. 'But, perhaps as long as a year . . . I'm so sorry, Mrs Peck. You will tell your family? You will need their support.'

'I will tell them when I feel ready to do so. Not yet.'

'Don't leave it too long,' he said, holding out the paper to her. 'These pills will ease the pain, don't be afraid to ask when you require something stronger.'

Susie was waiting anxiously outside. She couldn't recall the last time her mother had attended the surgery. Like most families, they had their own remedies for small ills, handed down. Her father was ill at times with recurring malaria, contracted when he was serving overseas. But her mother was rarely sick.

'Indigestion,' Mrs Peck said now, patting her chest. 'Slow down, I'm told, or I may get an ulcer, and as you know, I'm not a great lover of milk-sops.'

'So slow down you will, if I have anything to do with it,' Susie told her firmly. 'The brigadier's sloped off to the pub. Fancy joining him for a quick one?'

'I'd prefer coffee, my dear, and maybe one of those bread buns, with that synthetic cream that tastes of nothing in particular, but which fills the gap nicely.'

Who will fill the gap for me? Dear God, let me last a while yet.

Chapter Fifteen

Towards the end of 1943, things began to accelerate. Earlier that year the Russians had triumphed at Stalingrad, and in July there were the Allied landings in Sicily. On the fourth anniversary of the war, 3 September, Allied forces swept across mainland Italy, and the Italians surrendered five days later. Fierce fighting continued between the Axis and the Allies; the Germans captured Rome. Italy was still a war zone, so Gino and his compatriots would not yet be going home.

They were not the only ones who were homesick. Ket returned to London with Bekka when her husband was posted back. They were ignorant of the ominous menace to come in mid-1944, the flying bombs, tested and stockpiled by the Germans. The folk in and around Lynn grew attuned to the powerful roar of the great British and American bombers leaving base each night. The days of 'Got any gum, chum?' were receding fast.

The families in the cottages, and the staff at the mother-and-baby home became aware that kindly Mrs Peck was fighting a losing battle of her own. However, she saw a final Christmas, at which Susie and Burl, who'd conducted a quiet courtship, announced their engagement.

On the same day in January, 1944, the Allies landed in Anzio in the leg of Italy, and a historic battle ensued, Susie was wakened at dawn by her father.

Later, she boiled eggs and burnt, then scraped toast, for herself, Vera and her father. They toyed with theirs, while Vera, not knowing what to say, speedily finished her breakfast, and went off to the early chores, assuring them she could manage until Janet arrived.

'Would you like me to break the news, Susie?' Vera asked. She had news of her own, but this was not the right moment.

Something big was brewing, they all knew that. The Allied forces were grouping for the next attack, the invasion of Europe, which this time would surely mean freedom for the countries involved. But first, Vera and Chuck would wed, because Vera was pregnant, which to them was a cause for rejoicing, not recriminations. It also meant that she would shortly have to give up the heavy work when she was most needed, with the Italian labour no longer guaranteed.

'Please, if you wouldn't mind, though I'll speak to Wendy and Janet later, of course,' Susie said now. Vera closed the door quietly behind her.

Susie looked at the brigadier, sitting there, his egg untapped. 'It will all have to go,' he said. 'I can't carry on as we'd planned, not without her – or you.'

'But, Dad, you won't be on your own. You and I—'

'You'll go to America after the war's over.'

'How can I?'

'My dear, it's what your mother wished. I won't have to lose you yet, will I?'

Susie suspected Vera's secret, but kept it to herself. Sometimes she wondered, and worried, about how Wendy felt about herself and Burl, and whether he was still infatuated with Wendy. What would be his reaction if he discovered what had happened? They hadn't yet made love; she believed he respected her for holding back, because of her mother's illness. Anyway, she was her father's daughter; it was expected of her to behave with propriety. She accepted that Burl did not feel as strongly for her as she did for him, as she did, the fact that he could be drafted elsewhere at any moment. They could be parted for months. She'd shared her dreams with her mother of life in a new country, with a ready-made family, and the hope of children of her own.

At this moment, she longed to have the comfort of his arms around her; it was hard not to weep, but she told herself she must be brave for the brigadier. January was such a bleak month for a funeral, no flowers, and the earth, as Christina Rossetti lamented, as hard as iron.

They all missed dear Mrs Peck. Russ looked for her, when he was at the farm. They couldn't make him understand. And Rosanna also missed Bekka, but she still had Merle. Aunt Jan worked full-time nowadays, because Vera had got married and proudly carried all before her as Aunt Jan joked. Vera still lived at the farm, and helped Wendy with the housework. She was waiting for the day when she would travel to America as a GI bride. Susie too, Rosanna supposed.

Less often these days, Rosanna observed Burl's Jeep drawing up outside the farm. If she was seeing to the animals there, and he spotted her, he would come over and have a brief friendly chat, and maybe ask if she would like some spearmint gum for herself and Merle. She didn't chew in front of her mother, and Dad didn't approve of gum, he was old-fashioned like that, but when she and Merle were on their own they popped the sugar-covered strips in their mouths. The sweetness didn't last, but they chewed so determinedly their jaws ached. Aunt Jan was more tolerant: she pretended not to see the gum stuck to the brass knobs on Merle's bedpost. When she peeled it off and rechewed it, Merle told Rosanna:

'It's disgusting, I know, Rosy, but you don't think of it, after a bit.'

She didn't tell her mother of these encounters; she knew without anything being said that the friendship between Wendy and Burl was in the past. When she moved into the room she shared with Russ, she climbed on a chair and put Burl's banjo and Derry's puppets on top of the cupboard in the alcove, knowing that if Russ saw them, he would want to play with them, and might break them, and they were too precious to her for that.

Having Dad home meant so much. Sometimes he was withdrawn, and depressed, but these episodes were, thankfully, becoming less frequent. He even talked about returning to his old job, but the doctors told him he must be patient.

All through the spring of 1944, Rosanna and Baz, with the beaming help of Russ, worked together whenever they could, in the garden. Wendy discovered some packets of seeds, tucked away in a box still unpacked after their move from Lynn, samples which Baz had showed to his customers in the spring of 1939.

'They won't all germinate,' Baz told his daughter, 'but it's worth a try.'

Later on, Rosanna enjoyed seeing Russ rubbing a fresh-pulled carrot on his trousers, and crunching it with delight. 'Not too many,' his mother advised, 'Grandma Birdie knew a girl who ate so many carrots she turned bright orange!'

'Then why isn't Grandma Birdie shrimp-coloured?'

'You're getting saucy, you are, just like Merle!'

'Sor-cy,' Russ repeated, dribbling carrot juice. He'd started school last September, just mornings, because he needed individual attention and his teacher had thirty other children in her class. Wendy said it was enough, as he tired easily. He was shorter than average, but heavily built, and the other little boys in the playground learned to swerve when he charged after the ball with a husky cry of 'I kick!' They indulged him, he was everyone's friend.

Rosanna recognized the fear in her mother's eyes when he had one of his limp, lethargic days, and once she heard Wendy repeat to Baz the words of the sister at the hospital: 'Make the most of him . . .'

Wendy was roped in to help with several new arrivals at the mother-and-baby home, supervising the bathing of the babies. As she demonstrated how to support the back of the head, with the tiny limbs moving almost in a swimming motion, she soaped them gently with her free hand then encouraged the novice mothers to rinse them clean, lift them clear of the water and wrap them in a soft towel.

'Never wash your baby's face in the bath,' she said solemnly. 'Clean it before you immerse them, with cotton wool dipped in boiled water, wipe eyes to the outer corners, and gently roll a twist of cotton wool to clean each nostril – mind you don't poke, the same with the ears.'

This took her back to her own early mothering days, and how Jan soothed her apprehension. She thought of the lost baby, tears pricking her eyes, but this memory must be banished.

Despite its having been a warm May day, once back home she decided to cook a special supper for her family. Norfolk spoon-dumplings, lighter than the suety sort, served with rich, thick gravy from that skirt of beef, so tender it wouldn't take too long to cook, but which she really should be saving for Sunday.

She broke two of Rosy's bantam eggs in a bowl, added a good pinch of rock salt, then alternately shook in flour and milk until she had a thick whipped batter. She dropped spoonfuls into fiercely boiling water, watched as the dumplings plumped and rose. Fifteen minutes later, after testing with a fork to ensure they were cooked through, the dumplings were drained and kept warm while she served up the stew.

'These are good,' Baz said appreciatively and beaming, she counted the dumplings she had reserved for pudding, to be dribbled over with a butter-and-demerara sauce, eked out with a dash of boiling water, and decided he could have an extra one. 'Should sleep well tonight,' he added, patting his full stomach.

She thought of those words ruefully, as she pinned her hair in snail curls that night. Sleep: that was all, these days, though Baz had been home for sixteen months now. She yawned; it had been a full day. Then she settled in bed beside him. I'm too weary to read tonight, she thought.

Then the unexpected happened. He reached out, pulled her close.

He had recently grown his moustache again, and she felt a sense of *déjà vu* as he kissed her.

'Wendy – is it all right for you?' He'd asked that discreetly in the old days.

She wasn't sure what to say; it had been so long, too long, after all. But what would it do to him if she rejected him?

'I'll be careful, just as I was after Russ was born, because I knew you were afraid that it might happen again . . .'

'And later on, I *wouldn't*. Oh Baz I was so unkind to you . . .'

'You couldn't help it, it was all the strain you'd been under. I understood.'

Gone Away, her letter was marked. Janet was unsurprised, for Mrs N. Wallis had said that was what she intended to do. Janet didn't know what made her write. *Are you all right?* had been the gist of it. What would she have done if there had been a reply, asking for help? Was there out there somewhere the little son she knew Jim had wanted, to carry on the Bird name, the naval tradition; or a tiny girl with a look of Merle? It was unlikely she would know now.

Merle was blossoming, she thought proudly. In her fourteenth year she had a definite bosom, rounded hips and long, slender legs that any dancer would covet. She was a beauty, their daughter. When this war was over, clever Merle must be given her chance. University – now wouldn't that be wonderful?

Janet tore the letter into small pieces, poked them through the bars of the stove. *I love Jim, that's all that matters. He'll be coming home soon.* Before then they had an unexpected visitor, but a very welcome one; Derry, in his brand-new naval uniform and cap, grinning from ear to ear, standing on the doorstep, waiting for the door to open. It was a Saturday afternoon, and only Merle was at home, supposedly doing her homework. The others, including Grandma Birdie, had gone over to the farm to see Vera's new baby boy. Everyone would be vying to hold the baby, which was likely to do something smelly in its nappy at any moment, or protest if you didn't hold it just right. No fear, Merle thought.

She stared, speechless for a moment. Then recognition dawned.

'*Derry!*' she shrieked, and flung herself at him.

'Merle?' he said in her ear, hugging her in return, as if he couldn't believe it. 'How old are you now?' he suddenly sounded disconcerted; his hands were against the bare skin of her back, because she was wearing just a halter-neck sun-top and shorts which really were too short for her these days. He put her gently from him. 'Aren't you going to ask me in? Where is everyone?'

She tossed her glossy black hair, her face glowing, as she looked at him.

'Oh, they'll be back soon – yes, come in. Oh, we've got so much to talk about, so much to catch up on, haven't we.'

How old is she? he wondered.. Far too young to have that effect on me. I'm almost nineteen, for heaven's sake. Then to his relief he heard voices. He glanced back and then he was surrounded and hugged and kissed by them all, even Baz, except for a small person who stood to one side and gazed at him soulfully.

'Rosy?' he said at last, waving a hand at her.

She nodded. She knew she couldn't compare with vibrant, growing-up-fast Merle. She was still a little girl to him, but to her, Derry was still her hero. He'd actually called in to say goodbye, before he joined his first ship.

Shortly afterwards, there was Operation Overlord, D-Day. The Allies were on the way to winning the war, but it would be a long haul, with much bloody fighting.

Ket and Bekka would return for a while to Norfolk, after enduring the terror of the flying bombs, followed by the more sophisticated V-2s and Rosanna and Bekka would resume their friendship as if they had never been apart.

A year later came Victory in Europe, followed by Victory over Japan, achieved by a great mushroom of fire and smoke from what was called the atomic bomb.

The farm was sold when the brigadier unexpectedly died, and Susie and Vera sailed, a few months after peace was declared, to America on a great ocean liner, to join their American husbands.

It was time for the family to split up again. Jan, Jim, Merle and Grandma Birdie went back to the fens; Wendy, Baz, Russ and Rosanna to Lynn, where Baz rejoined his old firm, in the office now, and Rosanna in her turn went to the high school, and learned that it was not as daunting as Merle always said it was.

And she still dreamed of the floating moon, and Derry, and of being in a boat with him again travelling along the river.

PART TWO

Chapter Sixteen

1950

In the summer during which Rosanna reached the age of sixteen, she became suddenly, sharply aware that she was a couple of inches taller than her mother and rather more curvaceous. It was during this summer that she left school, heading quickly towards the time when she would leave Lynn, only she wasn't aware of that. There was the long holiday ahead of her, and she'd been invited to the fens. Merle was back from her first year at Edinburgh University, eager, it seemed for her company.

Having passed her school certificate, Rosanna wished to be free of further education and, as she reminded her disappointed parents:

'I'm not a swot like Merle, you know that. I wouldn't want to go far from home like she has . . .' She would recall those words so many times in the following years of separation.

'Anyway,' Rosanna said now, 'Derry's going to be there, too, for three weeks – his father's bought him a new boat, and he moors her by the river.'

'Fancy him going to Cambridge when he left the navy. I thought he was going to make that his career,' Wendy said.

'He must be coming up for his final year at university,' Basil thought.

'There's plenty for you to do in Lynn, and your friends are always welcome here,' Wendy said. She could do with Rosy's help with Russ. They lived in a modern house now, and enjoyed a comfortable style of living, because Wendy worked during term time in Baz's office. They didn't miss the car, because Lynn was so convenient for everything. There was a lively social scene for the young – not that Wendy encouraged her daughter to participate, with coffee shops and milk bars;

dance-halls buzzing with jazz music and jiving; all, so some older Lynn residents sighed, a legacy from those darned Yanks. Now our boys were off to fight another war, along with their American counterparts, in Korea.

Rosanna tried to say that as part of their extended family Aunt Jan seemed like a second mother to her, and Merle, the sister she'd never had. She recalled their closeness, despite their childhood wrangling. We're both grown up now, she thought. I've got a good feeling that this'll be a summer to remember.

'Oh, well, if you must go . . .' Wendy capitulated. 'You'll need some new clothes, I suppose.' There was still little on offer in the shops, even though clothes' rationing had ended. Dior's 'New Look' was not always achieved.

'Just shorts, shirts and sandals, for messing about on the river . . .'

Rosanna was glad, however, when Wendy came up trumps with a pair of *Slimma* slacks in the summer sales. She wore them with a pink T-shirt in soft chenille, self-conscious because it clung to her figure. However, she was blissfully free of suspender-belt, stockings and lace-up school shoes; she wiggled her toes happily in new sandals, with bouncy crêpe soles, so much easier on the feet than the wooden soles they'd put up with for years.

'Brothel creepers,' was how Baz described the crêpe soles, because, should you want to, you could sneak up on someone unawares. Rosanna didn't dare laugh when her mother indignantly batted him on the head with a cork table-mat, with the cry:

'None of your army expressions here, thank you very much, Baz!'

'Oh good,' Derry greeted her, just as if it hadn't been six years since they last met, as she stepped down from the train. 'I arrived this morning myself. Merle wasn't even up – and I'd only been in the house ten minutes before I was informed that I'd volunteered to meet you. I'm relieved you're properly dressed, Rosy.'

She blushed furiously. What did he mean? *He* certainly wasn't as smart as he had been when she'd seen him last, in his uniform, going off to war. He wore creased drill trousers, and his blond hair was crew-cut. But, as Aunt Jan had predicted when he was a gangling lad, he had indeed 'filled out.'

He bent to kiss her flushed face.

'You look as if you've got a touch of the sun already.' He took hold of her case. 'What have you got in here – it weighs a ton! Hope it'll go on my carrier. Got your ticket at the ready? Follow me!'

My entire wardrobe, she thought wryly, and that doesn't amount to much. It's the banjo and the puppets I added when Mum wasn't around, for old times' sake. That was naïve: I don't suppose Derry goes for home entertainment now.

She was glad she was wearing slacks when she sat on the hard pillion of the Royal Enfield 125cc motorbike. It was nippy, rather than fast, with a *putt-putt, pop-pop* sound, but she clung on anyway, with arms tight round his waist, quickly learning to sway with the bike as they rounded corners until they eventually bumped along the track to the house. Because it was a hot day the wind blowing in her hair was exhilarating, but now she wondered what on earth she looked like.

Even as she dismounted, on rather wobbly legs, and put up a hand to smooth her hair, she found herself enveloped in a warm embrace, and dear Aunt Jan was crying:

'Oh, Rosy dear, how lovely to see you, it's been too long, and just look at you! You're not a little girl, any more.' Janet had scarcely changed in appearance, Rosanna was reassured to see, although her hair was streaked with grey. 'Call me Jan, why don't you, "Aunt" makes me feel old!'

'You're right, she's all grown up,' Derry said lightly, but he was looking beyond Rosanna to the open door of the house.

'Hi, Rosy!' Merle ran towards her, hugged her, then held her at arm's length. 'Gosh, you look *smashing!*' Then she turned to Derry. 'Good to see you, too.' she added quite casually, as he unfastened the straps round Rosanna's case.

Rosanna suddenly felt overdressed for the heat of the day. Merle wore white cotton pedal-pushers, a sleeveless top with ties accentuating the swell of her bosom, revealing a tanned midriff. She was shoeless, with toenails painted scarlet. She, too, had grown her hair, but wore hers in a ponytail.

'So do you . . .' she blurted out.

Lunch was laid out invitingly on the kitchen table: a crusty loaf, waxy unrationed Edam cheese, a green salad with chives, new potatoes cooked in flaky skins, jars of pickles and a still-steaming plum pie with a jug of thick yellow custard, the sort you had to coax out with a spoon and a vigorous shake.

Rosanna exclaimed with delight: 'Oh, everything's *just* the same!' as Janet produced the familiar serviette ring, with:

'Not too old for this, are you?'

Grandma Birdie looked frailer but she was still busy in her vague way. She slopped milk in the teacups, and smiled at Rosanna.

'How are you, Wendy?' she asked, and Rosanna smiled, back, aware that she looked like Wendy when her mother was her age.

Then Jim came in and told Rosanna he'd give her a kiss when he'd washed his hands or he'd get into trouble with Jan, and 'just look at *you*, Rosy.'

'In your jim-jams,' she finished, then blushed again. 'I was just . . .' She floundered.

'Remembering the night we escaped from bed and walked the plank, eh?' Merle supplied. 'Move up,' she added, squeezing between Rosanna and Derry.

Derry reached past Merle and patted Rosanna's hand.

'Nice to be together again, we three, isn't it?' But again, she saw that he was looking at Merle.

Derry and Jim went on the motorbike to the popular Three Pickerels to sit outside with their tankards of beer, overlooking the river, swatting at the gnats which swarmed in the evening, yarning and watching the passing boats.

At ten o'clock promptly Jan yawned and said she was off to bed. Grandma Birdie had disappeared upstairs around 7.30, but that didn't mean she would stay put all night.

'You girls get yourselves a late supper, catch up on the gossip, eh?' Jan said.

Merle was still miffed that Derry hadn't stayed with them. But she brightened up when they were on their own; she wound up the gramophone.

'Seen *The Third Man* yet at the flicks, Rosy?'

Rosanna shook her head.

'Well you must have heard that gorgeous zither music, they play it all the time on the wireless,' she said, humming along to it, as the haunting *Harry Lime* theme began.

'D'you think we could have a glass of nice cold milk?' Rosanna asked.

'I can think of something better than that . . .' Merle gestured her out of the way, and came out with a bottle of cider. 'Fancy a drop of this?'

'I – don't . . .'

'You don't know, because you've never tasted it, right? And you're usually in your bed at this late hour aren't you? But we're not letting Derry get off lightly – we'll wait up for him, and tease him a bit, eh?'

Rosanna didn't like the cider much, being used to Tizer once a week with Sunday dinner. She'd only just arrived here, she thought ruefully, and already Merle was suggesting mischief.

'I'll leave you young ones to it, then,' Jim told them. 'I'd better get to bed; some of us have got to work in the morning. 'Night.'

' 'Night,' they replied in unison.

'Come in the other room,' Merle said. 'Then we won't disturb anyone.' She placed their half-full glasses on a tray, together with the bottle and a glass for Derry. 'You can bring the gramophone, Derry. The records are in there.'

'Hey, I've had my fill,' he protested mildly. 'And don't you think Rosy's too young for this stuff?'

'I'm not!' Rosanna retorted, the drink making her bold.

They plonked themselves down on the sofa, then Merle sprang to her feet again as the gramophone wound down.

'What do you fancy now, you two?'

Derry put his arm casually around Rosanna.

'One sleepy little gal, Merle . . .'

'I'm not – you said . . .' Why did her voice sound strange, Rosanna wondered? She closed her eyes, wanting to prolong her closeness to him.

'I know, but you *are*, Rosy.' Her hair was half-obscuring her face; he stroked it back gently. 'Stick to lemonade in future, don't let Merle lead you astray.'

'She's like Wendy,' she heard Merle say after a while, as if from a distance. 'She'll fall in and out of love and get hurt, you'll see. Don't you know she's always had a crush on you? Don't encourage her. What about *In the Mood* – Glenn Miller? Susie, at the farm, passed on her records when she left for America and married Burl, who was over here in the USAF during the war. I shouldn't really tell you this, but before he and Susie got together, Wendy and Burl had a bit of a brief encounter, like in the film, you know. Baz was in hospital at the time, and I suppose she was lonely.'

'They had an affair, you mean? You must be mistaken.'

'Nope. Of course, Rosy here was fortunately too young to realize what was going on, but I know my mum was worried sick. Something stopped it, though, before it got too serious. Wendy made herself quite ill over it.'

'So you don't think – anything much, happened?' Derry sounded concerned.

'I didn't say that. Burl sometimes stayed late at Wendy's, after Rosy and Russ were safely tucked up . . .'

Rosanna couldn't stop an involuntary movement, a sudden shiver, but she kept her eyes tightly closed. She knew they must be looking at her, because of the sudden silence, and wondering if she had heard what was said.

'She's still sound. Want me to carry her upstairs?' Derry asked.

'No!' Merle said, rather quickly, as if she didn't approve of the idea. 'Lay her down on the sofa and let her sleep the cider off, then rouse yourself to dance with me. I'll take her to our room when I feel like calling it a day, myself.'

'I'm not sure it's a good idea, the dancing, you and me . . .'

'You think we'll make too much noise?'

'You're not wearing shoes, and I can soon slip mine off – no, it's not that . '

'You've suddenly realized I'm all woman, eh?' Merle asked daringly. 'Don't be silly, we're cousins, after all.'

'That's what makes me wary.'

'You feel it's incestuous, do you?'

'Certainly not. Cousins can marry these days.'

'Then what are you worried about?'

'I don't think your parents would approve, Merle. We've both had a drink or two, that's when inhibitions fly out of the window.'

She snatched at the gramophone needle.

'You've made me scratch the record now! I'm not a novice, you know, I've seized my chances at university . . .'

He gave Rosanna's arm a gentle shake.

'Come on, Rosy, time to go to bed.'

Once Merle had turned the light out and punched the pillow before settling down in the bed they were sharing, just as in the old days, Rosanna gave up any pretence of sleep. It wasn't the first time she'd been an unwilling party, she thought, to secret goings-on; if only she hadn't spied on her mother and Burl that night, then she wouldn't be at last aware of the true facts. Her father worshipped her mother, they had a good marriage, that was all that mattered, she finally decided.

'You awake now, Rosy?'

'Yes.'

'I'm glad you're here,' Merle whispered. She sounded as if she meant it.

Chapter Seventeen

The boat was not quite as Rosanna had imagined; she wasn't a brand-new racing-dinghy, her sail faced with colourful nylon, but she was barnacle-free and painted blue, because Derry had worked on her during odd weekends since spring. However, the wrinkles and warts of age were still visible on close inspection. The canvas sail was neatly patched and the name, she thought was disappointing: *Agnes Bell*, or *AB* as Derry referred to her. Well, whoever was *she*?

'Wife of the original owner,' Derry told them. 'Old *AB*'s travelled widely in her time, so sailing along to the Wash won't be too challenging for her, or for us. Dad pointed out that she cost more than when she was built, thirty years ago. She was in dry dock all during the war, but was looked after well and I like her, don't you?'

They set sail, one promising-to-be-sunny morning, three days after Rosanna's arrival. Ahead was the cathedral, floating serenely in the mist. Merle promptly bagged her position in the prow, as look-out. Derry was at the mast, being experienced. Rosanna, being small, was left with the narrow space in the stern.

Earlier, they had humped the bare necessities aboard. There were blankets, change of clothing, waterproofs and wellington boots, a two-girl tent, lamp, portable stove, Swan Vestas, first-aid box, coil of rope. A shovel, buckets, pole, buoyancy-aid, string-and-hook for catching supper, and a can of drinking-water. There were also three green-and-white Penguin paperbacks, from the crime series, loaned by Jim, with a mild reminder that they cost two-and-sixpence apiece; a small battery wireless, and Rosanna's banjo, in case they needed a bit of light entertainment. Most of the foregoing had been packed neatly into oilskin bags with drawstring tops, 'knocked-up', as she put it, by Janet on her trusty sewing-machine, so that they could be stowed in odd corners. Oh, and a tarpaulin to cover Derry at nights, for he had opted to sleep in the boat. The vital tide-table and map were rolled and stuffed into the back pocket of his shorts.

'We'll nip ashore and get grub along the way,' Derry said. 'But I haven't forgotten the iron rations, as your mum insisted, Merle – I don't know what's in this old Mackintosh's toffee tin, but you can bet it's something to eat, eh?'

'I hope so,' Merle called back. 'Breakfast was at some unearthly hour. Why do expeditions always begin at dawn? And as a poor university student I've only got five bob on me – how about you?'

'Not much more. I spent most of my allowance on *AB* I've got a small reserve for the odd packet of fags. I daren't ask Dad for another sub. Forgive the pun, but you and I are in the same boat, dear cousin.' They both looked at Rosanna speculatively, grinning.

'Dad gave me two pounds for the holiday, will that be enough?' It was meant to last me a month, she thought, but I can't say that. But there's the emergency fund Jan gave me just before we left, whispering that I should hide that in my banjo case and not let the others spend it in the pub, or take *me* in there, either.

'It'll have to be!' Derry said blithely. 'But mind you don't get the notes wet!'

'Pity poor old Topper's not still around, he'd have made it all perfect,' Merle said, flicking her hair so that it hung in a slick down her back. She leaned over to dabble her hands, ostensibly to see how cold the water was, so that she presented a provocative view of her rounded behind in cut-off trousers. 'Then we would *really* have been like *Three Men in a Boat*.'

The pose was not lost on Derry.

'One Man and Two Pretty Girls, one with a big bum, seems more appropriate,' he said lightly. 'Right, all ready for the off?'

Rosanna rooted through the first-aid box: a strip of plaster, pink headache-pills, a roll of narrow bandage, small scissors and a wad of cotton wool.

'No calamine, I'm afraid,' she reported to a sunburnt Merle, who'd stretched out for too long in the rays of the midday sun when they moored at lunchtime. Rosanna'd rolled down the sleeves of her blouse, covered her head with a scarf and sought shade under a scrubby tree on the bank, but her own face felt taut as there was always a breeze on the river which reddened the skin. Gnat-bites too, she thought ruefully, scratching; darn it, there was no TCP either.

'We'll stop at the next outpost,' Derry said, 'and buy stuff there.'

Merle covered herself with a blanket, despite the heat, rested her head on one of the softer oilskin bags, and closed her eyes again as they cast off.

'First mate's planning a mutiny, I reckon. *You*, OK?' Derry asked.

'OK,' Rosanna assured him, fiddling with the wireless controls. *Oh What A Beautiful Morning* crackled, then briefly revived, on a truly beautiful afternoon.

When they moored again, Merle flung off the blanket and said grumpily that she'd go to the general stores as she couldn't wait to anoint herself. Rosanna gave her half-a-crown, and loaned Merle her head scarf. She didn't expect, or get a thank you. Merle was in a Mood.

Derry and Rosanna sat on the grassy edge, dangling their feet in the water, watching a pair of swans sailing majestically past and dipping their beaks occasionally. Behind them was a flat field, with hedges full of red and yellow berries, the portent of a hard winter to come, and a barred gate. He brushed an insect from her hair, she waved off something about to sting his leg.

'Oh, is that scar from that awful scab that landed you in hospital that time?' she exclaimed.

'You've got a good memory! Yes – that's a legacy of the op I had – the infection went down to the bone. Don't look alarmed, Rosy, it doesn't hurt now! Dear Jan was more concerned than my own mother – Jan brought me grapes.'

'She's always looked after us all. But you were passed fit for the Navy.'

'Of course I was; and playing energetic sport at school long before that.'

'Why did you leave?'

'School?' he joked.

'No! The sea, I mean.'

'I had no choice. I see you don't know. I guess my parents kept it quiet. Still a bit of stigma attached, I suppose. Mum was horrified. Dad was more sympathetic, being a Bird. Foreign ports and all that – I contracted TB in forty-seven. Spent a year in a sanatorium, not something I'd recommend, but I was lucky, I got better, despite snow blowing in open windows and patients shivering with cold. I gained another scar then. They collapsed one lung, to rest it, which was excruciating – but they reinflated it in due course!'

'Will you show me?' She surprised herself with this request.

He unbuttoned his shirt slowly, revealing a deep cleft below the breastbone. She put out a tentative finger, touched it lightly. '*Oh . . .*' She exhaled.

'This sort of sailing, now, that's fine, plenty of fresh air to breathe in and out. But I was advised that the stress associated with being a naval officer was no longer for me; look for a career ashore they said. If I pass my finals I suppose I might end up as something very minor in the City. London, that is.'

'I'm so sorry,' she said earnestly. 'I know how much it meant to you, to follow in the family footsteps.'

He leaned towards her, kissed her cheek.

'Dear Rosy, it was a bitter blow at the time, but I wouldn't be here with you now, would I? I really wished you were my little sister, despite having to look out for you, all those years ago.'

'I expect you thought the same of Merle, too.'

'Maybe then, certainly not now. Look, what I said, keep it between you and me, eh? Oh, here she is, covered in blotches of pink and looking decidedly cross!'

Chops charred on the paraffin stove, small potatoes and large tomatoes boiled together, in their skins, bread rolls, all eaten with the fingers, which could be wiped on the grass, tasted good, even without the salt they'd forgotten to bring. The milk had gone off, so it was black tea. For dessert, pineapple chunks, the tin opened with Derry's Swiss knife, then passed round, to save washing dishes.

Derry put up their tent in the field, to one side of the gate. Then, as the evening drew in, they sat under the green canvas, with the front flap open, and the lamp hanging from a stout stick at a safe distance. Moths fluttered round the light like shadowy dancers. Rosanna shyly produced the banjo, began to strum.

'Pass me a fag,' Merle said to Derry. 'The smoke will keep these darned mosquitoes, or gnats away.' She inhaled without spluttering.

Home on the Range, Rosanna played, for old times' sake. She pictured Burl, and Wendy, all of them singing along together on bath-night in the cottage. She tried not to think of what Merle had divulged recently, but it was difficult. Had Wendy actually been in love with Burl for a while? She realized now that he must have had strong feelings for her mother. Was that what desire meant? That you couldn't help yourself, that you couldn't control your emotions?

'Been a good day, hasn't it?' Derry stood outside the tent, stretching his arms above his head, yawning. 'Well, fasten the flap, girls, and I'll see you in the morning. Got your torch? Then I'll take the lamp, oh, and the banjo; you haven't room for that. I promise not to play it, Rosy! Remember I'm only a hundred yards away, and I'll hear if you call.

Goodnight. I'll make the morning tea.'

'You'd better, you're the only one who can manage the stove,' Merle told him. ' 'Night, Derry.'

' 'Night,' Rosanna echoed. They weren't undressing, just rolling up in their blankets on their waterproofs, spread out as a groundsheet on the grass. Surprisingly, Rosanna was asleep within ten minutes, despite the hard ground.

Merle had scrounged another cigarette. She lay with her arms folded behind her head, smoking and thinking wryly that it hadn't been a such a good day for her. She'd grown out of roughing it, whereas Rosy was now in her element. She hadn't managed to put Derry off by unkindly revealing that young Rosy had a crush on him; the joke about her 'big bum' still rankled, even though she'd caught his admiring glances when he thought she wasn't aware. She hoped he hadn't taken in the fact that Rosy, too, had suddenly blossomed in a womanly sense.

She threw back the blanket; better dispose of the cigarette stub outside, she thought. She didn't need the torch, for the moon had risen. On a sudden impulse, she closed the tent flap, climbed over the gate, and walked quickly over the silvered grass to the boat.

It was definitely lower down than it had seemed when they'd merely stepped across earlier on. She realized they hadn't checked the tide table. The boat swayed, and Derry stirred on the decking, mumbling something in his sleep.

Merle moved carefully over him, insinuated herself under the tarpaulin and blanket, wriggling close to his body, her face pressed against his back. Surely he would wake up properly, she thought, with mounting excitement.

'Merle?' he said uncertainly, after a long moment. He struggled round, in the confined space, to look at her. 'What are you doing here?'

'What d'you think?'

'Trying to seduce me, I imagine . . .'

'Surely it should be the other way around? *You* about to take advantage of *me*?' she whispered.

'You're quite brazen, and I'm not going to do anything of the sort,' he protested, yet he didn't push her away.

Emboldened, she slid her arms round his neck, pressed her lips to his and began to kiss him passionately. His resistance was abandoned, his ardent response was all she had imagined it would be.

Abruptly, it was over before it had really begun. He turned away.

'No, Merle, *no* . . . Go back to the tent. Supposing Rosy wakes and wonders where you are?'

'Why?' she pleaded with him. '*Why*?'

'Because this holiday is for the three of us, not an excuse for you and me to indulge in lovemaking.'

'But, I thought . . .'

'You thought I wanted this, as much as you did.'

'Don't you?'

'I'm too old for you, Merle.'

'Only five and a half years!'

'But I've seen a lot more of life, and whatever you may claim, I'm the one with the experience. Your parents trust me; I'm not going to betray that.'

'I can't go back to the tent yet,' she said in a small voice. 'We forgot the tide, we're rapidly going down, I suppose we'll be grounded in a few hours . . .'

'Lie down,' he said, resigned. 'All right, you'll have to stay here until the boat bobs up again. You have this space, and I'll go down the other end out of temptation's way.'

'Derry?'

'Yes?' He was covering her with the blanket.

'I'm sorry.'

'So am I, believe me. Forget it, Merle; no harm done, eh?'

'Derry?'

'What now?'

'I haven't really got a – big bum, have I?'

'Of course not, you've got a super shape.'

'That's all right then,' she said.

'Is it?' she thought he said softly, as he retreated, but she couldn't be sure.

At first light, Rosanna looked down in disbelief at the boat. It must be twenty feet below her, she thought, scared. She couldn't get down that slippery cliff side, and Derry wouldn't be able to climb through all that mud and muck to her.

She found her voice at last: 'Derry! Merle's disappeared!' she shouted.

Then Merle was waving at her and laughing.

'It's all right, Rosy, stop panicking! I couldn't sleep, I came to chat to Derry, and I was marooned!'

Derry was now standing beside Merle, his arm casually around her shoulders.

'Sorry to give you such a fright. Go back to the tent and try to get some more kip – I can't even pass you up a cup of tea, eh? Don't worry, we're six or so feet up on what we were, and rising rapidly; we'll get you aboard as soon as we can.'

She rolled herself up in the blanket once more. She'd run out of the tent without sandals, and her feet were wet and cold. She took Merle's discarded blanket and draped it over her legs. Merle, she thought disconsolately, no doubt kept warm and cosy all night . . . Am I to be a – a *gooseberry* from now on?

Chapter Eighteen

There were some evocative names along the Great Ouse, enchanting places, like Queen Adelaide, Prick Willow and Brandon Creek, where the Little Ouse wandered away from its parent, Denver Mill to Downham Market, past Wimbotsham to Kings Lynn, where they planned to spend a few hours with Rosanna's family before reaching the Wash, and about-turning to sail back to the pumping-station.

In a quiet stretch of river, with clouded skies above and a billowing sail, with not a soul to be seen in the fields on either side, or another vessel in sight, they moored in a natural harbour for a while.

They were suffering from hunger pangs, so Derry cast the line, even as the first fat drops of rain splatted on their heads. He was already wearing his waterproof and advised the girls to follow suit, and to spread the tarpaulin, too.

'Well, if I'm going to get wet anyway,' Merle said, 'I might as well have a dip – we haven't had a proper wash in days. Coming, Rosy?'

Rosanna shook her head. She wasn't much of a swimmer, having inherited her mother's nervousness around water, also the river was deep.

'I'll boil the kettle,' she offered. 'You'll need a hot drink when you come out.'

'Be careful,' Derry advised Merle. 'Keep away from the reeds, and don't stay in too long; I imagine the water's pretty cold.'

'Don't look, I haven't got a swimsuit, so I'm having to improvise!' Merle warned him. 'Be ready with the towel, Rosy, when I give the signal on my return.'

'My attention is well and truly on the task in hand, I'm watching the float. But take heed of the current and don't go far from the boat.' Derry cautioned her.

Rosanna was startled and embarrassed to see Merle stripping off completely, then diving off the other side of the boat. It all happened in a flash, with a splash, as she cleaved through the water; there was the pale, undefined image of her bare limbs moving rhythmically, her long hair floating out around her head like strands of seaweed in dark greenish brown rippling water, ruffled with rain.

'You *are* looking now,' Rosanna accused Derry.

'Can't help it,' he said simply. Then he grinned. 'Come on, Rosy, don't be a prude, you know as well as I do, she's done this on purpose. I'm not going in after her – yet! But, being Merle, I expect her to shout help any moment now . . .'

'You won't dive in with all your clothes on, will you?' she asked anxiously. He could sink, she, thought.

'What for? She's a strong swimmer, so I'll just chuck her the rubber ring, and haul her in, if necessary. Oh boy, I've actually got a bite. Stand back, while I pull that aboard first, eh?'

There was a growl of thunder, then the heavens really opened as Derry landed his catch, moderately sized, but, he hoped enough for three. Rosanna shoved the bucket over to receive the somersaulting fish. As he unhooked it, she realized that Merle was no longer circling the boat, but was apparently travelling fast downriver.

'*Help!*' Merle yelled, as Derry had predicted. 'I'm being carried away – *Derry!*'

Then it was Derry, discarding mac, jersey and boots, jumping rather than diving into the river, with the tow rope hastily knotted around his waist, and the buoyancy aid round his neck, shouting to Rosanna to let out more rope when necessary, to heave like mad when he waved.

Merle was clinging desperately to a root snaking out from the bank, when he caught up with her. He slipped the ring over her head, told her to grip the rope round his waist, and swim with him.

'Don't worry, I won't let go of you,' he promised. He lifted one arm and waved frantically at Rosanna.

They lay gasping in the bottom of the boat, shivering uncontrollably, while Rosanna covered them with towels, then blankets and lastly the tarpaulin.

'I'll get the tent up on the bank, it's almost stopped raining, thank goodness, and then you can get inside where it's dry, and I'll make you a strong cup of tea to warm you up, and I'll pass in some dry clothes for you both . . .'

'And then I'll cook lunch,' Derry said through chattering teeth.

'Sorry,' Rosanna apologized. 'But I had to throw that poor fish back overboard – I thought it might pop off, if I left it any longer.' Then she realized what she'd said. 'Oh no, we *could* have eaten it then! Still, there's eggs, and tomatoes – I'll whip up an omelette, but you'd better cook it, Derry, the last one I made stuck to the pan.'

'My staple diet at university,' Derry assured her.

He and Merle made their way unsteadily to the tent and crawled inside.

'You dry yourself first,' Derry insisted, 'and get dressed, and I'll keep my eyes tight shut, I promise.'

'You must have seen all there is to see of me,' she said ruefully. 'I'm sorry to cause all this trouble, Derry – I admit I was trying to get your attention in the beginning, but then, the unexpected happened . . .'

'Like this?' he said, his hands on her bare shoulders, drawing her even closer to him, as they huddled together under the coverings.

'Better close *my* eyes, I think,' she murmured, as he kissed her. It was a dangerous moment, they both were aware of that.

They rolled apart swiftly as they heard Rosanna call:

'Decent yet?'

'Almost, give us another minute or two,' Derry called back.

Merle fastened her bra with chilled fingers, pulled on her warm jersey. She wormed her way into her trousers and socks, under cover of the blanket.

Derry was similarly occupied. They stood up awkwardly at the same time, face to face, bending under the slope of the canvas.

There was the warning squelch of waterlogged crêpe-rubber soles approaching. Rosanna, in the sandals which had proved a bad buy, approached with two enamel mugs of steaming tea in her hands.

'Merle, forget that happened.'

'Why should I! All right, I supposed I asked for it, in a way.'

'Yes, you did,' he said frankly. 'But I should have said last night that there are other reasons why . . ' he cleared his throat. 'I'm not sure you'll understand.'

Rosanna was there. 'It's all *steamy* in here!' she blurted out.

There was a moment's startled silence, then they all began to laugh. Derry took the mugs from her quickly and said.

'Thanks, you're a treasure you are, Rosanna Bloomfield!'

Wendy, Baz and Russ were there to meet them when they docked at Lynn. While Derry lowered the sail and secured the tarpaulin, Rosanna and Merle stepped ashore.

Russ endeavoured to loosen the grip of his parents' hands as they held him firmly between them. He spluttered with excitement.

'Zanna! Come with me! Let go!' he scolded Wendy and Baz.

Folk along the quay turned to look curiously, but turned away quickly when they saw who was making all the noise. They don't smile at him as they did when he was little, Rosanna realized, feeling awfully sad. He ought to be like Derry was at his age, tall, wiry and athletic, clever and independent; but he's short, tubby and he, well, he looks different. He's trusting like a child, which makes us feel protective and love him even more, even though sometimes he can be a bit of a handful. Mrs Peck said he was special, and I try to think of him like that, but he'll always be my kid brother and I know Mum and Dad expect me to share the responsibility for him. Is it wrong for me to feel I'm not ready for that yet?

'He's really missed you, Rosy,' her mother said hopefully. 'Can't you stay, now you're home?'

It isn't fair, Rosanna thought, and Mum knows it, but she expects me to give in. She looked appealingly at her father.

'Now, Wendy, her holiday's just begun. We can manage, can't we?' Baz asked, looking at his daughter's glowing face and lightly tanned limbs.

'I'll have to, you mean,' Wendy replied.

She's feeling bitter about things nowadays, poor Mum. She's suddenly realized I'm grown up and one day I won't be around any more and she'll still have a child to look after, and worry about.

I ought to say OK, I don't mind, but I do.

Rosanna held her hand out to Russ. 'Let's walk along the quay, eh?'

'Want to take your banjo back to the house?' Derry called. 'It would save you carrying it on the train.'

Baz caught hold of it, as Derry passed it up from the boat. 'Never knew where you got this from, Rosy.'

Rosanna didn't look at her mother. 'From a friend, during the war,' she said. 'Someone who went home before we did.'

Derry left a clean plate. 'There, you won't need to wash mine, Wendy! You and Jan are definitely the best cooks in the family, you know, especially where steak-and-kidney pie is concerned. Mum's always on a diet at home, food at sea was of the stick-your-ribs-together variety, and I cater for myself at university, baked beans and sardines, that sort of thing; fortunately I like tomato sauce.'

'What are you studying?' Baz put in.

'Economics.'

'You're taking English, aren't you, Merle?'

'Yes. And drama.'

'Are you going to be an actress?' Rosy asked, in awe.

'She is one already!' Derry was awarded a reproving look from Merle.

'What about you, Rosy?' she countered. 'You won't have much choice of a job, you know, in these hard times, without extra qualifications.'

'I got a distinction in both English language and English lit in School Cert,' Rosanna said defensively.

'But you failed maths,' Wendy reminded her, collecting up the dinner plates. 'Who's for plums and custard?'

'I'm not going back to school, if that's what you're hinting at, Mum. I'll get a job where they'll give me further training while I work.'

'Oh, and where's that?' her mother asked. 'And you can't answer that one, can you, because you're too busy enjoying yourself instead of finding out.'

Rosanna flushed miserably, even as Baz remonstrated with Wendy.

'That's not fair, dear. She deserves a break after all that hard graft this year at school.'

Rosanna pushed her chair back, got up from the table.

'No, it's *not* fair, Mum!' Then she rushed out of the room.

'Leave her,' Baz told Wendy. 'I'm sorry,' he added to Merle and Derry.

'She'll get over it,' Merle said. 'I should know, I was just the same at her age. You just want to be allowed your head. But I was cunning; I let my mum and dad think they were pushing me into going to university; in reality, it's exactly what I planned to do. Rosy hasn't learned those ploys yet, but she will.'

'Plums?' Russ banged his spoon on his plate to attract attention, and from upstairs, they heard the fierce thrumming of Rosanna's banjo.

'Silly girl, she'll bust a string.' Wendy automatically took the stones out of Russ's plums, so he wouldn't swallow them and choke.

'Maybe she needs to,' Derry said quietly. They looked at him, startled.

'Don't worry about what Mum said,' Baz whispered, giving his daughter a farewell hug before she stepped into the boat, later. 'She didn't mean it.'

She did, Rosanna wanted to tell him, but she refrained. What had happened this last week, while she'd been away? Mum had bought her those new clothes, and not been too against the idea, before she'd departed, after all.

There was another, unexpected, hug that night, as she was about to follow Merle into the tent. Derry caught hold of her, so that her face was muffled against his ribbed jersey, which smelled of fish and, not unpleasantly, of sweat, for he did most of the strenuous work on the boat. She slipped her arms about his waist, comforted by their closeness. She felt warm and content.

'Rosy, you're not still upset by what your mother said, are you?'

'No . . . Yes! She doesn't understand, Derry, I want—'

'You don't know what you want, do you? No one does, at your age. But you'll find out, I promise you. Just don't get too hurt in the process.'

'Did – did you?'

He kissed the top of her head. 'I'm afraid so, and even at my advanced age, it's not all over yet. 'Night.'

' 'Night,' she said. As he released her she saw that he was smiling encouragingly at her, and she smiled back.

Wendy turned her back on Baz in bed. She'd guessed what he'd said to Rosanna. It's not on, she thought, Baz should support me where Rosy is concerned.

'Wendy?'

'What is it?' she said ungraciously. 'I'm tired, after entertaining, and packing them up more provisions – they've really no idea, any of them.'

'It's me should be asking that: what's up?'

'Can't you guess?'

'No.'

'I'm pregnant, after all this time, Baz. Doctor confirmed it when I went to collect your prescription at the beginning of the week.'

'You should have told me.'

'Is that all you can say?'

'I – I don't know how it could have happened.'

'Well it did. I'm thirty-seven years old, Baz.'

'That's not too old.'

'Maybe not, if we hadn't already produced a handicapped child. Doctor reminded me it was more likely to happen again.' she said flatly.

'It might not.'

'It's a risk we're going to have to take. And think how embarrassing it's going to be, to tell Rosy. At that age you don't like to think of your parents, well, you know. You saw for yourself she's about to go through a rebellious stage. I might have known Merle would encourage her in that. Just when I need her to be extra helpful at home, and to relieve me of some of the care for Russ . . .'

'You mustn't expect anything of the sort, old dear.'

'There you are – you *do* think of me as old!'

Baz sighed, attempted to put his arms round her, was repulsed.

'How far. . . ?'

'Three months, almost, so it's definite – and you never noticed a thing . . .'

'I'm sorry.'

'You're sorry! What d'you imagine I am? I was enjoying my job, and Rosy being almost off my hands, even Russ, settled happily at school. I don't know if I can cope. Oh, Baz!' She turned to him at last, and he patted her shoulder and wiped her eyes with the hankie out of his pyjama jacket pocket.

'Hope you hadn't blown your nose on that.' She sniffled.

'There, you almost laughed then, didn't you? Look, darling, I'm here, and I'm fairly fit again, thanks to all your loving care. I'll just be repaying some of that, by looking after you. All right now?'

'No,' she said, but she snuggled up to him at last, and gave him a grateful kiss. 'I do love you, Baz, you know that.'

'I know you do. We'll manage somehow, we always do, eh? Don't keep secrets from me, Wendy, sharing halves the worry.'

But there was still that secret, which would spoil everything, their life together, if she confessed it, she thought. The doctor knew of course, he'd read through her notes.

'I see you had a miscarriage seven years ago, Mrs Bloomfield. Again, you are, I'm afraid, in slightly more danger of this happening again. You should rest up. Would you like me to speak to your husband?'

'No, I'll tell him, he'll see I obey orders!' she said, as cheerfully as she could.

'It's hospital for the birth this time; the doctor insists,' she told Baz now.

'And I'll come with armfuls of flowers. It'll be a spring baby, won't it? Be wonderful if it was a little sister for Rosy, wouldn't it?'

Chapter Nineteen

The letter had been readdressed, in a different hand: *Try Bird, Pumping-station.* Janet turned it over twice before opening it, then looked again curiously at the original address. That too was incomplete, in shaky script, as if the person who penned it was old, or ill. *The Farm Cottages, The Common.* She sat down abruptly at the kitchen table, pushing aside a tray of rusks which were still hot from the oven, causing her to suck her scorched fingertips ruefully.

She had been busy as usual, while waiting for Jim to come in for his early break, his cup of Camp coffee, made with milk, the way he liked it, and was now about to call Grandma Birdie in from the vegetable garden, where she was picking runner beans. They planned to salt these down for winter. The jars were ready: washed and sterilized. They'd string and slice the beans to *Housewife's Choice*; they both liked Wee Georgie Elrick, the Scottish presenter.

Her own hands shook, as she tore the envelope open:

Dear Mrs Bird,
Sorry to trouble you again, and break my promise but I don't know who else I can ask. You were very kind to me, I don't forget that.

I have had a struggle, but I am glad I kept my little boy. Jamie has my late husband's surname. The fact is I am now in poor health, and have been told I must go into hospital next Tuesday for a big operation.

Please Mrs Bird, could you speak to your husband, and if you can take my boy for a while it would ease my mind so much. I will have him ready for you here on Monday afternoon.

I will tell him you are relatives.
Sorry again for all this,

Yours sincerely,
N. Wallis.

'What's wrong?' Jim asked, concerned on seeing her white, shocked face.

Silently she handed him the letter. It was his turn to show consternation. He passed his hand over his bald pate, and slumped down in the chair opposite. She pushed his cup over to him, spilling some in the saucer.

'Drink up,' she ordered.

Obediently, he took a gulp or two of coffee.

'You didn't tell me she wrote to you.' He sounded almost accusing.

'It was just after you'd gone back that time. She asked me not to tell you. I tore that letter up, I thought it for the best. But I can't blot out what it said.' She dug the knife in the butter, automatically spread some on a couple of rusks transferred them to a small plate. 'Here.'

But he didn't touch the offering.

'She told you about a baby – Jan, how could you keep *that* from me!'

'She didn't tell me – I *guessed*. I sent her money, the money you gave me Jim, I don't regret that, because it's obvious now she needed it, and she kept her promise and didn't contact me again.'

'Until now,' he stated flatly. 'Oh, Jan, what a mess.'

'Jim, can you forgive me?'

'Me forgive you? It should be the other way around. I've put it out of mind, you see, all this time, and you've never brought it up, never against me. How I must have hurt you – and her, poor girl.'

'It's today already,' she said, sounding anguished.

'What d'you mean?'

'Well, what with the letter going first there, then here, it's *today*, Monday, we have to fetch him, Jim . . .'

From the new portable battery wireless on the dresser came the strains of that old favourite, *On the Sunny Side of the Street* sung with great warmth by blonde and bubbly Dorothy Squires, just as Grandma Birdie toddled in with a trug full of long, tender green beans.

'More to come.' She beamed.

'I don't even know her Christian name,' Jan said, breaking a lengthy silence as they drove along and she studied the map. Fancy, she thought, mother and son weren't far from us, and we never knew. Wisbech was once a port like Lynn, but the Ouse was long ago diverted into the sea, and the marshes drained – it's such rich soil here for growing. But here's the river Nene, and on either side the North and South Brinks, and: 'We go over the town bridge,' she reminded him.

'Norah,' he said briefly, answering her previous question.

'Is she – younger than me, Jim?' She thought, I expect I look like a middle-aged mum – well, I am. . . .

'About Wendy's age, I think – I don't really know. That sounds awful, doesn't it? I can't really recall much about her, except she had long blonde hair, maybe not her natural colour; she looked sad and pinched in the face, but then she was recently bereaved. I was sorry for her. Jan, you don't want to hear all this.'

'Yes, I do. Take the left turning here,' she said, seeing the road sign. Then, 'This is it, I think. Number fifteen.'

It was a shabby little house in a rather run-down street. No fine Norman architecture here as in the centre of the town. No nineteenth century worthies had made their mark here, like Octavia Hill, she of the housing reform, who had been born at South Brink House, or Thomas Clarkson, campaigning son of the grammar school headmaster, who dedicated his life to the abolition of slavery. But the street was on the sunny side, even though the sunlight showed up the peeling paint on the door. When the car stopped, she was first out.

'Wait, Jim – she wrote to *me*, after all, didn't she?'

The woman who answered the door was mousey-haired, not blonde; thin and hunched, but with a swollen stomach. For an incredulous moment, Janet thought that Norah Wallis must be pregnant again, then she took in the yellow tinge to her face, the dark-ringed eyes. This was someone who was desperately ill. Not a rival for Jim's affections, but one in urgent need of help and kindness.

'Mrs Wallis?'

'You must be Mrs Bird. Thank you for coming. I was sure you would, but I wouldn't have blamed you if you'd ignored my letter. Will you both come in?'

Janet waved at Jim to join her, follow her inside. They went into a dark, small sitting-room off the narrow hall.

'I'll make a cup of tea,' Norah offered. 'I'll send Jamie in, he's upset, naturally, at leaving me. I've explained I'll be in hospital, that he can't stay here alone.'

'We can bring him to see you at the hospital,' Janet said impulsively.

'Thank you. We'll see. Depends how I am, doesn't it? Do sit down.'

Jim, so far, hadn't said a word, and Norah hadn't spoken to him directly. They sat, tensed up, on the hard chairs, waiting. Norah had left the door open. The boy peeked round at them, before he entered.

Janet's heart beat fast. Jamie didn't look like Merle, in fact he had a definite look of the younger Derry; floppy, straight fair hair, keen blue eyes, a skinny frame. He was tall for his age, which she estimated to be seven. He was a Bird, she could tell. This didn't upset her; he was a vulnerable child, who needed their support.

'Hello,' Jim said, rubbing his head again. 'I'm . . .' he hesitated, 'your Uncle Jim and this is your Aunt Janet . . .'

'I've got to go with you to your house, my mum says,' Jamie said ungraciously. 'You're not really my aunt and uncle, Mum says you're sort of cousins, but that's what I've got to call you.'

'Do you mind very much, about staying with us?' Janet asked. She suspected that he had been crying.

He nodded, looking mutinous.

Norah came in with a tray.

'Jamie, it's very kind of your uncle and aunt to invite you to their home. You'll have a good time, really you will.'

'We're back at our old place, on the fens – it's a lovely place for children,' Janet put in. 'I've written down the address, and our telephone number for you.' She took the sheet of paper from her handbag, passed it to Norah.

'How long have I got to be away? I'll be back for school, next month, won't I?' Jamie asked anxiously.

'I don't know yet. It depends on how quickly I get better, Jamie. It'll be a comfort, knowing you are being well looked after.'

'Have you got any children?' Jamie asked Janet.

'One daughter, but she's grown up, and at university. She's on holiday right now, sailing down the river with her cousins.'

'I wish I could do that,' the small boy said unexpectedly.

'I'm sure you will. Derry, he's – he's your cousin, too,' Janet floundered a bit, but at least that was true. 'He's got a nice boat. Look, ask Uncle Jim about it, while I go with your mother to collect your things, and then she can tell me what you like to eat, that sort of thing.'

Jamie's clothes, a book or two, and a few favourite toys, were packed in a white canvas sack familiar to Janet, because of Jim's kit bag. This one was labelled ABLE SEAMAN ALBERT WALLIS.

'His father,' Norah said, sounding very definite about that. Then, flatly: 'I've got to have a diseased kidney removed, Mrs Bird . . .'

'Oh, Janet, please.'

'They believe that the other kidney is dodgy, too. I lost a sister when she was young, to the same thing. Not a good outlook, is it. It's all right, I've cried all the tears I had in me, when the boy's asleep at nights. I went to a solicitor last week, it's all down legally, but I'll need to tell him your right address. If anything happens to me, I want you to keep him, bring him up as your own. You can tell him the truth, when you feel the time's right. Will you do it?'

'I hope it won't be necessary – I pray it won't – but you have my word, and – I can speak for Jim, too – that we would do our very best for him.'

'Thank you, Janet. Now, will you go, please? No drawn-out good-byes. . . .'

Wendy hadn't bothered with the treacle-and-vinegar concoction this time; when she saw the doctor he gave her a bottle of a chalky mixture to combat the nausea. She was aware that Rosanna had heard her being horribly sick early one morning a couple of weeks ago, when she'd emerged unsteadily from the bathroom.

'You all right, Mum?' she'd asked, concerned. Wendy couldn't answer because she'd had to turn and dash back to the basin. Now she'd have to tell her daughter.

I wonder if Princess Elizabeth suffered from morning, noon and night sickness, with *her* second baby? She thought ruefully. Anne, that's what the Royals have named their brand-new daughter. Little Charles is not even two yet, bless him. I wonder whether he knew his mum was having a baby? Not that we need tell Russ until much later, he's got no real concept of time.

When Russ dropped in action, and she'd covered him up on the settee with the small blanket which he used as a comforter, she decided to look up in the loft to see if the pram she'd used for him and Rosy was still serviceable. It had been used before them by Merle, and passed on to her by Janet. Now that she'd told Baz about her pregnancy, she could herself accept that the baby was a reality.

She stood on a chair, and hauled herself through the opening, torch in hand. She shone it in the recesses, careful not to tread on the weaker parts of the floor. There was the pram, which had been taken on all their travels, 'just in case'. She put up the hood. The material was a little worn where the steel points held it taut. The rain cover needed new elastic loops. She rocked the handle once or twice; the springs squeaked. Like the Tin Man in *The Wizard of Oz*, a favourite film with Russ, it needed the oil-can; she smiled to herself. She tried the brake. It held tight. Good. It would be a saving, using the pram, even if it did look old-fashioned. She'd better get down; Baz would be home shortly, it was early closing at the seed merchants.

She dangled her legs through the hatch, groped with her feet for the chair, missed, sent it toppling over. She took a deep breath. Turn around, she told herself, grip the edge with your hands, it won't be far to drop down. . . .

Baz knew something was wrong directly he opened the door. Russ waited at the bottom of the stairs, trailing his blanket in one hand. He was obviously agitated, pointing upwards. 'Mud-mud!' he shouted.

'My God!' Baz took in the situation immediately. 'Stay here, old boy,' he cautioned Russ. Then he took the stairs two at a time. Wendy was conscious, but lying in an undignified heap, her skirt rumpled round her waist.

'Are you hurt?' he cried. Then he saw the spreading stains on her pink petticoat.

'Don't touch me,' she said faintly. 'Call the doctor. . . .'

The doctor was reassuring; the bleeding had stopped, it looked worse than it was, he told Baz. Mrs Bloomfield must rest, flat on her back in bed for at least a week. This was a fairly common occurrence. He paused, noting the appeal on Wendy's face, directed at him. He put two and two together, as he and Baz stood by the window. The last time this had happened to his patient, he calculated, was during the war, while her husband was away. A common dilemma in wartime.

'The district nurse will call in daily at first, then can you make your own arrangements?' the doctor asked. 'Rosanna must be of an age where she could look after her mother, and her brother, if necessary, eh?'

'She's on holiday,' Wendy said flatly.

'Ah. But she'll be back before long?'

I'm sure she will, once she knows the situation, Baz thought. 'I'll see you out, Doctor. Thank you for responding so quickly.'

'Let Russ come in,' Wendy called after them. 'Tell him to bring his book, I'll read to him, before he goes to bed, I can do that, at least.'

'Hello young Derry.' Grandma Birdie greeted Jamie, without surprise. She stroked his cheek with a bony finger, despite his flinching, at this strange old lady who called him by another name. 'Did you remember the strimps for tea?' she asked Janet. 'The boy likes shellfish, don't you, Derry.'

'Sorry,' Janet apologized. 'But we'll have a nice cauliflower cheese, eh? Nice and simple. Quick, too.'

'I'm not hungry,' Jamie stated. He shuffled back from Grandma Birdie. He'd insisted on humping his bag indoors himself, and now he lifted it up and asked: 'Can I take this up to my room, please, Aunt Janet?'

'Your room . . .' She hesitated, then made up her mind. 'You can have Derry's bedroom, we can stow any bits and bobs of his away in the cupboard. Put that down, dearie, Uncle Jim'll carry that, he'll take you upstairs right away and show you where everything is, won't you, Jim?' They've hardly said a word to each other, she thought, this'll give them a chance to get to know each other a bit better. Jim must have looked like Jamie, when he was that age; he still had a mop of that fair hair when I married him, not that anyone would know now.

'Think you're going to like it here?' Jim asked awkwardly, as he led the way.

'Don't know yet,' Jamie replied. He followed Jim into the small room under the eaves. 'What's that?' he added, looking out the window.

'It's where I work. Care to look around there, after tea? D'you like to know how things work – engines and that?' Jim tried to sound casual.

'I took my mum's clock to pieces the other day. She wasn't very pleased.'

'Did you get it all back together again?'

'Yes, but it took a long time and I lost a bit, but luckily I found it before Mum got the carpet sweeper out and sucked it up.'

'Did the clock go again? That's the thing.'

'Yes, and now I know what makes it tick,' the boy said, and for the first time he smiled.

Chapter Twenty

Rosanna was having the time of her life, crewing for Derry on the way back. He was tolerant of her mistakes; they joked and laughed a lot. Merle, after plunging into deep water, both literally and with regard to Derry, was content to laze on deck in balmy weather, with a sprig of lavender pinched from a riverside garden to ward off the flies. She was 'reading with eyes closed', merely complaining mildly when the others tacked and zigzagged according to the prevailing wind and the vagaries of the river.

On the last morning, Rosanna caught Derry gazing thoughtfully at Merle: at her exposed, brown limbs, at the spread of liquorice-coloured hair on an improvised pillow; the skimpy sun-top and shorts. Seeing Rosanna watching him, he grinned and ruffled her hair, lank, because it needed washing.

'OK, Rosy?' he asked. 'Don't fret, you're beautiful, too, you know.'

I've got a horrible spot on my chin, he's being kind, she thought ruefully. It's nearly that time of the month, so maybe it's as well we're on the last lap of our expedition. Merle takes it all in her stride, I'm not that self-assured yet.

After tying up and helping to hump all the baggage out, Rosanna lingered for a moment in the boat with Derry, while Merle stood above them on the landing-stage, with her back to them, waving to her father, who, unexpectedly, was accompanied by a small boy whom they didn't recognize.

'Hi, Dad!' she called.

'Derry . . .' said Rosanna.

'Mmm?' He was hunting around to see if they had forgotten anything.

'I – had a really wonderful time. Thank you so much.'

He gave her an impulsive hug. 'Thank *you* for coming, Rosy. You're now a seasoned sailor, eh? I hope you'll crew for me again soon.' He paused, lowered his voice: 'You'll keep our secret, won't you? About you know what.'

'Of course I will, Derry,' she said simply.

Years later, she would realize that his next words were tender ones.

'You don't have to tell me how you feel, I *know*, and I'm flattered, Rosy, but before you know it, you'll be inundated with prospective boyfriends and you'll wonder what you ever saw in me! Come on, let's step ashore.'

'Had a good trip?' Jim asked. 'This is Jamie, who's staying with us while his mother is in hospital.'

Merle exclaimed: 'Good lord! He looks like you, Derry!'

'Well, you are related in a way – but it's rather complicated.' Jim had been rehearsing this. 'We won't go into it all just now.'

'*You* look like Aunt Janet,' Jamie told Merle. 'Can I get in the boat?' he asked Derry eagerly. He'd lost his initial wariness.

'Tell you what, after we've had one of Jan's bust-your-guts meals, if the ladies present will excuse such indelicacy, we'll stagger back here, hoist the sail and go as far as the bend in the river and back.'

'Not me,' Merle called back over her shoulder. 'I intend to have a bath!'

'Thought you'd had one already,' Derry teased.

'I'll come,' Rosanna offered, although a bath had been her priority, too.

'You haven't had enough of the river, then?'

'No, I'd like to live on a boat, one day. Just think, no housework . . .'

'No bathroom, and washing your smalls in the river, no fear!' Merle put in.

Merle came into the kitchen, where her mother was about to wash up. Grandma Birdie, asleep in her chair, mouth slightly open, emitted a little purring noise.

'Can I have that big towel off the airer?' she asked. 'Are there no bath-salts?'

'I'll look in the store; I used the last of them in the bathroom on Jamie last night. He gets filthy, pottering about in the pump-house – he likes being with your dad.'

'Who is he really?' Merle asked curiously.

'What d'you mean?'

' "Sort of related", Dad hinted. Come off it, he's a Bird, that's obvious!'

'He's Jamie *Wallis*,' Jan said firmly. 'Here, Nipper gave me these for

Christmas. Label says violets, but that's the colour – soda, probably, so don't overdo it, or your skin'll peel off.'

'Don't be evasive, Mum. Then he's related to us on his mother's side?'

'That's likely it. Don't let that water get cold, Merle. The new geyser in the bathroom costs enough to heat.'

'I'll find out, you know. I'll ask Dad when he gets in from work tonight!'

The telephone in the hall shrilled. Grandma Birdie twitched in her sleep.

'Haven't got used to having the phone here,' Jan said. 'I hesitated when your dad suggested it. It might be the hospital, ringing about Jamie's mother.' She picked up the receiver belatedly. '*Baz*,' she mouthed at her daughter.

As Merle went upstairs, she heard her mother say: 'Yes, she's back, but she's out at this moment, just for an hour or so – what's that? *Oh my dear!* We'll make sure she catches the first train home tomorrow morning.'

Jamie was eager to learn, so Rosanna relaxed as Derry obligingly ran the sail up and they cleaved across the sunlit water. He's good with children, she thought – then, wryly: he thinks I'm still a child, too. We didn't circumnavigate the world this time, but it's been an adventure and even Merle's moods added to it. I wonder, if I bring the puppets out after tea, will Derry agree to a show, for old times' sake?

'What are you smiling at?' Derry called.

'I'm remembering Captain Codswallop, the baby with the beard, and you—'

'Me declaiming those corny words, eh, in a voice veering between treble and bass: '*It's a wise child what knows its own father!*'

'Something like that.'

Rosanna stood apprehensively on the station forecourt the next day, waiting for her father.

'Don't panic,' Jan had tried to reassure her last night, 'but your mother's been told to rest up for a week or two, so your dad says he's sorry to cut your holiday short, but you're really needed at home. You can come again soon.'

'I had another ten days,' she sniffed. 'What's wrong with Mum, anyway?'

'It's best they tell you that, I think. Nothing dire, anyway!'

Then Russ was clutching her and his excitement melted her resentment, and she found herself giggling and saying:

'Anyone would think I'd been away months, not just a fortnight, Russ Bloomfield!'

'Got a hug for your old dad?' Baz smiled. 'Hurry, or we'll miss the bus.'

'Got a caseful of dirty washing, so don't drop it and reveal it to the world!'

'I'm sorry, but it couldn't be helped.'

'Not *your* fault, I'm sure, Dad,' she said, as they settled in the front of the bus so Russ could watch the driver, and the conductor pinged the bell.

'Don't blame your mum. You'll understand, after you've talked to her. I have to go back to work tomorrow, and Russ needs looking after, of course—'

'Of course he does! Let's not go on about it, eh?'

'You had a good time, anyway, on your sailing trip?'

'Yes, I did,' she said, as he squeezed her hand.

'There'll be other holidays,' he told her.

'I know, but I'll always remember this one, along our river.' And I'll remember this morning, she mused: Derry rising early from the couch where he'd spent the night, Jamie having taken over his room, to make toast for their breakfast, while Jan boiled the eggs. Riding pillion behind Derry, arriving as the train steamed in. A snatched kiss on her parted lips.

' 'Bye, dear Rosy, don't cry.'

Then he'd helped her aboard.

'Hello Mum, I'm back.'

Wendy opened her eyes. She'd been dozing while the others were out.

'You're tanned, I must say, but Rosy, your *hair*! What have you done to it?'

'Not washed or brushed it much recently,' Rosanna said frankly. She leaned over and kissed her mother. 'This is a bit of a shock, Mum, you being ill.'

'Rosy, not really ill. I had a scare that's all. You see, I'm having a baby. Now we've got used to the idea, your dad and I are pleased, and I hope you will be, too.' A rush of words from Wendy.

Rosanna was silent for a long minute. *Baby*, she thought, that explains a lot. It reminded her sharply of another time when her mother had been ill, when Mrs Peck was so kind, and Jan had held the fort. Dad hadn't been there. But Burl . . .

'Well?' Wendy demanded anxiously.

'If you and Dad are happy about it, that's all that matters.'

Wendy looked relieved.

'Maybe it's just as well, after all, that you insisted on leaving school. You needn't rush to find a job, Rosy. You can keep me company at home. I'll be very glad to have you around, especially when it gets nearer the time. We'll make you a proper allowance, naturally, that's only fair.'

It's *not* fair, I was looking forward to going out in the world, but I can't say that, with Mum like this, Rosanna thought.

She said instead: 'Don't worry, Mum, I'll do my best.'

'Thank you, darling. There's a lot of Jan in you, caring for us.'

'She's looking after a little boy at the moment while his mother's in hospital.'

'Oh, who's that?'

'Well, I wasn't back long enough to find out. His name's Jamie and the strange thing is he looks like Derry. Jan said he's related to the Birds.'

'That's odd. I know all the relatives on Jim's side. Derry's the only boy among his brother's children; I never heard of a Jamie.'

Rosanna rose, smoothed the bedclothes over her mother.

'You'll have to ask Jan about that, won't you.'

'What's all this about Jan and Jim, Rosy?'

'They said I was grown up enough to drop the uncle and aunt bit. I'll be up again later, Mum. I'm going to the shops for Dad, and I'll take Russ with me.'

'Thanks for not making a fuss. You *are* grown up, and I never realized . . .'

And I'm grown up enough to have my secrets from you, too, Rosanna thought. Especially about being in love.

Janet hadn't visited a hospital since Russ had been ill during the war, when Burl briefly entered their lives, especially Wendy's. Things had changed, mostly for the better, what with the National Health Service, she thought. The nurses were younger, slender and attractive, with wide elasticated belts nipping in the waists of their striped dresses, swishing starched aprons and black stockings, accentuating shapely legs. They smiled more; whisked about the long ward with thermometers and bedpans, briskly drawing curtains around patients, or smoothing the creases in sheets and plumping pillows.

'There's your mum,' Jan told Jamie, but he'd already seen her, and was hurrying along the polished floor, his shoes squeaking, to her bed.

As Jan followed she was touched to see him drawing a chair close to his mother's side, carefully holding her hand, for she was attached to a drip. Jan stood at the foot of the bed, not wishing to intrude on their reunion.

'Are you all right, Mum?'

'Not too bad, Jamie. And you? Enjoying your holiday, dear?'

'Yes – but I wish you were there, too.'

That decided Jan. She hadn't discussed it with Jim, but: 'She will be, Jamie. When the hospital says she can, she's coming to stay with you, and us, and we'll look after her and make sure she gets better, won't we?'

'There's the rent to pay on the house, I can't just leave it.' Norah faltered.

'We saw the landlord and had a chat, didn't we, Jamie, when we popped in to get the things you asked for. He said he'd waive the rent for another couple of weeks, and then take it from there.' She won't be going home, poor girl, Jan thought: she's put Jim and me down as next of kin, that's why the almoner rang to tell us that the operation had gone as planned, but there was nothing more they could do. If we don't take her in, and make her as happy and comfortable as possible, she'll have to stay here, until the inevitable happens. She should be with her boy, that's only right.

'Please, Mum,' Jamie said, 'You'll like it there. Rosy, that's one of my cousins, lent me her puppets. Derry, another cousin, only he's quite old, made them, oh, ages ago. They've both gone home now, haven't they, Aunt Jan, but Merle is there for a bit longer, until she goes back to Scotland.'

Janet helped Norah to take a sip of water, holding her head steady.

'Thank you, Janet. You're a real friend. I didn't expect . . .'

'I know you didn't. But there, you're both family now, aren't you?'

Janet couldn't know that around this time Jim had asked Grandma Birdie:

'You all right, old dear?' He touched her gently, and then realization struck. He was the only one around, for Merle had caught the bus to town, saying she was bored, and she might go to the flicks.

Grandma Birdie was in her usual chair, with the patchwork cushion she'd sewn in his youth, behind her head. Her fingers were always busy, however tired she was, he thought, beginning to sob, for there was no one to see.

He wasn't too sure how old she really was, but he had been the youngest of her boys, born when snow was falling in the first month of the twentieth century.

'I know what Jan will say.' He spoke aloud. 'As one goes, another comes to take their place . . .' and she'd add: 'That means Wendy's baby will be a girl.'

She'd had a good, long life, he told himself: Jan was like the daughter she never had. It just won't seem the same here without her.

Chapter Twenty-one

There was bitter weather and a fuel crisis when Marcia was born at the end of January. Wendy and Rosanna had pored over the baby names book which Baz had purchased in a rash moment, and had then wisely left his womenfolk to it. Journeying into space would be no longer a fantasy in this second half of the century, and Marcia, a name inspired by the planet Mars, would be part of it.

This time Rosanna was not 'sent out to play', but supported her mother and her father throughout Wendy's protracted labour. In rural areas all over the country where other women were about to give birth, doctors and midwives made heroic efforts to reach them through snowdrifts; wheels churned and skidded on ice and hospital casualty departments were busy plastering fractured limbs. Here, roads were spread overnight with coarse salt; the ice chipped away from paths and pavements by diligent householders wielding shovels.

'Thank goodness we're not still on the farm,' Baz told his wife, at just past midnight. 'At least we can get you to the hospital if needs be.'

'I'm not going to hospital!' Wendy wailed, gripping his hand through the next wave of pain. Then, 'Oh – *oh*, my waters have broken. *Rosy!*'

Rosanna replaced the drawsheet on the bed with a thick towel and assisted Baz in gently removing Wendy's soaked nightdress and replacing it with one of his pyjama jackets. Wendy shivered violently, despite the fact that both bars of the electric fire were glowing.

'Can you find her some bedsocks?' Baz asked his daughter. They both visualized Grandma Birdie in her pink ones, but couldn't muster a smile.

Baz had rung the midwife, and woken Rosanna at the same time, an hour after she had gone to bed, to warn her that Wendy was experiencing twinges. The nurse's calm advice was:

'Ring again when her waters go, or when the contractions become very close.'

The baby was arriving earlier than expected; the original plan having been for Wendy to stay, as before, with Jan for the final month and to have the baby there, but although the doctor reluctantly agreed to a home birth, he'd insisted she should remain in Lynn, to be monitored by the local midwife.

In any case, Janet and Jim had their hands full at present. Not long after losing dear Grandma Birdie, they were caring for Jamie's sick young mother, Norah. The relationship between the four of them was still a mystery, but Baz had an inkling. However, he wisely kept his thoughts to himself.

Rosanna had never seen her mother unclothed before. It was a shock to see her swollen belly, tight as a drum; the loose smocks Wendy wore during the latter part of her pregnancy made her look top-heavy, but concealed the reality.

At least she knew from where the baby would emerge, having learned the basic facts of life from Janet, and later the clinical side of things from biology at school. But she was unprepared for this. Why did the midwife talk matter-of-factly about 'contractions' when it was obvious that Wendy was in great pain?

Nurse Clarke, with over twenty years' experience of home deliveries, considered fathers to be an unnecessary nuisance when their wives were in labour. She briskly dispatched Baz to boil pans of water, for which there appeared to be no obvious need; instructing him to ensure that Russ didn't wander into the bedroom. Clarkie, as her patients affectionately called her, had taken up midwifery when her own four children were in their teens. She was big and bosomy with immaculately styled auburn hair and despite the unearthly hour, she wore what she called 'full war paint', wafting a flowery fragrance rather than antiseptic.

'Reassuring for the mothers,' she told Rosanna. 'It removes the barrier of fear, I find. Now, my dear, you don't feel faint do you, at the thought of what's to come? You know where babies come from, eh?' She had a throaty chuckle.

'Yes.'

'Then I'm promoting you to nursing aide, just for tonight.' Another chuckle, followed by a groan from Wendy.

'Shallow breathing, dear; *huff*, that's right. Let's see how things are progressing.' She gave a brisk jerk to the flannel jacket.

Rosanna stepped back. She thought, Mum won't like me intruding on her . . . well, privacy. She observed Wendy flinching at Clarkie's cold hands, but her touch was a soothing, gentle one; an art perfected because of her own memories of rough handling when she had given birth herself. Wendy visibly relaxed.

'Wring out a flannel in tepid water, dear; lay it on your mother's forehead. Don't worry about the strange noises she is making.'

But she's suffering, Rosanna thought desperately, doing as she was bid, because I can tell from her eyes. I'm *never* going to have a baby, not if it hurts like this.

Something was wrong, Wendy had been in the second stage of labour for too long. Rosanna was sent to tell Baz to call the doctor out.

He picked up the receiver, his hands shaking badly.

'Line's dead!' he almost shouted. 'Must have been more snow. I'll have to go for the doctor myself.'

'Dad! It's quite a way.'

'Can't help that!' He was struggling into his overcoat, winding a thick scarf round his neck. 'I hope he won't send her off to hospital, Rosy – you know the thought of that frightens her.' He sounded terrified himself.

'Dad! Get going! I'll see to Russ if he wakes up, don't worry.'

'How can I not worry? Where's my torch? The street lights are low . . .'

'In the hallstand drawer, with your gloves. Oh, please hurry!'

'Rosanna,' the nurse called urgently as the door closed behind him. 'I need you, dear! Couldn't your father get through to Doctor Brown?'

Rosanna took the stairs two at a time.

'Line's down,' she said breathlessly. 'He's going to fetch the doctor.'

'She's bleeding. She'll collapse, go into shock, if it goes on. . .'

Wendy's face was blanched, her limbs trembling spasmodically.

'The baby?' Rosanna asked fearfully.

'My first concern must be your mother.'

Just then Wendy gave an almighty heave, and the baby was propelled into the nurse's outstretched hands, an automatic reaction, for it took them all by surprise. The baby girl was not a pretty sight, being streaked with blood and a yellow greasy substance which Rosanna afterwards learned was vernix.

There was no panicking from the nurse. She swiftly cleared the baby's nose, snipped and tied the cord, dangled her from her heels and gave her a slap on the back. The baby gave an indignant cry. It all happened in seconds.

Mutely, Rosanna passed the warmed flannel sheeting, the baby was wrapped, and handed to her, with:

'Sit over there by the fire and cuddle her close, I have to deal with the placenta. Where's that doctor?'

As if on cue, they heard pounding on the stairs. Doctor Brown closed the door firmly on Baz, telling him:

'Make the tea, old man. Sugar hers well.'

Rosanna, seemingly unnoticed by the doctor, cradled her little sister in her arms, not daring to look towards the bed. There had been no time to clean her up, but the baby was alive and breathing and, from the brief glimpse of her that Rosanna was afforded as she shot into the world, she looked – *all right* . . .

The attention was naturally directed at her mother. Eventually, the doctor straightened up.

'She'll do,' he stated. 'But we'll have to get her to the hospital shortly. She may need a transfusion.' He seemed to see Rosanna at last. 'Bring the baby here; you've done well, I hear.'

Wendy was trying to say something. As the doctor gave the baby a cursory examination, Rosanna leaned over her mother and made out:

'Thank you, Rosy, I hope this hasn't been too – shocking, for you . . .'

Baz appeared, the tea tray rattling in his nervous grasp before he put it down.

'Here's your husband, my dear, come to see how you are, and to meet his new daughter. Has she a name?'

'Marcia.' Wendy even managed a little smile.

'*Marcy*,' Baz put in. 'Goes with Rosy, doesn't it.' He kissed his wife tenderly on the forehead, stroked her arm as she curled it round the baby.

Doctor Brown cleared his throat. 'I'll have to take you to hospital myself, drink your tea up. Just a precaution, you understand. And, I'm glad to tell you that the baby appears to be, ah, normal.'

Russ was calling out from his room next door: 'Mud-mud!' And Rosanna left her tea untouched, to go to her brother.

Wendy brushed the pulsing dark head, freshly washed but still greasy, with her lips. *Normal* Doctor Brown had said. She'd known instinctively that something was not right when Russ was born, twelve and a half years ago. This time, despite the discomfort of stitching, and the weakness due to the loss of blood, she had a feeling of well-being. 'Marcia – Marcy,' she whispered to the baby. In five minutes, the night nurse would take the baby to the nursery, then make Wendy as comfortable as she could for the remaining hour before the day staff arrived.

Tears trickled down her face. The baby looked much like Rosy when newborn. More like herself than Baz. Would that little lost one have resembled Burl? She shouldn't be thinking of him now. Nevertheless, she thought, there was something special between us. I've never again experienced passion like that. Not with Baz. Yet I do love him, I do, and surely Marcy will bring us even closer.

'Here, this won't do,' the little nurse said soothingly, wiping her eyes for her. 'You've had a busy night, Mrs Bloomfield, but isn't Marcy worth it?'

Wendy nodded. 'Yes . . .'

'Then turn over and get some shut-eye, there's a good girl. Before the whole nursery starts wailing, and we move you into the main maternity ward, eh?'

Marcy's crinkled little face was warm, slightly fuzzy, like a ripe peach. Wendy kissed her again, before relinquishing her to the nurse. Marcy was a gift, a precious thing, an expression of their love. She mustn't dwell on those dangerous, delicious moments again. They must be firmly relegated to the past.

'Aunt Jan!'

Janet stirred as Jamie plucked insistently at her sleeve. Beside her, in the bed, Jim also awoke. It was that dark time just before dawn.

'What is it, dearie? You'll catch cold. Where's your dressing-gown?'

'I . . . I had a nasty dream—'

'Shush, don't wake your mum, will you? Remember her door's open, so I can hear her if she calls. Here, under the covers, my side. Move up, Uncle Jim! Let's all get back to sleep.' He snuggled into the warmth of the feather mattress, allowed her to put her arm round his waist in that comforting way she had.

Then the phone shrilled downstairs. Janet nudged Jim.

'Can't they let me rest on my nights off?' he mumbled, but he half-rolled out of bed, then groped for his slippers.

He returned after five minutes, when Jamie was already asleep.

'Well, who was it?' Janet whispered.

'Baz. The baby's here – arrived a couple of hours ago. I nearly said, couldn't you wait to tell us until morning?'

'I'm glad you didn't! Come on, boy or girl, and is all well?'

'It's a girl. Didn't catch the name, sorry. The baby's fine apparently, but Wendy had a rough time and they've both been whisked off to hospital – Baz said not to worry. He'll ring again in the morning, the phone was off at the crucial moment when he had to phone for the doctor, but he just tried it again and—'

'Managed to get us! Well, now we can relax. Cuddle up and get warm again.'

Sandwiched between them, Janet was cosy, but resigned to being wide awake. She wondered how her sister was feeling at becoming a mother again after such a big gap. It was too late now for Jim and herself to have another baby, but she had Jamie to care for now, and she loved him. Norah needed her, too: she believed Jim when he said he felt friendship and concern for Norah but that *she* was the love of his life. She guessed, however, that he wanted the family to know he was Jamie's father. One day, she yawned, *one day*.

Russ held Rosanna's hand as she coaxed him towards the hospital bed. He was nervous of doctors in white coats and nurses who smiled at him and said; 'Aren't you a lucky boy. A dear little sister!' Hospitals meant injections, and lying on a couch while a doctor listened to your heart. The needle hurt, though the examinations didn't, and he didn't like the hospital smell.

Wendy was sitting on a rubber ring to ease her painful posterior, with Marcy in her arms.

'Russ, come and see what Mud-mud's got!' she encouraged him.

'It's a baby,' he said gruffly. Dad had brought flowers, hot-house roses, closely budded, and after kissing Mud-mud he'd gone in search of a vase.

'Rosy, fetch that chair nearer, dear, will you? Then he can see properly.'

His mother unwrapped the bundle, laid it on the bed between them, still holding on to the baby.

'Your new sister,' she said, 'Marcy.'

Russ looked at Rosy. *She* was his sister.

'Marcy,' he repeated, then he smiled because that always made Mud-mud happy.

'Would you like to hold her? If Rosy helps,' she qualified.

Rosanna laid her in his lap, keeping hold of her, so that she was secure.

'Marcy,' he said again, to please his mother. He looked over at the door. 'Where's Dad?' He hoped that his father had not gone away and left them here.

'To put my flowers in water.'

'Mud-mud come home?' he asked hopefully.

'Soon, darling, soon. Rosy is taking good care of you isn't she, while

Dad's at work?' Wendy patted her elder daughter's shoulder, as she knelt beside Russ and the baby. 'I don't know what I'd do without you, Rosy. I thought I'd miss Jan this time, but you've taken her place very nicely.'

Baz, coming back with the roses, caught both these words and Rosanna's beseeching look, directed at him.

'When everything's back to normal, when you're able to look after the baby yourself, Wendy, and to manage Russ, we must let our Rosy loose in the working world, don't you agree?'

Chapter Twenty-two

Rosanna celebrated her seventeenth birthday in April, when Marcy was three months old. She read the Sits Vacant, while her mother nursed the baby, ostensibly 'listening with Mother' on the wireless, now referred to as the radio. Russ also enjoyed this new programme for under-fives when he was home.

'I wish we could afford a television,' Wendy said. Rosanna wished her mother would nurse the baby in the privacy of her bedroom, not in the living-room. Marcy was a noisy feeder, hiccuping from time to time, and when Wendy requested: 'Pass me a muslin, Rosy,' to mop her up, Rosanna felt again, *she* wouldn't want to cope with all this one day!

'We could get one if you didn't have to keep me,' Rosanna hinted. There were one or two copy-typing jobs, but she couldn't type. She didn't regret leaving school, but she hadn't much to offer in office skills, apart from good spelling. Dad said he'd ask at work, but that still smacked of dependence.

'What did Bekka say in her letter?' Wendy asked, rubbing Marcy's back, which action produced a satisfying belch, but more regurgitated milk.

Rosanna seized her opportunity.

'Oh, she was full of that Festival of Britain the King's opening on the third of May. The Dome of Discovery sounds well worth a visit. The whole thing's costing millions and millions! She's decided to leave school, too, and Ket's disappointed because she wanted her to stay on, go on to university, but Bekka prefers the University of Life! She's got a job lined up already in a publishers', because she's bilingual and she's going to enrol at Regent Street Poly for evening classes in shorthand – she can type because she got a portable last Christmas, and she can use all her fingers . . .' She paused for breath.

'Like her mother she's a perfectionist. What's all this leading up to?' Wendy said warily, pinning a fresh nappy on the baby.

'Bekka says there's another job going, and she's told them about me, and my distinctions in English, and I love books, and—'

'You're not thinking of going to *London* surely?'

'Well, I wasn't, but there's nothing here and Ket has offered to have me there. You like her – and she's strict, so I'd be unlikely to stray.'

'What a silly expression! You'll have to discuss it with your father tonight. Now, take Marcy, then I can think about lunch.'

When Jamie came out from school that afternoon, he found Uncle Jim waiting for him, instead of Aunt Jan. He knew instinctively that something had happened, and he glanced warily at Uncle Jim, as they drove back to the pumping-station.

After a while Uncle Jim said:

'I've got something to tell you, Jamie, and I just don't know the best way to do it . . .'

'Mum's bad, isn't she,' Jamie demanded. Norah had been confined to bed for the last few weeks; the doctor and the district nurse made frequent calls. When he'd kissed her goodbye this morning she'd been too weak to raise her head from the pillow. She'd managed a smile, said as usual:

'Be a good boy for me . . .'

They drew up by the house. 'Wait,' Jim said. 'Your mum . . .'

'She's – died, hasn't she. She told me it would be soon, Uncle Jim – she said I must be brave . . .' Jamie faltered. He looked stricken, old for his seven years.

Jim put his arm round the boy's shoulders.

'Yes,' he said simply.

Jamie didn't cry then.

'Is she – still here?'

'No.'

'I can't see her, then?'

'Later, if you wish. She's – in the chapel of rest. Where Grandma Birdie was taken – you remember? It's very peaceful there . . .' What else could he say?

'Where's Aunt Jan?'

'She's here for you.'

Jamie shrugged off Jim's arm, scrambled out and ran to the open door. Jan enfolded him in her arms, comforted him, without words.

'Your mother wanted us to continue looking after you, Jamie,' Jan told him. They sat quietly in the best room, with the curtains still drawn, in respect. It was a quiet service, with Baz present to offer moral support, and Merle and Derry – Derry'd driven up from London to Edinburgh to fetch Merle. He'd take her back tomorrow, Friday. She had essays to complete, so couldn't stay the weekend.

Baz excused himself, after a cup of tea and a sandwich, saying he must get back to the family, and return his boss's car. The other two quietly withdrew at a signal from Janet. Merle knew what her father was going to tell Jamie; he had spoken to her, and to Baz earlier. She was now permitted to tell Derry.

'I know,' Jamie said to Jim. He was quite composed today, but Jan had had to comfort him twice last night. He preferred to cry his heart out in the dark.

'This may upset you, Jamie, but I think you are old enough to under-stand.'

'You're my real dad,' Jamie stated.

'How did you know that?'

'I guessed. I look like you. Mum said – you'd be my mum and dad when—'

'D'you mind?'

'No. Because she was glad about it.'

'And so are we.' Jan broke another lengthy silence. 'We're glad, even though we're sad. She was so ill, Jamie, so uncomplaining; you can be very proud of your mother . . .'

'I am. I always will be,' Jamie cried fiercely 'Do I call you Dad now?'

'Only if you want to.'

'You're *Merle*'s mum and dad: I suppose she's my sister. Can I keep on with Uncle Jim and Aunt Jan?'

'Of course you can,' Janet said for them both.

'But I'll *know*,' Jamie said again, 'That's what counts.'

Merle and Derry walked hand in hand towards the river.

'This is, nice, despite the occasion,' she said, looking up at him. She wore a pencil-slim black skirt, a white blouse with a black bow. It had taken ages to achieve the smooth french pleat at the back of her head, but now he stopped abruptly, unceremoniously pulling the restraining pins from her hair, so that it tumbled in loops to her shoulders.

'Now you look like *you*,' he said.

There was no one about. Merle smiled; it was an 'I dare you' look.

'You know how hard it is for me to resist you,' he said gruffly.

'Then don't.' She sat down on the bank, slipped off her court shoes, rolled down her stockings, aware he was watching. 'I intend to cool my feet, if not my head.' She tested the water with her toes. 'Come on, sit yourself down, Derry.'

'I'm wearing my best suit,' he reminded her, 'and the grass is a bit damp.'

'I'll clean any marks off for you, I promise.'

He sat down then, leaving a space between them.

'Derry, Dad said to tell you, he is Jamie's father.'

'That's not really a surprise. How do *you* feel about that?'

'At first I suppose I felt – a bit cheated, maybe a trifle jealous, having always been number one. Mum said they both wanted him, that Dad had been honest with her about what happened at the time and she'd forgiven him, but they hadn't known about Jamie until just before they brought him and Norah here to live.'

'And now?'

'I reckon I'm a bit old to have a little brother, but then, Rosy's got a baby sister, and there's an even bigger age difference, and Jamie's feelings are what matter, not mine, and at least Dad won't have to explain it all, just yet.'

He moved closer. 'You're being very generous, Merle.'

'Am I? Did you really expect me to be selfish and mean about all this?'

'I love you the way you are. You're impulsive, demanding and – desirable.'

'She looked at him in disbelief.

'You mean that?'

'Yes, I do. I know it's not possible, and I shouldn't tell you, but I wish—'

'You could make mad, passionate love to me?'

'It isn't only that – and this is not the time—'

'Tell me!' she demanded. 'I've never made any secret of how I feel, Derry.'

'I thought you'd grow out of it.'

'I'm twenty years old! I know my own mind. If you asked me, I'd throw up my studies, move in with you, *marry* you—'

'That's not possible!'

'That stupid cousin thing, I suppose. I told you, there's no legal bar—'

'No, and if things were normal, we could take our chance, but . . .'

'But what?'

'I haven't told anyone – well, Rosy knows, but not all of it.'

'*Rosy*? Why would you confide in her, and not me?'

'She – she had a crush on me, as you suspected that time; I had to warn her off. I had TB, Merle, quite badly, that's the real reason I jettisoned the Navy, or rather they decided to dispense with my services. It might recur, I can't be positive that it won't. I've only one good lung. Maybe I won't make a great age. I shouldn't marry anyone, least of all you, because if *we* were to have children, well, they'd be twice as likely to inherit any genetic defects. Now, you see why I have to hold you at arm's length, despite admitting my feelings for you.'

'I don't see anything of the sort! If – we *did* marry one day, we needn't reproduce, to put it bluntly. I *won't* give up, Derry. You're right, of course, today is not the time for abandonment – but there's always tomorrow.'

'We'll be driving back to Edinburgh—'

'Yes, but you're staying with me overnight, aren't you, as it's the weekend?'

He groaned. It was madness, he knew it.

Rosanna couldn't believe it had been so easy to sway her father. True, he'd insisted on a trial period, say three months.

'You're far too young to leave home,' Wendy worried.

'You were only two years older than me when you married Dad!'

'But that's different – I was mature for my age!'

'Darling,' Baz reminded her gently, 'You weren't! We were both a couple of kids playing at marriage – look how we relied on Jan and Jim early on.'

'That's not fair!'

'It's true. Nowadays, girls want a career before they settle down. If Rosy is prepared to continue her education while she's working, well, London's not a bad idea, is it? Let her go, Wendy. She can always come back if it doesn't work out.'

Derry's in London, Rosanna hugged the thought to her. Now I've got an excuse to write, and say I hope to see him soon!

It had been a long, tiring drive in the rain. Merle lived at the top of a town house converted into what were called apartments, but were really bed-sits, with a gas ring and gas fire and a share in the bathroom on the floor below.

'Not sure I've got anything much in the grub stakes,' she said. 'Got a match? We'd better light the fire, it's never warm in here, not even in the summer.'

'We had a good lunch,' he said, looking at the sofa, wondering if it was long enough to accommodate him. Merle's bed was curtained off at the back; her books and papers heaped untidily on the table. It was a typical student's room.

'Pickled onions – well, two in a sea of vinegar looking a bit green round the gills; two rashers of bacon and two eggs.'

'You'll recall omelettes are my standby; I cook for myself, too, you know. I'm more adventurous nowadays, like spaghetti and a spicy meat sauce.'

'No spaghetti, but at least we had the sense to buy a loaf along the way.'

'A cup of tea would be nice,' he said, then, seeing her rueful expression: 'Don't tell me, you're out of tea.'

'I'll borrow some from the girl in the next room, or will coffee do? Mum usually sends me back well provided for, but—'

'She was too preoccupied. Coffee will be fine. Now, got an apron?'

'You must be joking! No casual clothes in that bag to change into?'

'Nope. Just a clean shirt and underwear, and a towel.'

'Use that, then! I'm retiring to get changed myself. This is my only decent outfit, and I'm renowned for spilling things down my front.'

He was flipping the omelette, when she re-emerged, wearing pyjamas.

'It didn't seem worth getting properly dressed again.' She came up behind him, wrapped her arms round his waist, intent on disturbing him.

'Watch out,' he said as lightly as he could. 'Cooking is dangerous work, you know. Go and lay the table, girl.'

'Oh, can't we just slum it on the sofa, and balance our plates on our laps?'

'You make the coffee then. The kettle's boiled.'

She released him. 'Breathe again! Did I say I've run out of sugar, too?'

'I'm not surprised. Plates? Ready to serve up.'

'Delicious,' she approved, a little later. 'You'll make a good husband, Derry.'

'No, I won't. I told you—'

'It doesn't matter what you told me, Derry. The dishes can wait 'til morning.'

'In the morning,' he said, aware that he was fighting a losing battle, 'you'll be in your bed, and I'll be on the settee.'

'In the morning, maybe,' she said dreamily, She slung her dressing-gown over the back of the settee. 'But now ... flip the switch, eh?'

The situation was saved by a knock on the door and a female voice crying:

'Anyone at home? The light bulb's gone in the bathroom and I'm dripping water everywhere.'

'Time I was going,' he said, ushering her friend in before Merle could protest. 'Kind of you to offer me the use of your couch, Merle, but I did tell the hotel I'd be back late this evening. I can see myself out, so I'll say goodnight. Glad I could help with the chauffeuring. You help your friend with *her* problem . . .'

She couldn't resist it, of course: 'Sorry I couldn't help you with *yours*, Derry!' and he knew the sarcasm was to conceal the hurt she felt, and despite his relief at his timely escape, he hated himself for causing that.

Baz laid the replete baby in her cot, climbed back into bed. He yawned widely.

'Sorry,' Wendy said, 'I should have done it, you've had a long day, dear.'

'Poor girl. A short life and not a particularly happy one, it seems. But at least the lad's got a good home and a new family.' He paused, then: 'The riddle's solved: Jim's his real father, apparently. Hard to take in, isn't it? He seemed like the last person . . . Jan forgave him long ago. Did you know anything at the time?'

Wendy felt sudden fear.

'No.'

That wasn't really a lie. Jan had guessed Wendy's own predicament but Wendy hadn't realized Jim had been unfaithful too.

'All water under the bridge,' Baz said comfortably. 'You'd have done the same as Jan, the difference being I could never make love to another woman, my darling.' His hand gently caressed her bare arm, moved over her breast. 'Wendy, don't you think it's . . . well . . . time we resumed our normal married life?'

She clutched him convulsively. 'Oh Baz. *I love you*, you know that.'

Chapter Twenty-three

Bekka was waiting, as promised, on the platform at Liverpool Street station when the train steamed in. Rosanna was travelling light because the big trunk, with most of her possessions, had been sent on ahead by rail, already collected.

They clattered up the winding stairs to the top deck of the 137 bus where Rosanna rubbed the window with the rolled-up early edition of the *Evening Standard*. The terraces of shops, the advertisement hoardings, people crowding the pavements, rival newspaper vendors, whining trams, flashed by; then, at the traffic-lights, Rosanna observed a red milk-cart, drawn by a brown horse taking the opportunity to deposit a steaming pile of manure in the road.

There were yawning gaps between the buildings where bombs had blasted, colonized by buddleias – butterfly bushes, along with toadflax. The latter was not yet in pink bloom and Rosanna was suddenly reminded of country strolls with Susie, when fluffy seed balls from this flew around in autumn and she and Merle jumped up in the air, with Topper nipping at their heels, to try to capture them. She recognized dandelions, ragged robin and nettles jostling with the brambles, too. These wild plants had appeared out of the blue, like the poppies in the muddy fields in France following the First World War.

'Oh, I *love* London!' she exclaimed enthusiastically.

'This is Streatham Hill,' Bekka pointed out. 'There's Pratts store. Ket reckons it's almost as classy as Oxford Street without the flashy prices. There's the dry-cleaners where she's manageress. There's the Gaumont: we have all the latest films there, but we also go to Streatham Hill Theatre, I adore live performances, don't you? Sometimes they have old-time music hall. Wait until we explore the heart of London though! There's so much you can see for free. All the galleries for a start.'

'There's lots to see in Lynn, too!' Rosanna said loyally. 'Everyone talks about the Whisky à go-go club; not that I'm allowed there, though the strongest drink they serve is cappuccino.'

'Why did you move from North London? You said your dad liked it in Highbury because of Arsenal FC and his compatriots round and about!'

'Ket persuaded Dad to invest in property, while it was dirt cheap because of bomb damage, or people deciding not to come back. Wait 'til you see our house, it's *super!*' Bekka enthused. 'It's at the back of Streatham Common, up the hill – the bus stops at the end of our road. It's still nice and green there, though it's getting more and more built on. There are even cows in the fields at Valley Farm Road – you saw the United Dairies cart? That's where we get our milk from!

'I *must* introduce you to the tennis club. We go on afterwards to the Olympus Café, still in white shorts and believe me, mine *are* short! I made them myself. The boys are rather sweaty and spotty, but eager to chat you up over cups of coffee, which they pay for – the muddy sort, not frothy like your old Whisky-wotsits. Ket would probably put the Olympus out of bounds, like your mum, if she knew, but she's pleased I'm getting some exercise at last!'

Bekka was transformed from the studious youngster Rosanna remembered, to a vivacious teenager with bold lipstick and mascara.

'D'you like my hair?' she enquired cheerfully. It was cropped above her ears. 'It's the urchin cut,' she added, 'it's meant to look as if you've chopped it yourself. No perms, no pinning up. Shampoo, shake your head and it's dry in no time!'

'You'll look as if you haven't any hair, under a hat,' Rosanna ventured. She hoped Bekka wouldn't say she must follow suit. Mum and Dad wouldn't approve.

'Who wears hats these days? Not *our* generation!'

Wendy had bought a brimless light-weight hat for her daughter to wear to the office, and cotton gloves. Now, Rosanna thought, oh dear! Would her boxy jacket with three-quarter sleeves look 'old hat', too? Bekka had a casual shoulder satchel; she had a square bag with a handle, a mirror in the lid, and ruched pockets for cosmetics, comb and purse. It had seemed modern back in Lynn.

'You've changed,' she said.

'In some ways I suppose I have. I made up my mind some time ago I was going to be a free spirit and unstoppable! I imagine you felt the same, when you said you were leaving home. I haven't left home, because it suits me to live in the lap of luxury, and there aren't any younger ones fighting for my parents' attention! I bend the rules when it suits me. Well, our stop; come on! Ket will have lunch ready, something from the deli and a green salad. We eat our main meal at seven.'

To Rosanna, used to a high tea around six, rather than dinner, this sounded rather daunting, but naturally she'd have to adapt to their ways.

It was a double-fronted house in an avenue of thirties mock-Tudor detached properties, with wide steps up to the solid oak front door. Trees were planted at intervals along the pavement, thick hedges screened the front gardens with their square lawns and rose bushes. The Maestri family had really gone up in the world.

Ket looked youthful in a circular skirt patterned in swirls of orange and emerald, and an orange blouse. Her hair was worn in a sleek chignon. Her husband was reassuringly much as Rosanna remembered him, with curly grey hair and a kind smile. He waved a friendly hand at the guest.

'*Ciao*, Rosanna!'

Ket kissed Rosanna.

'How like Wendy you are! Fancy, a baby! I thought that, like me, she was past all that lark. Bekka will show you your room, but don't be long, lunch is on the table.'

'Mum and I decorated the room for you,' Bekka said proudly, ushering Rosanna within. 'She did the distempering, she likes plain cream walls, not wallpaper, but I chose the blue for the ceiling, stuck on all the silver stars – and even a full moon to remind you of that floating one when you were little! I stood on the bed to reach that high, but I don't think there are footprints on the bedspread. Like it?'

'It's beautiful!' Rosanna said, in awe. She thought it resembled a Hollywood boudoir, with snowy draped window-nets, and tasselled cords to swish the dark-blue curtains at night. The lampshade was covered in matching material; there was a fluffy mat by the bed which had a padded headboard and patterned coverlet. This was sophistication, London style.

'Glad you approve! You can unpack later. Now let's relax until Monday!'

Rosanna decided to travel with Bekka first thing to London, as she wasn't sure she could find her way to Fetter Lane alone.

'You'll have time to fill,' Bekka reminded her, 'before ten.'

'I don't mind, I'll get a chance to tidy my hair and compose myself, won't I.'

'Don't worry, I've told the boss you're just right for the job, and that you're going to enrol at night school, which he approves of. Ask questions, he'll like that.'

'I don't know if I dare.'

'Don't be silly, Rosy. Your staying here depends on it. Mum and Dad can't keep you for nothing, although they don't mind for a bit, until you're earning.'

'Of course they can't! But I do feel rather nervous.'

'You needn't! If the boss approves of you, well, you can start today.'

Rosanna immediately dubbed it the Windy Corner as they turned into Fetter Lane. The area had obviously endured its share of bomb damage. A breeze caught at the hem of her skirt, lifted scraps of paper which twirled round her ankles. As she bent to remove the debris, she heard Bekka indignantly remonstrating with a man who had almost cannoned into them:

'Here, just you wipe that off my shoe!'

And the chap in the bowler hat actually apologized as he removed the spittle from her shiny black pump with his handkerchief. Then he hurried off.

'That's how you catch TB, through people spitting. That's why the buses have notices saying they'll fine anyone they catch doing it. Filthy habit!'

'He didn't look the sort to spit on the pavement,' Rosanna ventured.

'You'd be surprised,' Bekka said enigmatically. 'You'll learn. Don't go into the stationery room unaccompanied, that's all I'm saying.'

Rosanna was disappointed when she saw the rather decrepit building where the publishing company was housed. There was little light in the entrance hall, the lift was an antiquated cage, with a thick, dangling rope hauled by a little grey man in a grey uniform, with one empty sleeve tucked into his pocket.

'New?' he asked Rosanna, as the mesh doors clanged shut.

'I – hope to be!' she said shyly. She studied the notice stuck to the inside of the cage door, as they swayed and inched upwards.

> DEAR MADAM/SIR. SHOULD YOU LOSE YOUR RIGHT
> GLOVE, ITS PARTNER WOULD BE MUCH APPRECIATED
> BY YOUR LIFT ATTENDANT, YOURS RESPECTFULLY,
> TED HEAD.

Donatti Directories, publishers of business listings, guide books, Italian phrase books, technical manuals and other prosaic paperbacks, were on the top floor of the building. Here things were brighter, due to white paint and colourful prints on the walls in the reception area, where Rosanna awaited the call from Mr Donatti.

The receptionist had obviously been to the same hairdresser as Bekka. She chewed gum incessantly and assumed a posh voice when she answered the telephone calls constantly buzzing on the switchboard.

'Jest one mo-ment please! Will you hold the line, please – Mr Don-atti is busy at this mo-ment!' Then, relapsing into her normal speech: 'Oh hi, Nina. I'm sorry, but I can't help out with any typing just now, as I'm looking after a client . . .' She glanced at Rosanna, who pretended to be reading a magazine. 'Like a cup of coffee, Miss Bloomfield?'

Rosanna hesitated. Her throat was drying up in her nervous state, but if she accepted, she might want to visit the lavatory, and she hadn't been told where that was.

'No thank you,' she heard herself say.

It seemed a long hour. Monica Long, as the card on her desk informed the curious, answered a buzz with: 'Rightyho, sir,' and beckoned Rosanna over.

'Through the end door, down the corridor, swing doors on the right, notice saying 'Boardroom' – OK? A word of advice, dear – take your gloves off before you shake hands with Mr Don-atti. Good luck!' Monica unwrapped another piece of gum. 'Hello? Mr Don-atti is busy right now. Will you call back later?' Through startling upswept glasses, she winked at Rosanna.

Rosanna swallowed. She hoped her voice wouldn't come out all squeaky.

The boardroom was unexpectedly large, the walls lined with leather-bound tomes. Behind a long mahogany table was another diminutive grey-haired man in a grey suit, with small hands resting on and reflected in the polished surface. Rosanna studied his protruding white cuffs, the pearl links, rather than his face.

'Do please take a seat,' he said, and his voice reminded her instantly of Bekka's father. Precise English but with that slight intonation. Mr Donatti was of Italian origin too.

'He's nice,' Bekka had reassured her earlier. 'Old college friend of Dad's, but despite knowing me all my life he never uses my Christian name in working hours. He even calls his daughter Miss Donatti!'

Belatedly, Rosanna tugged at her gloves. They were difficult to budge because her hands were damp. Mr Donatti pretended not to notice.

'We have received a good testimonial from your school.' Mr Donatti tapped a sheet of paper. 'You know how to punctuate?' He tapped the paper once more as if illustrating a comma or full stop. 'I am sure you do. You are prepared to learn the mechanics of the typewriter in your own time, at the polytechnic? You will be paid weekly, four pounds ten shillings, with annual increments; two weeks' paid holiday a year, usual bank holidays; nine to five-thirty, one Saturday morning in four. Any questions?'

'I – have I got the job?' It had all happened so quickly.

Mr Donatti smiled, rose, held out his hand. He was no taller than Rosanna, but still imposing.

'While you were coming along the corridor, Miss Long buzzed me to say I should offer you this position, which I must tell you is a very junior one, but with good prospects as you proceed through each department, find your forte as it were. I always trust Miss Long's judgement, it saves a great deal of time. Also, there were the glowing comments of your friend, Miss Maestri, whom we will now ask to show you around.' He pressed the buzzer before him.

There was a large workroom with trestle-tables end to end down the centre; books from ceiling to floor on three walls here too, of the well-thumbed variety, untidily replaced, but obviously in some order or category, with cards in faded ink. On the wall at the far end was a door to another room, and a row of metal filing-cabinets where the drawers were opened and slammed alarmingly every five minutes or so.

Immediately on entering the workroom Rosanna saw the glassed-in cubicle within which the single telephone continually rang. Now and again, a middle-aged man wearing a green celluloid eyeshade, who sat at a desk within, opened the door and shouted, above the hubbub of voices:

'For you, Val – Joan – Mr Tiplady – Miss Donatti – alert Terry, Mr Donatti wants him to take a message.'

There were half a dozen busy people seated, or moving around the table. Rosanna saw long sheets of paper spread in what seemed to be a haphazard manner; pots of paste and brushes; curved scissors; dip-pens and bottles of ink, as they waited at a respectful distance for someone to address them.

'Galleys – proofs,' Bekka explained. 'These are the proofreaders, they check and correct. It's a rush job – the printers want all this back by tomorrow. You won't be working in here yet – you'll be in the general office next door, with the copywriters, Mr Donatti's secretary

Nina, and her assistant, me! Oh, Miss Donatti, please can you spare a moment? This is Rosanna, who's joined us . . .'

Miss Donatti was small and pretty, younger than the other girls, but obviously their senior. She evidently had a habit of running her often sticky fingers through her short chestnut coloured hair, so that it stuck up at angles.

'It is a pleasure to meet you,' she told Rosanna. 'We will talk later; for now, as you can see, we are working against time.'

Val and Joan, in their early twenties, Rosanna guessed, waved languid hands in her direction, called hello, then bent again over their work. Mr Tiplady looked very superior and merely glanced at the new recruit. Above the constriction of his collar, his prominent Adam's apple bobbed up and down. The older women at the table were having a heated discussion and a tussle over one of the galleys.

Rosanna followed Bekka meekly into the adjoining room, which was furnished with desks and typewriters.

'Stationery cubby hole – remember?' Bekka indicated a door, with a giggle. 'Watch out for old Tiplady.'

It obviously helps to be of Italian origin to work here, Rosanna thought, when she met Nina, who was to supervise her metamorphosis from schoolgirl to junior clerk with aspirations.

'There isn't much you can help me with until you can type, but practise on the old Underwood whenever you have a spare moment. Miss Morris,' she said sharply, to a woman in a green overall seated at a desk by the window, causing her to swivel round in her chair. 'Mr Donatti and I have decided that Miss Bloomfield will assist you for the time being. But bear in mind, I may have need of her services from time to time.' Nina had a husky voice and exquisite features which reminded Rosanna of one of her favourite film stars, Gina Lollobrigida.

Just then a buzzer sounded on Nina's desk; she swept up her notebook and pencil and departed smartly, leaving Rosanna standing there.

Bekka gave her a push in Miss Morris's direction.

'Better get on with my work, I suppose – see the look Nina gave me?'

Miss Morris's worried expression cleared with Nina's departure.

'Rosanna, isn't it? Anyone under thirty automatically gets called by their first name, except for Miss Donatti, of course. I won't divulge my age, but you may call me Morry. Miss Donatti, Mr Tiplady and I are the chief copy-writers. Now, I've a tedious task for you, but a very necessary one. Just pull up a chair next to mine.'

For the rest of the morning Rosanna was busy with a large business

dictionary carefully tearing out the pages, then cutting each advertisement and sticking it on a separate piece of paper.

'These are last year's. We're now collating them for the new issue.
I'll check them for errors or alterations which are necessary, then you
address the envelopes and post the copy for approval and renewal.
Don't look so mystified, I'll go through it with you, step by step.'

'Cloakroom,' Bekka informed her, opening a door with a flourish.
'Unmodernized, but Dot, the cleaner, mops the floor at least twice a
week! We have to bring our own soap. I buy a Fairy green bar and cut
it in three – here's your share!'

'Was it Dot who brought round the morning tea?'

'Yes, that's her. She's a bit sloppy, but good-hearted. Nina had a go
at her the other day about dust on top of the filing cabinets well, you
saw how short Dot is, but she said: 'I don't do nothin' above shoulder
level. It's in me contract!'

'Good for her.' Rosanna grinned. The lavatory doors had big gaps at
bottom and top, which Bekka pointed out was useful, for you could tell
by the shoes who was ensconced and then you didn't . . . well, put your
foot in it with your gossip. But she didn't add that, sometimes, you
could be left with the chain in your hand.

'Now, let's get cracking, Rosy, to Jolley's, where they make super
sandwiches. It's in Fleet Street next to Ye Olde Cheshire Cheese pub.'

Chapter Twenty-four

'Only my fifth day,' Rosanna lamented to Bekka in the middle of the morning. 'And I've got a permanent dent at the base of my thumb from all that scissor work.' I'm only on letter D, too, she thought. The book's not much lighter.

'Cheer up, it's pay-day! Mr Greene, he who hasn't yet emerged from his glasshouse to make your acquaintance, is Accounts, you know, and he'll be making his rounds before lunchtime with those little brown packets.'

'Maybe I won't be lucky, I haven't worked the full week 'til this evening.'

'Did Mr Donatti say anything about working a week in hand? No? Well, then, that's been calculated, as you'll see.'

'Shush,' Morry mumbled, her mouth full of questionably acquired chocolate, of which she kept a seemingly unlimited supply in her desk drawer and to which she was obviously addicted. 'Nina's back.'

'Haven't you any work to do?' Nina's remark was vitriolic. As Bekka had told Rosanna ruefully at the beginning of the week, 'She's more Beast than Beauty!'

'She's frustrated, working here,' Rosanna imagined. 'With her looks she could have been a film star, or an air-hostess, or—'

'Or nothing. We all know we're lucky to have a job these days, don't we?'

Now, Morry dabbed her lips with her handkerchief, and behind this cover, whispered:

'Watch out, here comes old Tiplady! Get the key!'

Rosanna unlocked the walk-in stationery cupboard.

'After you,' Mr Tiplady said, in his dry way.

Was this what Bekka, and later Morry, had hinted at? Rosanna had no choice. She glanced at Morry, who mouthed at her.

'Don't let him get away with it!'

167

As she stepped forward, notepad in hand, for all requisitions must be recorded, she anticipated the sly pinch on her behind. She whirled round. Mr Tiplady merely looked superior, distant, as usual.

Aware of the pregnant silence in the office behind her, she hissed: 'If you do that again – *I'll report you!*'

A slow tide of red suffused Mr Tiplady's face, spread down his neck. His Adam's apple worked overtime. He pointed to her notebook.

'Ream of quarto, bottle of blue/black ink, box of pencils, two paste brushes – got all that?'

'That's worth a buttered bun from you to me at elevenses,' Morry whispered approvingly when Mr Tiplady had departed with his box.

Then, surprisingly, Nina said from behind her desk, where she was absent-mindedly linking together paper-clips while reading through her shorthand notes:

'Good for you, Rosanna. That man's a menace.' Then she buzzed Monica in reception to tell her the news.

Mr Greene did not make his rounds until it was almost time for Rosanna to ease the scissors from their cruel grip on her thumb. They waited for him to leave before they tore open their envelopes. Nina put hers unopened in her bag.

'She doesn't want us to see how much she gets,' Bekka whispered to Rosanna. Morry checked the chocolate drawer and then departed smartly for the cloakroom.

'My treat,' Bekka said grandly. 'We're going somewhere special for lunch today – we can expect grilled fish this evening, no chips, because Ket says she has to watch her figure, so we can eat our fill. Actually the rule on fish on Fridays has been relaxed since the war, and Ket knows I take full advantage of it. Come on!'

'I'm not dressed up, if we're going somewhere posh—'

'Who said anything about posh? I want you to meet the current object of my affections and to taste his sublime cooking!'

They were trailed down the road as usual by fifteen-year-old Terry, the office-boy, who liked to be called Tel. Despite its being a warm May day, with all the girls going out for lunch in pretty, full-skirted cotton dresses, the men sweltered as usual in suits, and tightly knotted ties. Tel went one further, in that he slouched along in a belted white mackintosh, collar turned up, to catch the drips of Brylcreem from his slicked-back hair, the girls decided, giggling helplessly.

'He thinks he's Dick Barton, Special Agent,' as Bekka said. This was one of their favourite radio programmes. 'Don't worry, he's got his cheese-and-pickle sandwiches in his pocket, and when we turn right, he'll guess where we're going, and he'll veer off and make for Lincoln's Inn Fields, to gawp at the office-girls there playing netball in their lunch hour, and get pickle on his mac.'

Bellini's Italian restaurant certainly wasn't posh; from the outside it appeared to be just a café, with quickly prepared food for workers in a hurry to reach the nearest park bench to soak up the sunshine and fresh air for an hour. But as the door opened, the ambience was different. There were a half-dozen small tables, for two, or four at a crowd, with green-and-white gingham tablecloths and matching serviettes, in which the cutlery was neatly rolled. Despite it being noon, candles flickered in round wine-bottles sitting in baskets. There were crusty rolls on side plates, a silver-plated cruet set, with a handwritten menu propped against it. Behind a counter, cooking took place in full view of the customers; a great vat of spaghetti steamed away; to the pan of sauce was added chopped tomatoes and fresh basil by a middle-aged man with a striped apron strained round his ample middle. An equally plump woman was absorbed in grating parmesan cheese.

'Mamma and Papa . . . And there *he* is,' Bekka actually pointed at the smiling young man who lifted the spaghetti strands, tossed them and returned them to the pan. 'He'll come over in a moment, and take our order – isn't he *beautiful*?'

Rosanna felt rather uncomfortable at that description, although he was indeed very good-looking, with an abundance of black hair: irresistible curls you could twiddle your fingers through; she felt embarrassed by this outrageous thought. Also, it was all too obvious that he'd overheard what Bekka said.

'We met at the poly. He works here during the day in the family business, but he is studying management, he wants to work in a big hotel.'

'Who are you telling all my business to, Miss Maestri?' he asked, smiling, so that Rosanna could see that he had a perfect set of gleaming teeth.

'You startled me!' Bekka reproved him mildly. 'Rosanna, this is Daniel.'

'They call me Danny, of course.' He looked at Rosanna. 'And you. . . ?'

'Rosy,' she said, and she thought with a start, I really don't mind being called that, after all.

'We've known each other since we were little girls, haven't we, Rosy? She's living with us now, we're working together at Donatti's, and she's joining the poly, too. Secretarial, like me.'

'That's nice,' he approved. 'Now, your orders please. May I recommend the spaghetti à la bolognaise, today's special offer and our family recipe, but more herbs than meat these days, Papa sighs. We are not licensed to sell wine, Rosy, but you will enjoy our coffee.'

'Is it frothy?' she asked, surprising herself with the question.

'You like that? I am sorry, but we don't have an espresso machine.'

'I don't mind, really, as long as there is sugar!' she assured him.

'I'm hungry,' Bekka said plaintively. 'And,' she looked at her watch, 'we only have thirty-five minutes to eat, then we have to rush back to work!'

'You know how to manage the spaghetti?' Danny asked Rosanna.

She shook her head. 'I've . . . never had it before,' she said truthfully.

'Just chop it, don't let it dangle from your fork,' Bekka told her, jealous at the attention Danny was paying to her friend.

He ignored this. He took up Rosanna's fork and twirled it in the pasta strands. 'See, just a little practice makes perfect. You try. Easy, really, isn't it.'

Oops! He's affecting my concentration like Derry does, when he gets close to me, Rosanna thought, surprising herself again. I mustn't encourage him, because I can tell Bekka doesn't like it.

'Thanks, I think I can manage now,' she said.

'Danny' called his mother imperiously. 'Customers are waiting!'

'Well, what d'you think of him?' Bekka demanded as he went.

'He's – nice. I'm not too sure about the curls.' Rosanna floundered, managing to lose most of the spaghetti from her fork as she lifted it to her mouth. That came of telling little white lies. She really didn't care for the rather sickly smell of the cheese, either. She couldn't say that, of course, because her friend was paying for the lunch, and three-and-six for two would make a hole in her pay-packet.

'He had a short back and sides when I met him at the beginning of this year after his National Service. I suppose it's a reaction to that.'

'Your coffee,' said Mamma Bellini, placing their cups on the table. 'I will bring your bill; my son has to learn that too much talk does not earn the money.'

Danny whispered in Bekka's ear in passing a little later.

'Want to know what he said?' Bekka looked pleased. 'He said, when he introduces me properly to Mamma, she'll approve, as I'm a good Catholic girl!'

Wendy put the phone down. She was last in line to speak to Rosanna, because Baz had answered the call while she was putting Marcy to bed. Then Russ had been eager to listen to his sister; he didn't say much himself, but he obviously recognized her voice.

'She's having a good time, then.' Wendy sighed.

'You don't sound too pleased about that, old dear.'

'Don't be daft, Baz, of course I am.'

'But you rather hoped that she'd be homesick. Come on, admit it!'

'So did you!'

'Maybe. Still, she's being well looked after at Ket's, and she likes her job. Fancy, her first wage-packet today, and more than she would have got here, eh?'

'Money's not everything.'

'Of course not, but when you're young it's nice to have it to spend! Come on, Russ, time for your bath, old fellow.'

'Mud-mud,' Russ insisted, pouting.

'She's tired, missing Rosy's help, I reckon. I'm ready to do my bit.'

'Mud-mud bath me!' He pulled at Wendy's sleeve.

'Oh leave him, Baz. We're all missing Rosy, aren't we. Somehow, we've got to get ourselves in a new routine.' Now, they could hear Marcy grizzling upstairs. 'She senses things are a bit upside-down, and no, Baz, I can't just leave her to cry . . .' Her voice rose rather hysterically.

'I'll go,' Baz said firmly.

'You haven't had your supper yet.'

'I can wait. Russ can do without a bath tonight, and tomorrow he can have a go at bathing himself. Maybe we don't allow him to do enough for himself. Like Rosy he should be given the chance to be more independent – didn't the school tell us that? Read him a story instead, or better still help him with his reading-book.'

Things were gradually falling into place at Jan and Jim's house. Jan knew that she could never take on Norah's role with young Jamie, but she hoped that their affection and compassion would help him with his loss. When he needed a hug, he instinctively turned to her; when he had a bad headache and a raised temperature, she took him to the doctor's, to be sure it was nothing more serious. Sometimes she experienced a little pang at how his relationship with Jim was developing.

This Friday evening Jim came in with a surprise for the boy.

'You said when we were talking of old Topper the other evening that you'd always wanted a dog. Well, what d'you think of this little chap? Reg got him from the same place as Topper came from. Might even be related.' He set the wriggling pup down at Jamie's feet. As he stroked him, the pup straddled and let loose a big puddle.

'Whoops! Don't tread in it,' Janet cried, seizing the floorcloth.

'Thanks, Dad.' Then Jamie realized what he had said, and looked at Jim.

'That sounds good to me,' Jim told him quietly.

Janet made no comment, just busied herself with the mopping up. I'll always be Aunt Jan, she thought, and that's right, but I have to admit it makes me feel, well, a little odd, to hear Jamie call Jim by a name that only Merle has used until now. What will *she* think about it?

She sorted out a cardboard box, lined it with an old woolly. 'There. Will that do for a bed? How old is he, Jim?'

'Ten weeks.'

'How big will he grow?' Jamie asked, screwing up a ball of newspaper for the pup to chase.

'Topper size, I reckon. He'll still fit in a poacher's pocket.'

'What's that? Have you got one?'

Jim laughed. 'No. How about a tool-bag?'

'What are you going to call him,' Janet wanted to know. She was a little put out because Jim hadn't discussed the dog with her beforehand.

The pup scrambled into the box, scuffled up the bedding, then tipped it up on its side and bounded out again to chase the paper ball under the table.

'Well, I can't call him Topper, but I could name him Tipper – 'cos he just tipped the box over! Is that all right, Dad?'

'Just right, I reckon,' Jim said. 'Don't you, Jan?'

Rosanna was lying in bed, with the bedside light still on, gazing up at the stars on her ceiling, when Bekka looked in, after cleaning her teeth in the bathroom.

'Good day, wasn't it, Rosy? Payday always is, and guess what, Nina told Miss Donatti that she thought you'd be a real asset to Donatti's, and that's really something! And thanks for sharing the chocolate Morry gave you.'

'And thanks for the lovely lunch. It'll be my treat next Friday, I promise.'

'But before that, it'll be Thursday, and I'll see Danny again. Well, goodnight. Lie-in tomorrow, thank goodness, not our Saturday on duty.'

' 'Night.' Rosanna yawned, as Bekka closed the door.

Rosanna clicked the light-switch. I'm looking forward to seeing him again, too, she thought, but I've got to remember that Bekka laid claim to him first. She'd intended to write to Derry this evening, with her new address, but she hadn't given it another thought.

Chapter Twenty-five

She may have left school, but Rosanna was aware that learning continued, and for some she must pay herself. This made her concentrate on her course. She was not a natural like Bekka, who was fluent in shorthand in six months, but as Bekka said, 'It's just another language, and I'm good at those.' She'd be armed with her certificates soon and free from evening studies. Rosanna would have to continue by herself, so Danny offered to meet her after classes.

'We'll go to the milk bar, then I'll wait with her for the bus, so she won't get lost in the smog, Bekka.'

I mustn't give him any encouragement, Rosanna resolved.

Then there was the studying required at work. Rosanna had a booklet compiled by Morry for marking up copy and correcting proofs. There were tea stains and smears of chocolate throughout, so there'd really been no necessity for Morry to write her name on each sheet in black capitals, double underlined. Testing time came at tea-breaks, when Morry snatched the precious document, cream bun in hand, and Rosanna dipped her mapping-pen and made the mark demanded of her.

Despite all the hard graft, Rosanna enjoyed her new life to the full. She felt guilty, but not too much, when she spoke to her family or read Wendy's weekly letters, that she didn't miss them as much as they missed her. When she broached the subject to Bekka, she observed:

'It's the heady taste of freedom, Rosy, despite having to work for our living. It's good for me now you're here, because Ket imagines you'll curb any rebellion. Ha ha! That's a laugh, isn't it? She trusts you to see I don't do anything I shouldn't when we're out in the evenings!'

Chaperon, Rosanna thought ruefully; I'm the one who tags along, just as I did with Merle and Derry. But I'm having a good time despite it!

The tennis club was one of several which shared facilities rented from the council: three hard courts with rather droopy nets and a club-house where a non-playing member would make the tea or coffee, invariably wet and weak and accompanied by a stale biscuit, for threepence. The changing-rooms were not places to linger; they reeked of sweaty socks, as Bekka forewarned Rosanna, and there was no prospect of showers for another decade. One or two players would go on to better things long before that, even achieve Wimbledon, if not the headlines.

Rosanna refused Bekka's kind offer to make her a matching pair of shorts, but Jan sent her a pleated white skirt, and her modesty was preserved.

The girls blancoed their plimsolls and practised service and returns in the back garden over Ket's lowered washing line, with their new Slazenger rackets and an ancient tennis-ball, which the next-door children had lobbed over the fence and not bothered to reclaim, the bounce having gone out of it.

One summer's evening, the tennis captain, with inter-club championships in mind, decided that the inexperienced players should have coaching from those dedicated to the sport.

'Too much larking around,' he said sternly. He paired them randomly. Rosanna was partnered by Ray; she was in awe of his reputation both at tennis and with the girls. Ray was tall and handsome, pursued by them for his athletic prowess and sex appeal but was an easy going, cheerful chap.

He was patient too, helping Rosanna to correct her serve; sending an unerring stream of tennis balls which bounced off her racket however wildly she swiped. At the end of their session, when she shyly thanked him for his help, he asked unexpectedly:

'Fancy coffee at the Olympus? I'll hang on while you change.'

'I came like this,' she faltered.

'So did I! Saves time, doesn't it, and who wants to linger in the changing-rooms, eh?' He wrinkled his nose expressively, making her laugh.

Bekka came off court. She was surprised to see them still together.

'We're going to the Olympus – would you like to come?' Ray asked gallantly. 'Then I'll walk you both home, if you like. I live quite near you, I believe.'

They were aware of envious glances as Ray escorted them from the club, and Bekka waved goodbye airily to the remaining members: ' 'Bye, see you next Tuesday!'

Ray did most of the talking. He told them he lived with his widowed mother, that he was a trainee accountant, which paid next to nothing until he was qualified. He was studying for his exams by correspondence course. Playing tennis was a welcome break. He'd played cricket and football during National Service.

'Now I appreciate how important exercise is to combat mental fatigue, not just to escape fatigues,' he joked.

He's not only clever, he's genuinely amusing, Rosanna thought. I like him.

At the gate they continued talking for a few minutes, until Bekka spotted the lace curtains in the front bay window moving.

'Oops!' She went up the path.

Ray said to Rosanna: 'Just a sec. Fancy coming dancing at the weekend?'

'I . . .' This took her completely by surprise.

'I won't suggest the Locarno, though that's quite an experience, but how about the Grandisom? That's only a short bus-ride away. There's a new band playing there this Saturday. Bekka can come too! She's got a boyfriend, hasn't she? A foursome would be fun. You ask her, then give me a ring, eh?' He took a little card from his blazer pocket. 'There's my number.'

Bekka was holding the door open.

'What were you gassing about, Rosy?'

'He's asked us to go dancing on Saturday night! Would Danny come, too?'

'Can but ask! This might just be the opportunity I've been waiting for. Rosy, you're a dark horse! Now we've *both* got an admirer, as Ket puts it!'

In the privacy of her room, Rosanna looked at Ray's card. RAMON STEPHENS: No wonder he preferred Ray. A memory stirred, of Jan talking of the film stars of the late twenties, early thirties. Ramon Navarro! That could be it, if Ray's mother was around Jan's age.

Bekka knocked on the door, came in.

'Don't faint, but Ket said we can go! I've never been to a public dance-hall before, either. I can't ask Danny until poly night, but even if he can't make it, I'm not going to be left at home, eh?'

'Just one thing, Bekka, I can't dance! Any bright ideas?'

'My dear Rosy, we've got time to practise, and as long as you can waltz, one-two-three, one-two-three, turn, you can adapt that to the rest.'

'And what can I wear? I don't have a dance dress.'

'Oh, it's informal these days, just wear something nice, although you'll need dancing-shoes, they won't allow you on the dance floor, else.'

'I haven't got those, but will my green-and-white striped dress do?'

'I'm sure it will. Oh, and I believe Ket might be able to find the silver sandals I wore when I was thirteen and first went to dancing classes; she never throws anything away, a wartime habit she says. Size four; now, alas, I wear a six.'

Rosanna was cheering up again. 'I take fours.'

'There you are then! Rosy, why d'you think Ray took a shine to you?'

'I – I don't know.'

''Cause you're little and cute. Like Danny, he thinks you need looking after.'

'Danny's only got eyes for you!' She hoped she sounded convincing.

'He'd better have, that's all I'm saying. The difference between us was obvious tonight; my partner slammed the ball straight at me, I used my racket as a shield. Ray was more considerate! Ket says to ring him tomorrow; we don't want to appear too eager.'

Ray called for them at seven on Saturday evening, and they went off with Ket's strictures ringing in their ears:

'You will look after them both, won't you, Ray? Remember I'm responsible for Rosy's welfare, too, I promised her parents. Don't hang about afterwards, there might be Teddies around—'

'Teddy *boys*, Ket,' Bekka told her. 'They only push you off the pavement.'

'Oh, dear!'

'They'll be OK with me,' Ray assured Ket. 'And Danny will be with us, too.'

'I haven't met Danny yet.'

'We'll miss our bus and he'll wonder where we are if we don't go now, so 'bye!' Bekka did a bit of pushing herself. 'Come on you two!'

They sat on the back seat of the bus, a bit of a squash, so Ray linked arms with Rosanna.

'There, is that better?' He gave her a special smile.

Danny was waiting outside the hall. He looked smart in his sharp navy pinstripe suit and shiny patent shoes. Ray wore his blazer and flannels, but a tie, instead of his usual cravat, as requested by the management.

The two young men jiggled the coins in their pockets and, discreetly, Danny passed his share to Ray, who bought their tickets. Then the girls went into the cloakroom to change their shoes, leave their jackets with the attendant, and to apply more colour from new long lip pencils in gilt cases.

Rosanna looked at herself in the big mirror. The room smelled of powder and excitement. She wasn't sure she felt comfortable with coral lips, or the hairstyle devised by Bekka, but she was eager for dancing to begin. The band were warming up; snatches of music made her feet tap in the borrowed silver shoes.

Ray's hand was firm on her bare arm, as he led her to a row of chairs.

'I like your dress,' he approved. It was a simple style from Marks; cap sleeves, round neck; Ket had provided the green beads, and Morry had kindly given her a little silver lamé evening-bag. Inside, she'd discovered a bar of fruit-and-nut.

'For energy,' Morry had whispered. Rosanna would share it with the others in the interval.

The band played with extreme verve and much use of saxophone and drums. They wore evening-dress with bow ties, and between vocals the lead singer smoked a cheroot. Each dance ended with a roll of drums, then he blew smoke rings to the ecstatic girls crowding below the stage.

'Take your partners, *please.*'

Ray soon twigged that Rosanna really had no idea; he guided her round the periphery of the floor so that they didn't tangle with the other dancers, twirled and lifted her round the corners, so that her feet didn't touch the french chalk. When Bekka and Danny passed them, Bekka gave a little shake of her head, but Danny called: 'Change partners?' at the drum tattoo.

Ray held on to Rosanna. 'Jive coming up; the management don't really approve, but times are changing. I'll show you a few easy steps . . .'

Here Rosanna at last came into her own, for she and Merle in the farm days had begged Burl to show them how the Yanks jived.

Danny and Bekka watched from the sidelines. When they returned, breathless and laughing, Bekka remarked disapprovingly:

'You learned that from your mother's American friend, I suppose.'

Rosanna felt immediately deflated. Sometimes she thought of Burl and Wendy and the friendship which she now guessed had been more than that . . .

Danny claimed the first dance after the interval, when he and Ray rather obviously vied for Rosanna's attention. She was aware that Bekka didn't like this at all, although she rose obediently at Ray's invitation.

'I can't dance,' Rosanna told Danny and, with him, this was true. He drew her closer, ignoring her resistance.

'Follow my lead,' he murmured in her ear. He had obviously visited the barber, but the waviness of his hair was irrepressible, and so was he. He wasn't being fair to her best friend.

She felt exasperated with herself. How can I be attracted to two such different chaps at the same time? she asked herself.

But it was Ray who partnered her for the last waltz, when the lights were tactfully dimmed, a winding-down for the dancers after the energetic *Twelfth Street Rag*, which had several encores. It was Ray who kissed her goodnight, having escorted them home. Bekka left them to it, under the front porch. Not because she was tactful, but because she and Danny were denied the same opportunity, Rosanna thought ruefully, as she closed her eyes and felt his breath on her face before their lips met. It was OK, as Burl used to say.

'Goodnight. We must go out again,' Ray said. 'Thanks for a lovely evening.'

'Thank you,' she said sincerely. He kissed the top of her head this time.

'Rosy,' Ket called from the hall. 'Time you came in, dear.'

Chapter Twenty-six

Janet was mixing up a batch of scones, with the lightest of flicks with her fingertips, mingling the grated margarine and aerated flour. She shook in a good pinch of cream of tartar, a little bicarb, added a gill of buttermilk, kneaded the ball of dough. She recalled that she had been baking when Norah's letter unexpectedly arrived. She gave a little shake of her head to banish the thought. Merle sat at the table.

'Pass me the rolling-pin and a cutter from the drawer, will you, dearie?'

Janet floured the shiny Formica surface with which Jim had recently renovated the old table. Jamie's becoming part of the family, for adoption papers were being processed, seemed to herald a period of change all round. She'd chosen buttercup-yellow paint in here, and painted the hard Windsor chairs to match. The larder remained in use, but now housed the crocks and preserves. Janet's latest acquisitions were an electric Burco boiler, neat fridge and a kitchen cabinet with a pull-down working surface.

Jim was indulging her, which was very nice, she thought gratefully. Plastic fittings were all the rage, standard, in the new houses mushrooming everywhere, even if the houses were square little boxes. She appreciated the space in this house, though the empty rooms upstairs reminded her of losing Grandma Birdie and, even though she'd only been with them a short while, Norah.

Merle had been uncharacteristically silent for some time. She'd declined to go down to the river with Jim and Jamie to sunbathe while they fished. Now, she asked suddenly, as her mother filled trays with fat little scones ready for the oven:

'Don't you mind, Mum, Dad going off with Jamie in his spare time?'

'D'you mean, am I *jealous*, Merle? No. D'you feel miffed by it?'

'Well, it's just that—'

'You think he's a bit too fond of the boy, is that it?'

179

'Perhaps. I don't think he's being really fair to you.'

'You know me. Or you should! It's good to have a young 'un around again; you're all grown up Merle, and you're restless when you're here. Oh, I understand, I know you could have gone backpacking with your university pals, though I'd have been worried sick thinking of you thumbing a lift in foreign parts.' She dusted her floury hands on her apron, then sat down opposite her daughter. 'Still, I know the real reason why you came home instead.'

'To see you and Dad, of course.'

'Be honest. You hoped Derry would arrive, sail off with you, with no dewy-eyed young cousin in tow to spoil your chances, this time.'

'You *do* know me too well.' Merle sighed ruefully. 'But as for chances, well, he made it clear when he took me back to Edinburgh in the spring, that there was nothing doing. Sorry Mum; I'm really not one of those girls-who-do-but-ought-to-know-better, as Grandma Birdie used to say.'

'I always say you can cope with the truth; better to come straight out with it. Well, you know how much we think of Derry, don't you? I imagine young Jamie replaces him, for us, in a way. But is he reluctant – I'm sorry if this hurts – because you are fonder of him than he is of you?'

'It's not that. We – we're both *passionate* people – it would be so easy—'

'Then what's holding you back!' Jan surprised herself. 'Cousins do marry, and we wouldn't object. Of course, I don't know how Derry's parents would feel, but they've always been, well, rather detached from him, eh?'

'Mum, I'll be breaking a confidence, but I think I should explain . . .'

'I'm listening, dearie. Take your time.'

'The scones!' Janet cried, as she became aware of the smell of burning. She snatched the trays from the oven and looked at the contents in dismay. Then, practical as always she began to scrape the tops of the scones.

'Not so bad as I thought. Edible, I reckon.' This broke the spell; the confidences were over.

There was one last thing to be said. 'It's Saturday, he should be in his flat, ring him now and say you're catching the next train to London, and for him to meet you. If the mountain won't come to Mohammed, as they say . . .'

'Mum, you're wonderful and I love you,' Merle said.

*

Jamie felt a nibble, a tug at the line. He turned in excitement to Jim.

'Dad! I think I've caught one! What do I do?'

Jim still gripped his own rod, but he was hunched up, his head slumped on to his chest. He didn't answer; his breathing was stertorous.

'Dad!' Jamie said, in alarm. The rod ceased jerking, the fish had got away. He scrambled to his feet, 'Dad! Please speak to me.' He shook Jim's shoulder. Tipper was fooling around his feet, thinking it was some sort of game. 'Tip! Home, boy. Let Aunt Jan know,' he blabbered.

Tipper rolled on his back, paws in the air.

'No, Tip! I'm not playing with you – home, boy!'

Tipper at last recognized the command, usually given when he was sniffing about at the end of a walk. Home meant food, maybe a meaty bone, a long drink of fresh water, and a tussle with the latest cardboard box. He bounded off, but was soon diverted by the smell of rabbit. Clods of earth and tufts of grass were disturbed by his burrowing feet.

'Tip, stop it!' Jamie shouted. But Tipper was too engrossed to hear. Jamie said urgently: 'Dad, what's wrong?'

Jim was groaning, straightening up. Jamie saw the shocking greyness of his face.

'Jamie?' he said uncertainly. He slurred the next words: 'Wassa matter?'

'I don't know – you went all funny. Shall I fetch Aunt Jan?'

Jim struggled to his feet. His colour was returning, his voice suddenly back to normal.

'No, I had a bad pain in my chest that's all; indigestion. No wonder, boy, when you made me bolt my breakfast because you wanted to get down to the fishing, eh?' He smiled at Jamie. 'I'm all right now. Want to carry on, or shall we go home for elevenses? Aunt Jan promised us scones, remember.'

As they walked slowly across the field, Tip ran up, his nose caked in dirt.

'He's awfully hard to train.' Jamie sighed.

'He's the most loyal friend you'll ever have, you can forgive him a lot for that,' Jim said, adding, with studied casualness: 'Don't tell Aunt Jan I had a bit of a turn, will you? It was nothing, really. I'm not as young as I was, you know.'

Jamie nodded, relieved. 'I won't say anything.'

'Good lad.'

*

'You've come to stay?' Derry asked, hurrying Merle towards the tube.

'Overnight, if you'll have me. Too far to come for just a day.'

'You realize that you got me out of bed, when you phoned, and I was forced to tidy up the flat in your honour?' he joked.

'I hope that, while you wielded your feather duster you were thinking of all the exciting places you could take me to.'

'Aha! We'll start with the Tate Gallery, and lunch in the restaurant there.'

'Do I look tidy enough for that?'

'Of course you do. Dazzling, as always.'

'Oh I intend to dazzle you, Derry, I certainly do.'

'What would your mother say, if she knew?'

'You may be surprised to know she does! Her advice is to follow my heart.'

'*Instinct*, more likely! Quick, the doors are opening, jump aboard before they close and one of us is left behind on the platform!'

There were all the wonderful murals painted by Whistler on the walls to marvel at, and more to see in the gallery later. They sat at the table, facing each other.

'I'm still not ready to rush into anything, Merle,' he said quietly. 'You haven't forgotten what I told you in Edinburgh, have you?'

'No. I just want to be with you, at this moment. That's enough for now.'

The waitress was waiting for their order, pencil poised above her notepad. She whispered conspiratorially:

'Wouldn't have the rissoles if I were you. I can recommend the omelette ' She looked at them in surprise as they laughed. 'Chef's speciality, I assure you,' she added.

'Omelettes will be fine, thank you,' Derry managed.

'They're *his* speciality, too!' Merle choked, indicating Derry.

Lovers, they must be, the waitress decided. The choosing of food was a serious business; only lovers saw the funny side. She winked, to show them she understood.

The bus went along the Waterloo road, passing the Old Vic and The Army and Navy Stores *en route*. Rosanna and Ray, Bekka and Danny were going to Battersea Fun Fair, and to see the sights of the Festival of Britain.

The former bomb-site next to Waterloo Station had truly been transformed. Their escorts, who had been there before, were eager to tell all they knew.

Ray pointed out a tall, red-brick chimney.

'That's the old shot-tower, that's where . . ' He paused to marshal his facts.

'They what?' Rosanna asked. 'Why didn't they demolish it?'

'Not sure, but it's certainly redundant. They let molten lead rain down inside from top to bottom of the chimney and as it cooled, it separated into lead shot.'

'Sounds odd, Ray, you must admit. Are you sure you've got it right?'

'Well, there must be a bit more to it than that, but I'm training to be an accountant, remember, not a scientist.' He grinned.

She was walking between the boys, with Bekka on the other side of Danny. She wore the striped dress because Ray liked it, and the crêpe-soled sandals from last summer, which were OK as long as it didn't rain. She wished that Danny would pay more attention to Bekka, who was casting reproachful glances at him. Rosanna stumbled, and was instantly grabbed and steadied by Ray and Danny.

'Little and helpless,' Bekka said crossly, stalking on towards the funfair.

Rosanna flushed. 'Let go, both of you, I'm not a baby.'

This is what she'd protested so often to Merle in the past, when, really, she wasn't much more. She was reminded of something else, too. Merle and Derry talking when they thought she was asleep that night they'd played records. When Merle had said she was like Wendy, and would fall in and out of love too easily.

Well, she didn't *love* either of these boys, she decided now, and a goodnight kiss once a week from Ray didn't give him the right to be proprietorial. She didn't want to lose Bekka's friendship.

'Wait for me,' she called to her friend.

There was Roland Emmett's amazing clock to exclaim over, with its wonderful automata, particularly the cyclist in a pith helmet, balancing a table covered with teatime paraphernalia; the clock whirred and clicked and held them spellbound. Then there were the Guinness models, among them, the giant toucan. These displays were all so extravagant, so bright, like the crowds, who wore their most colourful clothes. The Festival of Britain was a real inspiration, and made everyone feel that things were getting better at last, after years of war and the continuing deprivations, the struggling back to normality, since.

The girls giggled and swayed their way over the rope-walk between the trees, well aware that they were being followed at a distance by the disconsolate Danny and Ray. Rosanna felt a little giddy and she clutched at Bekka.

'Who needs *them*?' Bekka said.

'Why did they have to get so serious so soon?' Rosanna asked.

'Fancy a go on the dodgems?'

'Why not!'

'Bet they'll go on it, too, and crash into us.'

'Then we'll bump 'em hard back!'

They couldn't keep this up all afternoon, of course. At some point they found themselves walking along together, the boys eager to please them by allowing them to choose the rides. It was good to have Ray's arm round her, Rosanna had to admit, when screaming and being whirled round upside down.

Travelling home in the bus, Ray asked Rosanna tentatively:

'Fancy going to the pictures next Saturday evening?'

Rosanna made her mind up instantly.

'Oh, I'm going home next weekend, I haven't seen my family for over three months.' I've been selfish, she thought, telling them how much I'm enjoying life in London; they let me come here with good grace. Suddenly, I want to be with them again so much.

'She's crawling!' Rosanna could hardly believe it. Marcy pulled herself up by her sister's knees and her happy little face made Rosanna smile back, even as her eyes filled with tears, as she realized just how much she had missed her.

Russ vied for her attention, too, waving his reading book.

'Zanna, look!'

'Sit beside me, let's see how well you can read,' she offered.

'Lunch in five minutes,' Wendy reminded them. 'I made your favourite, Rosy, steak-and-kidney pudding.'

Not exactly a good choice for August, but Rosanna appreciated the thought.

'Nice to have you home,' Baz said gruffly, passing her the dish of potatoes. 'D'you want to go out this afternoon, Rosy?'

'No, I just want to be here with you all. Oh, I've got so much to tell you!'

'I understand from Ket,' Wendy said later, in a deliberately casual way, when they were replete, 'you've acquired a nice boyfriend – anyway, she approves!'

'Oh, Mum! He's just a friend, that's all. His name is Ray and we play tennis together, but he's much better than I am. He can't take much time off because he's studying. So must I, if I want to pass my RSAs in the spring.'

'You still like the job?' Baz asked.

'Yes, I do! It's a lot of fun, as well as hard work.'

'A family firm, like mine, that's why. They really care about their staff.'

Marcy was weaned, Rosanna was glad to see. Her mother handed her the baby and a bottle half-full of juice. Her little sister fell asleep in her arms.

'Let's take her upstairs, lay her in her cot,' Wendy whispered. 'Look, the pud's sent your dad and Russ to sleep. Seen anything of Derry?'

'I haven't rung him yet,' Rosanna admitted.

'He was always your hero wasn't he?'

'Oh, Mum! He'll never look at *me* in a romantic light, you must know that.'

'Others certainly will, dear Rosy, in the next few years, I'm sure of it.'

Chapter Twenty-seven

'Mr Donatti wants to see you, Rosanna, in his office, *now,*' Nina said, coming back into the room with her notebook. 'I need a bit of hush,' she added. 'I've got a million letters to get off by the afternoon post. D'you have to keep opening and slamming your drawer like that, Morry?'

'Sorry, I'm sure,' Morry said through a mouthful of chocolate, despite its being but an hour since lunch. She scrawled a note to Rosanna and Bekka, who were sitting alongside. *Someone didn't get to bed last night*, it read.

This didn't make sense to Rosanna, so Bekka pencilled under this: *Man trouble*! She said aloud: '*Now.* Rosanna – didn't you hear? You've had the call!'

Rosanna, feeling apprehensive, whispered: '*Wish me luck!*'

Mr Donatti's desk was by the window.

'Do sit down, Miss Bloomfield,' he said kindly. 'Now, it has come to my notice via our Miss Long, that as Miss Maestri has successfully completed her secretarial course at the polytechnic, you would start the new term alone. The evenings are drawing in, and I am sure your parents will be anxious to think of you travelling home in the dark. As a father myself, I am concerned for your welfare. I have talked to my secretary and she has agreed to assist you with your shorthand, for two hours each week, at her discretion. I am asking now if you are in agreement before you pay the fees.'

In her relief, because she was worrying about seeing Danny on her own, Rosanna did not stop to think what being tutored by the temperamental Nina might be like.

'Thank you, Mr Donatti,' she said breathlessly. 'I accept, thank you.'

He rose, to indicate their talk was over.

'I am glad to hear it. Miss Bloomfield, this seems an appropriate occasion to tell you that, ah, we at Donatti's are very satisfied with your work here.' He held out his hand. 'Good morning.'

There was a quick wave from Monica, busy plugging in or pulling out, as Rosanna passed reception, and the whisper: 'You made the right choice . . .'

'Can't you close the door quietly?' Nina snapped, as Rosanna came in, ready to say she appreciated her kind offer. Rosanna swallowed the words, went to her desk, and wrote another secret note to put her friends in the picture. It was like school, she thought, with Nina as head prefect.

By the beginning of December, Rosanna was actually up to sixty words a minute with her shorthand, and Nina had proved a surprisingly patient instructor. Twice a week they sat together at Nina's big desk in the quiet hour after lunch; in their office they all went out between twelve and one – the rest departed promptly on their return and took their hour off between one and two. Mr Donatti, Mr Greene, Mr Tiplady and, surprisingly, Monica, visited Ye Old Cheshire Cheese. There was plenty of office gossip in the washroom regarding that! Still, Mr Donatti was a widower of long standing, and Mr Greene was a confirmed bachelor. Mr Tiplady's wife was always ringing the office, and he answered the phone in Mr Greene's cubicle, with the latter pretending he couldn't hear the line literally crackling. But Monica certainly couldn't fancy *him*, the girls conjectured.

Nina glanced at her gold watch. This was a recent acquisition which coincided with a more relaxed Nina.

'Time's up, Rosanna. You've done very well today, hardly a single hiccup. Are you looking forward to the Christmas outing?'

Rosanna had heard about this annual treat from Morry, of course.

'Oh, yes. Are we really going to Bertram Mills' Circus at Olympia?' she asked hopefully.

'I believe so, although I would have preferred a show; but there, we have to cater for the majority.' Nina looked as if she could already smell the performing animals. She added: 'Mr Donatti is most generous; we may each bring a guest.'

Later, on the bus home, Rosanna discussed this prospect in some excitement, with Bekka.

'Shall I ask Ray? Remember, I'm getting off the bus at Streatham Hill, we're going to the cinema this evening and I'm meeting him there.'

'Shall you ask Ray! Who else? Though it's a bit of a statement, if you do.'

'What d'you mean?'

'You'll be announcing to the world, well to Donatti's, that he's your intended.'

'Intended what?'

'Don't be daft, Rosy. Your partner, not only for the circus, but for life!'

'You must be joking.'

'I'm not.'

'What about you and Danny?' she retaliated.

'I'm not so keen as I was. He's got a roving eye, as you jolly well know. I might play safe and take my mum!'

'Well, I can't take mine, can I? So I'll mention it casually to Ray tonight.'

They had a milkshake and a bun, all they could afford in the middle of the week, before they dodged the rush-hour trams and joined the lengthy queue at the pictures. *The African Queen* was in colour, starring Humphrey Bogart and Katharine Hepburn. The reviews had been glowing. Ray was particularly keen to see it, being a fan of C.S. Forester, the author, and his *Hornblower* series.

'Don't overdo the snogging,' Bekka said, before they said cheerio on the bus. 'I want to hear all about the film. Maybe I can persuade Danny to take me, although he says Bogart and Hepburn are not his cup of tea.'

The snogging was unlikely, Rosanna smiled to herself now, as the usherette flashed her torch and they made their way down the aisle. They couldn't rustle up enough cash for the back row, where all that sort of thing went on in earnest.

The majestic organ rose into view and seated in the spotlight was popular Jess Yates, acknowledging the applause of the audience, and playing like a dream. Ray was not engrossed in the film as she was. Not his sort of boat, the old *African Queen*, being a rust-bucket; no dashing hero, no beautiful heroine; it had nothing to with the Napoleonic Wars: the action was set in World War One in Africa and the river journey was full of hazards, and sexual tension between two unlikely lovers thrown together by circumstance.

Rosanna was caught up in every aspect of the story, the unexpected tenderness between Rose and Charlie. She shuddered as brave Rose, who had previously led a sheltered life as a missionary's sister, pulled leeches from Charlie's quivering bare body after he'd dived in the water among the reeds; she marvelled at Charlie's ingenuity as he somehow kept them afloat and moving towards their impossible target, a German patrol boat. And she thought how Derry would have been as involved with the story if he'd been sitting beside her.

At one point, she was momentarily distracted when Ray daringly let his fingers stray under cover of her coat, draped over her shoulders. Rosanna silently and firmly pushed his hand away from her breast, and moved to the far side of her seat. He didn't say anything, but she guessed that he was hurt by the rebuff. Couldn't he understand that she was not ready for that, even after six months of going out together? She made up her mind then and there that she wouldn't mention the Christmas outing. He might read too much into it.

On the afternoon of the staff treat, they packed up working at one o'clock. It was the day before Christmas Eve, when they were also working a half day before the two-day holiday. A late lunch was provided for everyone in the boardroom, where the great table was protected by a thick linen tablecloth. There was grapefruit with a glacé cherry; slices of cold turkey, ham, tongue with salad; an ice-cream *bombe* which when sliced burst and overflowed with peaches, smothered with whipped cream. The real stuff, not evaporated. They were served squash, or light wine, and senior members were permitted a tot of something stronger with their coffee.

There was no pulling rank regarding the seating. Mr Donatti sat between Monica and Morry, Nina, looking grim, between Mr Greene and Tel, with Rosanna on Tel's other side, next to Dot the cleaner. Bekka flashed a silent signal, *Oh no!* at Rosanna when she discovered that she was beside Mr Tiplady, but at least she had a nervous looking Ted the liftman on her left, sandwiched between her and Miss Donatti. Rosanna didn't know that Val and Joan, the galley-slaves, as Bekka cheekily referred to them, had switched a place-name or two, so that they could sit together near the drinks trolley. From the bursts of laughter at their end of the table, it was obvious that they'd managed to have an extra glass or two.

Tel gave Rosanna a nudge.

'Who you bringing with you tonight, then?'

'Er, no one.'

'Thought you had a boyfriend? Seen you once, meeting a chap, like.'

'Trailing us, were you?' she asked ruefully. It was hard to be cross with Tel.

'Well, had to guard your honour, didn't I?' he returned smartly.

She was flushed, and it wasn't just the wine.

'I can look after myself,' she rebuked him, but she couldn't help thinking of the furtive fumbling in the cinema. She and Ray hadn't met up since; when they'd said goodnight, he'd said stiffly:

'See you some time.' It was her turn to feel rejected.

'I ain't got a partner, neither,' Tel told her, looking rather disconsolate.

Rosanna felt a rush of sympathy. Poor boy, his face was covered in acne, disguised with dobs of calamine cream, his nails were bitten down to the quick. She couldn't help herself.

'You can be my . . . escort . . . if you like,' she offered.

Before he could answer, Dot, who was listening in, said:

'Ooh, that's nice! I got my better half coming, pity we couldn't bring the kids, they love the circus.'

'You mean it?' Tel asked Rosanna, thinking it must be a joke.

' 'Course I do. Well, what d'you say?'

'Cor! Not half!' Tel grinned.

Miss Donatti rose, calling for attention. As everyone was chattering away, it was a few minutes before they noticed.

'I have a toast to make, please rise . . .'

Tel managed to spill his drink on the table, which Rosanna quickly dabbed at with her napkin. There was scraping of chairs and a little coughing, then glasses were picked up in readiness for the next comment from Miss Donatti.

'I have a most important announcement to make – I am happy to tell you that Mr Donatti, my father, and Miss Long, Monica, have just become engaged. Congratulations to the happy pair from all of us!' Her voice rang out in the sudden silence. It was obvious that she meant it.

It was Tel who began the clapping, soon followed by all present; then Mr Greene encouraged the united shout of 'Congratulations!' followed by: 'Speech!'

A broadly smiling Mr Donatti gestured at his very new fiancée. Monica rose to the occasion.

'As most of you will know, I have been with Donatti's for twenty years. I was with the company during the war when we moved to a secret location and worked for the government.' She paused while her colleagues let rip with a resounding cheer. Mr Donatti, whose head barely came up to her shoulder, patted her arm encouragingly. She continued: 'Recently, we have become more than friends,' she paused again, perhaps aware that this could be misinterpreted. Another cheer, led by the inebriated galley-slaves. 'Well, anyway,' Monica concluded hastily, 'we are very happy to share our good news with you, and to celebrate on this special occasion.'

'Nice lady,' Dot said hoarsely. 'Like me, she must be dyin' for a fag. But her intended don't approve of smokin' as you know.'

'Follow *that*!' Morry observed, back in their office, where they were waiting for their evening companions to arrive in time to embark on the hired coach to the circus. Despite all she had eaten, her hand strayed to the chocolate drawer. 'Where's her ladyship? In the cloak-room I suppose.' Nina was missing.

'I'd better tidy up too, before the queues start, before the guests arrive and everyone has the same idea,' Rosanna said.

As she washed her hands, she wondered about Monica and whether she called Mr Donatti Raphael. She turned to yank the roller-towel and recognized the feet visible below the first cubicle. Stifled sobbing emanated from within.

There were only the two of them in here, thank goodness. She hesitated before tapping on the door.

'Nina? Are you all right? Rosanna, I'm on my own . . .'

The door opened slowly. Nina stood there, her face blotched with tears, in her elegant red-wool dress with tiny gold buttons and wide gold belt.

'No, as you can see, I'm not all right.'

'Can – can I help?'

'No.'

'Shall I call someone?'

'Who? You must know I haven't got any real friends here.'

What could Rosanna say to that? She tried: 'Your guest will be here soon.'

'He's not coming,' Nina stated baldly. 'He can't get away. His wife obviously has something planned for this evening. He asked Monica to pass on his regrets, just before we went off to lunch. Shocked, little Miss Bloomfield?'

'I know I'm young, but—'

'You can learn a lesson from this. Never fall for a married man. Now, off you go, and don't worry, I've learned my lesson at last, too. Our secret, eh?'

Rosanna nodded mutely, and picked up her washbag.

The excitement and colourful circus acts took Rosanna's mind off Nina's predicament. Tel was a lively companion, with his mischievous asides about others' guests. Some they had accurately predicted, like

Mr Tiplady's overbearing spouse, but Miss Donatti's attentive woman-friend was a surprise.

Ket was enjoying herself hugely too. At the end of the evening, when they boarded the last bus home to Streatham she said to Rosanna:

'What a kind girl you are, Rosy, letting Terry sit with us. You know, you fit so well into our family.'

'I'm glad,' Rosanna said sincerely. She couldn't worry about Nina tonight.

She wasn't to know that Nina wouldn't return to Donatti's after the Christmas break. Bekka, to her surprise and delight, was given her job. Eventually, via Monica, the news filtered out. Nina had gone away. She was having a baby.

Chapter Twenty-eight

1952

The news stunned the nation in the cold, grey February of this year when the King died in his sleep at Sandringham during the early hours of the sixth. Now there was a second young Queen Elizabeth; a new era was about to commence. A few months later, for Janet and her family, there would be a personal bereavement.

It had been the usual anxious winter, watching the water-levels like a hawk, for Jim at the pumping-station, but he soldiered on as always. He was pale, his face uncharacteristically bloated; short of breath and continually yawning. His loud snoring disturbed Jan at nights, but she didn't consider moving into another bedroom. What if he was taken really bad one night, and needed her?

Reg, his colleague and friend, who'd been Jim's apprentice as a lad, when he was known as Nipper, had a quiet word with Janet regarding his own misgivings.

'I don't see how he can go on like this, Mrs Bird,' he said. 'He has a look about him like my dad had, before he had his heart attack.'

Despite her urging, Jim would not see the doctor.

'He'll tell me to retire, and I've got a few years yet left to go before I get a decent pension.' However, he agreed to take time off at the start of the school holidays. Merle would be home then, after taking her finals and leaving university. Her new relationship was quietly accepted by her parents. Derry would be with them, too, that week. Jim and Jamie looked forward to spending time with Derry on the river; he'd visited them twice since spring when Jamie helped to get the boat 'ship-shape'.

At least Jamie was doing well, Janet thought; he'd come to terms with losing his mother, over a year ago now, and he and Jim were inseparable, something Jim had never quite achieved with his beloved Merle, maybe because she was a girl, but probably because she was always so self-willed.

Merle and Derry arrived in time for Sunday lunch. It was an oppressively hot day, with the threat of a storm later. Jim went out to greet them. Merle gave him one of her exuberant hugs.

'Dad, how are you?'

He embraced her back. 'Not too bad, how about you?'

'Happy as a lark,' she almost sang out. 'Thanks to Derry.'

'Time you tied the knot, isn't it?' her father said in her ear.

'Oh, Dad! I want to work abroad for a year or so, I've had a good offer. I can hardly do that, now can I, if I'm a married lady.'

'I'm old fashioned—'

'You certainly are, darling! But I wouldn't change you for anything.'

'*We* used to be like that,' Jim said reflectively to Janet, when the young people went for an after-lunch stroll with Jamie and the dog.

'Like what, dear?' They were close on the settee, sharing the footstool. One trouser leg was rucked, and she lightly caressed his bared shin with her stockinged toes. 'Like *that*?' she asked, tongue-in-cheek.

'Mmm. *They* can hardly keep their *hands* off each other!'

'Jim!' She blushed. Then, 'I can't bring myself to let them share a room officially, but we'll have to turn a blind eye, if . . .'

He turned to her suddenly. 'I do love you so much, Janet, it was the best thing I ever did, marrying you. Dear old Mum used to say so, too.'

'What brought that on?' she teased tenderly. Even as she reached out to give him a kiss, he doubled-up gasping, then he slumped and went limp. There was a look of surprise on his face, his eyes were open, staring, but she knew that he had gone. It had all happened so quickly, yet it seemed a terrifying eternity.

She unbuttoned his shirt, pummelled his chest, unaware that she was screaming: '*Jim, Jim, speak to me!*' It was no use. Eventually, she eased his head against a cushion, walked slowly away into the hall and picked up the telephone.

Comforting phrases were spoken by the doctor, then the undertakers. Reg, from the pumping-station window, saw the cars come and go, and waited anxiously for a call. After a decent interval he came over to the house to have his fears confirmed. All he could do was to promise to take care of everything over the way, and to inform the river authorities. As he left the house, the rain began, and he saw three figures running towards him. He hurried himself, away to the engine-room. It was not his place to tell them the dreadful news.

Derry took Jamie away out of sight and sound of all this. Merle stayed with her mother, to offer support, although she was too shocked to do much.

Janet, amazingly, was calm now.

'Merle, will you ring Baz for me? If you get Wendy, ask to speak to him first. You know how she panics. Derry must contact his dad. I don't suppose Wendy will be able to come, because of the little ones, perhaps that's just as well – but I hope that Rosy will come with Baz.'

'Mum, please don't talk about – you know – yet,' Merle pleaded.

'I can't grieve until that's over. I'm only glad that Grandma Birdie went first. But Jim, at fifty. Cry all you want, my darling, I just wish I could.'

'I'm sleeping with Mum tonight,' Merle told Derry, when they met in the kitchen.'

He nodded. 'That's best. Not that I think you'll get much sleep, either of you. What about Jamie? There's the spare bed in my room.'

'Ask him. He'll want to be nearer Mum, I guess. She's all he's got now. She clutched at Derry. 'She's all I've got, too – I can't believe it, Derry.'

'You've got me,' he assured her.

'Have I? You and I haven't committed ourselves to anything, have we.'

'You've broken down my resistance this far, isn't that enough? I want to see you achieve your goals first. You deserve a brilliant career after all that studying.'

'I've just realized that I can't leave Mum to cope on her own. I don't even know whether she'll be able to stay on here – it's hardly the time to ask. I certainly can't go flying off half-way round the world; I've got responsibilities now.'

Rosanna and Bekka spent Saturday afternoon at London Zoo, after eating a packed lunch on the steps of the National Gallery. Now that they were fancy free, as Ket put it, they were enjoying going out, two girls together. As Bekka said, most of the interesting places to visit in London were free, but they paid to see the animals. It was worth it, but Rosanna couldn't help wishing the big mammals did not have to be caged, and she thought that the hot weather and crowds added to the mingled odours. They departed from the giraffe-house smartly when they saw a man in a bowler hat sketching one of the lofty creatures and, despite the fug, nibbling at a cheese roll. They were always full of mirth, when out and about.

'Let's rest our feet, after all that walking,' Bekka observed, as she opened the front door. Neither of them noticed the car parked past the garage entrance. 'First some tea; eating those peanuts we bought for the monkeys has made me thirsty.' That made them giggle again, recalling the reproachful looks of the chimpanzees.

Ket came quickly towards them along the hall.

'Rosy, your cousin's here! He telephoned first, and I said come over, you'd be home late afternoon. I put him in the study, he has something to tell you, not good, I'm afraid.'

'I'm so sorry, Rosy,' Derry said, after Ket left. He held out his arms to her, 'Jim died yesterday, your parents asked me to break the news. They hope you can get the day off work to be with Baz at the funeral next Wednesday.' He gave her a brotherly hug. 'What scent are you wearing?' It was something to say.

'Zoo, probably!' She sniffed. Then: 'It's lily-of-the-valley, my favourite.'

'They must be devastated,' she said, after a while, when she'd managed to compose herself. They sat in the small, book-lined room, he in the chair swivelled round from the desk, herself on the library-steps, so that for once she looked down on him. 'Dear Jan, one loss after another – how *can* she bear it?'

'Merle's with her for as long as she needs her, she says.'

'When did you hear about this?'

'I'd just arrived there, with Merle, for a holiday – don't you two keep in touch these days? She's finished at Edinburgh, hopefully gained a good degree.'

'Maybe she was too busy to write,' Rosanna observed, not really believing that. More likely she was too preoccupied with *you*. she thought.

'And you, were you too busy with your new life here to contact me? I had no idea we were so near each other all these months,' he reproved her gently.

'Merle must have known that,' she said. 'Are you two together now?'

'I'm not sure what you mean exactly.'

'Aren't you?'

'Ah, I see you really are grown-up at last, Rosy Bloomfield.'

'I'm eighteen years old, and you didn't send me a birthday card, nor did Merle, and I've had a boyfriend my own age as you said I should, but he's given me up because . . .' Why on earth was she blurting all this out to him?

'Because you kept him at arm's length, is that it?'

'How did you guess?'

'I've known you always, Rosy, remember.'

Ket looked in. 'Would you care to have some supper with us, Derry?'

'Thank you, but I should drive back to the fens, now. Will you ring your parents tonight, Rosy, then let us know sometime Monday which train you will be catching on Tuesday after work, so I can meet you? It will be best for you to stay overnight. Baz will come as early as he can on Wednesday morning.'

When he'd gone, Ket gave her shoulders an unexpected squeeze.

'I must write to Janet. She and Wendy were good friends to us in the war. I didn't get to know Jim so well, him being away, but they were obviously a devoted pair. You're a close family, aren't you? I could see that, with you two.'

'He's only a cousin by marriage.' Rosanna didn't know why she said that.

'That explains it,' Ket said enigmatically.

Dear Uncle Jim, Rosanna thought. You were almost, but not quite faultless. But unlike my mother, with my father, you were honest with my wonderful Aunt Jan. And I'll always remember you swinging me up in your arms and carrying me home, the night Merle teased me when we saw the floating moon.

'Are you awake Merle?' Jan whispered. She herself had gone to bed exhausted at ten but had been unable to get to sleep.

'Yes. D'you want to talk? Shall I make a cup of tea?'

'Don't disturb the others. Poor Jamie cried himself to sleep, didn't he? Derry's been so kind to the lad.'

'He's a very caring person, Mum.'

'So are you, my dear.'

'I haven't always been like that, I've been selfish, and I'm sorry – but I always felt close to Dad, and—'

'Now you feel closer to me.'

'How well you know me!'

'Well enough to say that you mustn't sacrifice your youth, your future, to me. It means so much to have you with me at this time, but when things have settled down, you must go off as you planned and make me even prouder of you.'

'Mum, no. You'll have a struggle bringing Jamie up, especially as he's not—'

'He *is* my son, now. That's a promise I made Jim. I'll have a word with Baz tomorrow, tell him that when things are settled up here, when the insurance is through, we'll move back to Lynn, to be near them. They'll offer me support, I'm sure of that, and in turn, I can help Wendy out with her children when necessary, because Rosy needs some space, a life of her own, too.'

'I don't know what to say.'

'Shush. I've said it all, haven't I? Just don't let Derry down, will you?'

Derry and Jamie were whispering, too. 'You OK, Jamie?'

'Not 'zactly . . . Derry, was – was my dad in a lot of pain, like my mum?'

'I hope not. This was obviously coming on for some time and he wouldn't do anything about it, but he was enjoying having a son at last. He was like a dad to me as well, you know, before the war. Now you've got to be brave, and look out for Aunt Jan because that's what he would have wanted, eh?'

'I don't feel very brave,' Jamie admitted. 'I wish he didn't have to die. I wish my mum was still here, too, but I *will* look after Aunt Jan, promise . . .'

'Try to sleep now. We'll all need to be strong for her, come Wednesday.'

Under her starry ceiling, glimmering from the shaft of light from the streetlamp outside, Rosanna turned over in her comfortable bed and cuddled her pillow. It was still damp from her tears. Derry, she thought: I can't ignore it this time, tell myself that first love fades and can't be rekindled. He's not for me, but he'll always be there, in my life. Please God, don't let Merle hurt him. Maybe one day I'll find someone, even if I can't forget Derry.

Chapter Twenty-nine

1953

Janet was relieved when Christmas was over. It would have been even more of a strain if they'd been in their old home, crowded with memories, so full still of the presence of Jim. Early last December she and Jamie moved into a top-floor flat in London Road in Lynn. It was important to her to be within walking distance of the the river. That was a link with Jim, too When things were sorted out financially they would look for a place big enough to share with Wendy and Baz and family. It would be like the old times, she thought, all together again, well, not *all*, of course. She might even try applying for a job at the old Muck Works again.

Merle wasn't with them. She'd helped with the move, the settling in, then she spent the New Year with Derry. Then she went to the States to take up a teaching post in English and drama. It was a wonderful opportunity; it would give her time to evaluate her ambitions, to decide, with Derry, if they were to be together.

On the last day of January, a Saturday, while Jamie was at Wendy's, Jan sorted the last unpacked boxes, then resealed them with brown parcel-tape, which tasted foul when licked. Merle's books were in one container. She stacked them methodically. The slim volumes of Shakespeare; how grateful they'd been when Susie passed these on to Merle.

'I hope you're happy in America with your Burl, Susie,' Jan mused aloud. 'Did you know about Wendy?' She thought she did.

She held *The Tempest* in her hand, Merle's favourite, she was an inspirational Ariel in the school production; I was so proud of her that day.

Jamie came thumping up the stairs. Why did children, despite their lack of weight, always sound *heavy* she wondered idly.

'Time for a cup of tea?' she asked Baz. He'd walked him home.

'No thanks. We're in for some bad weather shortly, I think. I'd best get back, you know storms upset Wendy. See you tomorrow? Come for lunch.'

'Love to,' she replied. 'See you then. 'Bye!'

'What's that book?' Jamie asked curiously. 'Can I read it?'

'Well, it's a play, Shakespeare, surely you've heard of him?'

'Yes, 'course, but we haven't done him yet. My teacher says that'll be a treat for us when we go in the top class. What's a tempest?'

'Well, it's what Uncle Baz predicts – a storm – but a real big one, I reckon.'

'Dad said Merle was a bit tempest-uous.' He stumbled over the long word.

'Look it up in the dictionary, you'll see he was right!' I'm glad, she thought, he mentions Jim so naturally, I wish Jamie could have known his father much longer, but I believe his influence will live on, and that's a comfort to me, too.

At six-thirty in the evening, the South Dock Master, Captain Jack White, noted that the tide was over the dock-sill and that it was 'a funny old night'. High tide was not due for two hours, but the water-levels rose so rapidly that the river overflowed and flooded the south beach.

Several worrying elements came together: the high tide was unprecedented, there was a tidal bore and the cruel north-east wind and torrential rain were whipping the water into a frenzy. It was truly a tempest.

Warning sirens blared, sandbags were piled in vulnerable doorways as the floodwater raced along London road, residents fled upstairs. Janet answered the frantic knocking on her door of her downstairs neighbour, an elderly woman, and pulled her inside. Water was ankle-deep in the hall and lapping the bottom steps. The electricity abruptly failed. In the local cinema the lights cut out, too, and there was a star-tled silence, before the rush home began. Parked cars were soon waterlogged, an ambulance was stranded. The floodwaters rose to several feet high.

Already there had been several fatalities, and the death toll would eventually reach fifteen. A new tidemark would be recorded on the stout pillars of St Margaret's. All along the Norfolk coast the floods and terror was repeated.

The Red Cross rose immediately to the emergency. A centre in a dry area was opened up for casualties. Among the rescuers was one who'd become a legend. He was an American from the local base, six feet seven inches tall, named Reis Leeming. He waded through the flood for hours, carrying those who were stranded, calming them with his words, reassuring them with his strength.

Around eleven at night he staggered as he brought in his final burden, then collapsed from hypothermia and sheer exhaustion. The Red Cross ladies tried to revive him as he lay unconscious, cut off his soaking clothes and wrapped him in blankets. He was in grave danger of losing his life, after heroically saving so many. Half a century later he returned to be fêted by the grateful residents of Lynn.

To Janet, offering reassurances to Jamie and to Mrs Cramp, it was a time for silent prayer. She kept the door firmly closed, lit the candles, and they huddled together, waiting for morning and what that might bring.

At dawn, they shifted stiffly. There was that evil smell Jan recalled all too well from the flooding on the fens. The stench of muddy water, of ruined furnishings; the chill of despair and destruction.

She peered out of the bedroom window. The water was still there. There were flashing lamps, and to her astonishment, men in small craft, some rowing, others with sputtering outboard motors. Voices booming from loud hailers:

'Are you all right? Do you need help? Open your windows and shout.'

'*Here!*' she cried, leaning perilously out of her own window.

'You can't go back there,' Baz stated, as he stirred the living-room fire into a blaze, and urged them to sit over it. Sunday lunch was as yet uncooked, it could wait until the evening; soup was all the two of them could manage. Their neighbour had gone to a relative. They'd been among the last to be evacuated, for others were in dire straits. 'It never gets flooded in this area,' he added.

'Our furniture,' Jan worried. 'We are so lucky nothing was damaged, but poor old Mrs Cramp, her stuff must be ruined. She was worrying about the insurance, thinking it'll probably be called an act of God.'

'As soon as it's possible, I'll get your possessions brought here. We'll store them in the garage. You see, it's fortunate I haven't got a motor nowadays, eh?'

'Thank you, Baz, you and Wendy are so good.'

'Our way of saying thank you for all you and Jim did for us over the years.'

'We wanted you to come here to start with,' Wendy put in.

'But it'll be a bit of a squeeze.'

'Nonsense. You can have Rosy's room, Russ will enjoy sharing with Jamie, and the dog can come here, unlike where you were, that will please the boys.' Tipper was being looked after by Reg back at the pumping-station.

'I know you were thinking of moving Marcy from your room into Rosy's . . '

'We'd miss the cheeky little blighter amusing us first thing, eh, Baz?'

'She looks like Rosy, but she's a performer, like your Merle,' Baz said proudly. 'Anyway, we'll look for our new home in earnest now, eh?' Marcy gave Jan a cuddle, which was exactly what she needed right then.

'Glad you could make it, Rosy,' Derry said, on Sunday morning as she got into the car beside him. 'Ket and Co didn't mind you going out for the day, did they?'

'They're at church, I've left them a note. They won't object as it's you.'

'Cousins are acceptable, then?'

'Of course. Anyway, I don't think of you as my cousin any more.'

'Oh, why's that?'

They were turning into the main road now; it was not a very nice day, cold and bleak, but they were going to London, for lunch in Derry's flat, and maybe a stroll in Green Park scuffling the leaves, if it wasn't raining. She'd jumped at the chance when he rang her earlier. They hadn't met since the sad occasion of Jim's funeral; he and Merle had sent her a joint Christmas card and present and Merle had actually phoned her to say goodbye before embarking on her travels.

Now, she said: 'Cousins have to be nice to each other, but if we're *friends* it's because, well, we've chosen to be so, don't you agree?'

'You're a funny little girl.' He laughed. 'Particularly wearing that red stocking-cap: makes you look like Father Christmas!'

'A Christmas present, knitted by Jan.'

'You liked our present, did you?'

'I'm wearing it, aren't I? Red lips like Joan Crawford, Dad said.'

'That's why I couldn't kiss you, because it looks very transferrable.'

'It is,' she said complacently.

'I hope they're all right in Lynn,' he said.

'Why d'you say that?'

'I heard the news on radio first thing. Terrific storm and flooding in Norfolk.'

'They'd have rung me, wouldn't they, if there was any trouble?'

'I imagine so. No news is good news, as they say.'

'I'll phone them tonight as usual. What's for lunch?' she enquired.

'Wait and see.' They were turning off into what had once been a slum area, but now consisted of purpose-built flats, part of the resettlement after the war.

There was already an appetizing aroma in the functional little kitchen.

'Casserole,' he said. 'A week's meat-ration. You'd better eat up and enjoy it.'

'Smells wonderful,' she murmured.

'You can have a kiss for saying that, even if it proves indelible.'

She took a deep breath, closed her eyes and waited. His breath was sweet, whereas Ray's was sometimes sour. It began as a cousinly kiss, but became rather more. She saw the surprise in his eyes, and knew he was shaken, too. She rubbed at a smudge at the corner of his mouth. He caught her hand, held it there.

She had to say something. 'That was nice . . .'

'It was *disturbing*. Maybe I shouldn't have brought you here, after all.'

'I'm not Merle, I won't . . .' she faltered, then wished she hadn't.

'Try to seduce me? No, but can I trust myself? ' He smiled. 'Only joking!'

That wasn't what she wanted to hear, but: 'I know you're spoken for.'

'But things have changed, whatever you say. Merle was frank with me before she left; she said we should both feel free to date other people. So, you see, I can flirt with you, Rosy, but the last thing I want to do, is to *hurt* you . . .'

The phone rang just as they were sitting down at the table.

'It was Baz,' Derry reported. 'He tracked you down here. He said you weren't to worry about them, as they weren't affected personally by the flooding. Jan and Jamie weren't so lucky, but they're fine, too, and staying with them for the foreseeable future. They'll ring you tonight at Ket's. He said, "enjoy yourselves today!" ' He looked at Rosanna reflectively. 'So, shall we do as we're told?'

She nodded. Who knew where it might lead?

'You'll never guess,' Bekka told her, when Derry had departed, with a toot-toot on his horn, which Rosanna interpreted as 'see you again soon!'

'Tell me,' she said absently, her lips tingling from his kiss in the car.

'Danny came over here this afternoon, without ringing first, and he got me on my own and confessed he'd really missed me, he was sorry for messing me about, and could I go to his place for lunch next Friday, and he'd make sure he introduced me properly to his parents and maybe, just maybe—'

'I'm happy for you, Bekka, if that's what you really want.'

'It is! Giving him the push did the trick, eh? Why not make up with Ray?'

'I don't think so. Can you believe it, he was lurking nearby when Derry and I were saying goodnight. He's getting just like Tel. You said so, when we turned round in the pictures last week, and he was sitting two rows behind us.'

'Poor chap. The tennis club heart-throb thrown over. Can't you be kind?'

'I did like him – oh, I still do, and he made me feel adult at last. But—'

'Aha! It's that old cousin of yours, I bet—'

'He's twenty-seven. That's not so old now I'm getting on for nineteen, is it?'

'I'll say no more about Ray then! Isn't it exciting – a man for each of us!'

'I thought you liked us being just girls together.'

'Yes, but nothing beats falling in love, does it? Shush! Here comes Ket, to see what we're whispering about in the hall.'

She's right, Rosanna thought. It's wonderful.

Chapter Thirty

Bekka had a heavy cold; Ket insisted she must stay in bed. It had snowed a lot at the beginning of the week, but the main roads were clear. However, Ket repeated her warning to Rosanna:

'Watch out for the slush on the pavements, as often there's ice underneath.' She added to Bekka: 'I shall have to go into work later, but I'll leave you sustenance, and don't forget to take the aspirin every four hours.'

'I'll buy you a cream bun from the trolley,' Rosanna offered her friend.

'That would finish me off! Leave me to my misery, you two. Oh, and remind Dad to ring Danny and tell him I'm on my sick-bed.' She coughed and groaned.

'He's got a busy schedule today,' Ket reminded her. Often, Bekka's father worked at home on his translating, but today he was going to Buckinghamshire by train.

It was the first time for twenty months that Rosanna had caught the bus on her own. There was more coughing and sniffling to endure from her fellow passengers, and a slow journey as the bus-driver took extra care.

Journey's end at last; Rosanna hurried along. She crossed the road to the honking of vehicles and stepped on to the pavement, aware that Mr Tiplady was about to turn at Windy Corner. Thank goodness, she wasn't the only one who was late, she thought, not that she wanted to catch *him* up. The next thing she knew she was skidding inexorably across an icy patch in what seemed like slow motion, then her head smacked into something and she slumped to the ground.

Disembodied voices floated over her; she seemed to be in a fog, unable to comprehend what had happened. Then she was vaguely aware of being lifted, carried into a building, and laid down on a long bench against a wall, panelled in dark wood. Blurred faces gazed at her from behind a grille, there were exclamations, some not in English.

She said the classic words of one briefly concussed:

'Where am I?'

She was in a foreign bank, a building she'd never really noticed before when she and Bekka were chattering and on the last lap to the office. She'd knocked herself out on the front wall. Those who rushed to her aid, slipping and sliding themselves, hammered on the door and the security man opened up, before hours.

Then she saw Mr Tiplady hovering anxiously nearby.

'This young lady works in the same offices as me. I can take her there . . '

'Not fit enough to walk, sir,' said the security man. 'Better call an ambulance, miss,' he called over to one of the faces behind the mesh.

'I'll wait with you, Rosanna, until it comes,' Mr Tiplady assured her. Belatedly, he removed his bowler hat, and sat on the end of the bench. 'Then I'll go on to Donatti's and explain. Miss Long will telephone your home . . .'

'No point,' Rosanna said faintly. 'They'll be out all day – except . . .' Her brow furrowed. Her brain still seemed fuzzy.

'Where's Rebekah?' Mr Tiplady suddenly realized she wasn't with her friend.

'She – she's at home, but she's ill – please don't . . . ring her . . .' Rosanna's eyes closed. I'll have a little nap, then I'll feel better, she decided.

She was lying in a hospital bed, her right arm supported by a sling, wearing an unfamiliar short white gown tied at the back, feeling groggy because of the injections which diminished the pain and shock for the time being. There was someone sitting near the bed. It was Derry,in his dark Crombie overcoat, despite the warm air circulating the ward. What was he – what was she – doing here?

Seeing that she was aware of his presence, he rose, looking down at her with concern. He took her free hand in his.

'Rosy darling, how d'you feel?'

The unexpected endearment registered, but:

'Why am I here?'

'You had an argument with a stone wall.'

'Why are *you* here?'

'Your friend Morry called me. She remembered you saying where I worked. I'm your nearest relative, so to speak. The hospital say you can go home, if someone keeps an eye on you for the next couple of days. You've had an X-ray. No skull fracture, thank goodness, but slight concussion. You're going to have a great black eye, Rosy, and you've badly sprained your wrist, but you'll live.'

'Thanks,' she said, managing a wry grin. 'But I can't go home because Ket's at work, and they're short-staffed due to all this flu about, and her husband's on a business trip and – and Bekka's in bed, feeling awful, too.'

'You'll have to come to mine, then. I'll look after you. I told you what a dull job I have, they won't miss me. Don't worry, I can lend you some pyjamas! A bed's a bed, isn't it, and I can cook, as you know. Not to worry if we do get snowed in, eh? I'll explain all to Ket when she gets home this evening.'

'Derry – don't ring Mum and alarm her, and tell Ket she mustn't either. They've had enough troubles in Lynn recently.'

'I won't, but I can't speak for Ket. Look, I'm going home to get things ready, then I'll be back with the car when you get the OK to leave. Have another nap now, best thing for you, they say.' He blew a kiss to her. 'See you soon, Rosy.'

She was propped up in his bed, with his pyjama jacket round her shoulders leaving her injured arm free; the trousers were slipping round her hips, but fortunately she was decently swaddled. He combed her hair gently, then tied it back off her face with a shoelace. He was good at improvisation, she thought gratefully.

'Had a letter from Merle today,' he said in a matter-of-fact way. 'She's loving it in the States, although they've got snow in Oregon, too'

'You must miss her terribly.'

'I suppose we've been apart more than together since the three of us were on the river; remember she was in Edinburgh for three years, and I've been in London for the past two. We had just those two weeks before she left me.'

'Not for ever, though, Derry.'

'Who knows? Merle's the one who decides what will be.'

By the weekend, Rosanna was well enough to be taken to Lynn for a further week's recuperation. Derry went to Streatham to reassure her friends and collected a case that Ket had packed for her.

'Don't get too near any of us,' Ket told him huskily. 'We've all succumbed to whatever Bekka has. Thank you for looking after her, Derry.'

'She's an uncomplaining patient.'

'Unlike my daughter, then,' Ket said with feeling.

Rosanna was a worrier though. As they drove along in more clement conditions, she wondered:

'How will they fit us in? Jan's got my room.'

'I'm sure she'll be glad to share it with you. And as for me, the settee will do. I've had enough practice in that respect this week, haven't I?'

'Sorry.'

'What for? I've enjoyed your company, despite the reason, Rosy.' They'd played cards or records, listened to the radio, and talked. Certainly nothing more.

She nodded, but she thought; there's more to it than that. For me, anyway. Merle's far away, and I'm going to make the most of my chances.

The family made a great fuss of them both. Wendy worried whether Derry would get the sack; taking time off when he wasn't ill himself; Derry said blithely that he'd been thinking of making a change, especially as his firm didn't seem to miss him too much.

'Anyway, I'll be back at my desk on Monday.'

'We all have to settle for earning a living,' Baz said quietly. 'When you've got a family to care for, who appreciate you, it hardly matters if you don't achieve the ambitions you had when you were young.' He, too, through Merle, knew why Derry had discarded his boyhood dreams.

'Want to talk, or go straight off to sleep?' Jan asked Rosanna that night.

'We haven't had a good old chinwag for ages, so yes! I never asked how you were, seeing as you were all concerned about *me*.'

'I'm coping well most of the time, Rosy, I think, until something knocks me back, like that wretched flood. But even that's had a positive outcome. I feel so much happier here with Wendy and Baz, I'm needed. It's helping Jamie, too, being part of a family again, not just him and me. I miss Merle, of course.' She paused. 'I don't think she'll be back for a while, and then, I don't expect she'll stay.'

'What about Derry? I – I thought they were in love, Jan.'

'I'm sure they are, but, well, they can live apart, as you can see. Every time Jim had to leave me during the war, I carried on, because I had to. You're worrying, aren't you, Rosy, because now *you* love him in a grown-up way . . .'

'How did you know that?'

'I just do. Are you going to do anything about it?'

'I'm not sure.'

'Well, I am. I backed Merle in her quest for happiness, but she chose to go in another direction. Derry may try to resist it, but I believe he's on the verge of falling for you, given time. Just wait and see, that's my advice.'

1953 was proving to be an exciting year. Rationing was finally relaxed, there was the coronation in June, and television sets appeared in many homes, maybe bought on the never-never, for a great occasion, added to by the news that Edmund Hillary and Sherpa Tensing had conquered Mount Everest.

One day in July Monica relayed a message to Rosanna in the quiet period after lunch.

'Derry's meeting you from work tonight, OK? Like to see our wedding photographs?' She and Mr Donatti had spent their honeymoon in Rome, where else? She perched on Bekka's desk, something she wouldn't have done in Nina's day. There was no news of Nina, and the others in her office wondered what had become of her. She hadn't kept in touch, which was sad.

'Hang on, 'til we've looked through these,' Monica said cheerfully, turning down the offer of fruit-and-nut from Morry; 'I won't be too popular with Raphael if I get chocolate on 'em.' He hadn't put a stop to the chewing-gum, though.

They weren't the sort of wedding photographs that Rosanna had envisaged. No bridal gown: Monica wore a pretty dress with a ruffled neckline and a big smile, while Mr Donatti was sober in a dark suit. Staff had clubbed together to buy a pair of sheets and pillow cases. *Double-bed size*, Monica had suggested demurely. It was a quiet wedding, and the girls also gave the bride three pairs of nylons, and a saucy suspender belt, which Monica accepted without a single blush.

Derry was waiting in the entrance as she stepped from the lift. Bekka promised to tell Ket she wouldn't be in for dinner.

'Taking you back to my place, all right?' Derry told Rosanna briefly.

'Leave the washing-up,' he said, after supper. 'I want to read you this, from Merle.' There were pauses where she'd obviously written things he did not wish, or perhaps found too painful, to share with Rosanna. But the gist was as follows:

Dear Derry,
There is no easy way for me say this, probably a letter is the coward's option. I haven't stopped loving you, and I don't believe I ever will. What we had ... thrilling ... but it's a destructive kind of love. ...

Please forgive me, but I have a chance to stay, have a wonderful life, I can continue with my career here, for I have accepted a proposal of marriage from my Head of English, a really good chap and quite a catch, I'm told ... Grant is offering to pay for Mum to come out for the wedding, which will be before my work permit runs out ...

Derry looked up, and Rosanna realized he was in shock. She took the letter from his shaking hand.

'You comforted me, now it's my turn,' she said softly. She held him close, his head against her breast, and they wept together.

Eventually he apologized.

'I'm sorry, Rosy, I shouldn't have upset you, too. I know in my heart that Merle and I, well, it wouldn't have worked. Maybe it's time for me to settle down, even with my medical history.'

'It *is* history!' she put in fiercely, startling him. 'You're being the cowardly one now! You could still sail away. *I'd* go with you ...'

'We don't have to do that, to be all right together, Rosy. I haven't faced up to the truth, have I?' He brushed away her tears gently with his lips.

'What d'you mean?' The tender gesture thrilled her.

'That I love *you*! I'll let her go, with good grace, if you'll give me hope.'

'I can give you much, much more than that,' she cried. 'If you ask me to marry you, Derry Bird, I won't stop to consider it, I'll say *"yes, oh yes!"* '

Much later, he whispered in her ear: 'Now, you'll *have* to marry me, won't you, and you'll still be Rosy B, only Rosy Bird not Bloomfield, and we'll sail down our river on our honeymoon, and live happily ever after.'

Chapter Thirty-one

1959

In September, Rosanna and Derry moved into their first real home, although they faced months of renovations. The two neglected cottages on the edge of the common would become one; the small estate had been sold off in lots in the spring. Jan heard about this at the Muck Works and alerted them to the auction.

They'd saved hard over the past six years while staying on in Derry's small flat and made sacrifices with this in mind. Holidays were the twice-yearly forays along the river to Lynn. Parting with the old *Agnes Bell* was sad but enabled them to acquire the five-acre field at the rear of the cottages.

The pump was redundant; there was now mains water and electricity, but the range in one kitchen was retained and was the main means of cooking and heating. This was the cottage they'd occupy first – Rosanna's old home – while working on the other, so for her it really was 'coming home'.

After they'd unloaded their modest possessions, with the help of fifteen-year-old Jamie, and Jan, it was time to take stock, to realize what they'd taken on.

Janet recalled the storm of the first moving-in.

'Wendy almost decided to move out again! D'you recall how the army came to our rescue, Rosy?'

'Yes, I do. All those tents disappearing like mushrooms picked at dawn. And Grandma Birdie demonstrating how to "squeeze and pull" – oh, can we get a goat, Derry, and maybe a Shetland pony, like the one I learned to ride on—'

'You're too big now for that,' he said fondly, 'but, one as a pet – why not?'

'I could have bantams – Dad'll get us seeds and plants at a discount, and—'

'There's a lot to do inside before we tackle the wilderness; we'll have to leave that 'til next spring, I reckon. I must get some sort of job to eke out the budget.'

'We've got all the time in the world,' she said. 'We'll be here *for ever*.'

Rosanna and Jan made up the bed, while Derry and Jamie unpacked downstairs.

'Sit down and take a breather,' Jan advised. 'You don't want to overdo it.'

'You know, don't you!' Rosanna challenged her aunt.

'I know *you*, Rosy Bird. You're very determined, in your quiet way. I can see you on your wedding morning, and me helping you dress, because Wendy was running round after Russ, intent on mussing up his new suit. You asked me, "D'you think Derry has any regrets?" and I said, "He knows he's marrying the right one, Rosy. It would never have worked out between him and my Merle."

'You looked beautiful, dearie, only nineteen, like Wendy was when she married Baz. And Derry, well the look on his face when he saw you in that lovely long dress with all those teeny pearl buttons, told me he loved you . . .'

'Those wretched buttons, Jan! You did them up, but I couldn't undo them; Derry had to, when the party was over in the hotel, all the guests had departed, and we were ready for bed. He was all fumble-fingers and heavy breathing!'

'Wendy and I worried about you. She hadn't a chance to tell you anything—'

'She didn't need to, I have to admit. Our first time – was when Derry had that letter from Merle . . .' Should she have said that?

'He looked to you for comfort, was that it?'

'I've never regretted it, because he realized—'

'You were the one. Of course he did. And now, you won't fit into those tight jeans in another month or two, will you?' Jan gave Rosanna's tummy a gentle pat. 'Though I don't imagine you'll ever have curves like Marilyn Monroe.'

'I haven't told him yet. I might tonight, if it seems right. You know of course why he said we shouldn't have children. But this seems the time and place.'

'Good luck, dearie. I'll keep my fingers crossed. I think it's wonderful news! I'll keep quiet where Wendy's concerned – you'll want to enlighten her yourself.'

'It's so kind of you, Jan, to come and help us like this when you're going to America next week. I suppose . . . Merle. . . ?' Rosanna paused.

'No. My turn to tell a secret. A baby's not on the cards. Grant's a nice chap, very kind, paying my passage over there every year. I'm able to go, because I can leave Jamie with your mum. Not that he isn't becoming an independent young man, eh? So like Derry! But Merle can't be fulfilled, despite her lovely home, her career. You see, Grant, although he's fond of her, as she is of him, wouldn't have married if pressure hadn't been put on him when he became Head of School. His preference for male company, however discreet . . . well, there were rumours.'

'Did Merle know?'

'She says so. They obviously came to an amicable agreement. She mentions younger men friends who escort her to functions when Grant is "too busy".'

'Does she ever think of coming home?'

'I don't think so. But I may learn more when I see her. Now, more tidying up, eh, before your family descends eagerly on you tomorrow!'

'You look about fifteen,' Derry observed fondly. He was already in bed, watching her as she gave her hair a perfunctory brush and divided it in childish bunches.

'I'm all hot and sticky; no chance of a bath for weeks maybe.' She climbed in beside him. 'At least the mattress got turned.' She yawned.

'You're not going to sleep already? Don't you feel like . . .'

'A chat?'

'Don't tease. You know. A cuddle.' He nuzzled her cheek with his chin. He needed a shave, there hadn't been time this morning.

'That leads to other things . . .' His caressing hands were distracting.

'What's wrong with that? We've been too busy, with the move—'

'Derry, you may turn your back on me, when I say—'

'Come here, you silly girl,' he said firmly. 'Now I've got you in my arms, you can confess. I'm sure I'll forgive you, unless you've hidden that awful chamberpot we discovered, under the bed. Who knows who used that last?'

'All right. *We're going to have a baby next April.* Remember when we were on the boat last July, it was raining, so we found a B and B for the night?'

'One night of love, like the film, eh,' he said wryly. 'A sort of second honeymoon, as I recall very well.' The thought of this was obviously pleasurable.

'We didn't hear the landlady's call to breakfast – she looked at us coyly, said she'd guessed we were newly-weds – *so* embarrassing!'

'But great. We could do with a repeat tonight.' he teased.

'Derry, aren't you upset? Didn't you take in what I said? It'll mean I can't tackle all the heavy stuff here, I've only just realized that—'

'Stop clucking, Rosy B. I've just realized something, too. Moving here and us having a baby – most of all, me having *you* – what more can a man ask for?'

As always, life was about to deliver a mixed bag of highlights and sadness. Only a month later, Rosanna suffered a miscarriage, like her mother before her. The only positive thing she could salvage from the pain and shock of this was that she knew how much Derry had been looking forward to the baby, too. When they felt braver about it, she thought, they could plan another pregnancy, and when she was stronger there was so much to do here, which would take her mind off her loss. The doctor had been very reassuring, but his advice too, was to wait a while.

A friend of Jan's at work told her about a boatyard which built small craft in the traditional way; Derry applied for work and was successful in being initially offered three days' work a week. With his great interest in sailing and knowledge of boats, his practicality, this was an unexpected but uplifting turn of events.

Then it was April, 1960, and Rosanna was twenty-six years old. She was relieved when the date the baby would have been born had passed. Now they could really look forward to the future, she thought.

It was time for scything down the long grass in the field and planting up the vegetable garden with help from her father, Russ and Jamie, and discovering, with delight among the weeds, the clump of rhubarb, which they had planted long ago. She kept an eye on young Marcy, enjoying her company: her sister was the same age as she had been when she first lived here. Wendy and Jan seized the opportunity to go shopping, unencumbered, in the Saturday Market, and would arrive later, in Jan's little car. After supper they'd watch *Juke Box Jury*, with David Jacobs and pop music celebrities, like the the oddly-named *Beatles*. The four young men were fascinating, amusing, with talk of 'sarnies' and 'ciggies'. Like the expressions used by the Yanks during the war, this vernacular would be adopted by their fans and then spread countrywide.

Russ was getting on for twenty-two, but he was a still a loveable child to them all. He attended a daily sheltered workshop, with trained helpers, and was learning to assemble simple wooden toys. Jamie was a naval cadet and longing to join the Navy, like his father before him. Jan said she knew that Jim would have been very proud. She was the only one to correspond with Merle; letters between her and Derry and Rosanna had long ago dwindled and then ceased.

The merging of the two cottages was at last taking definite shape. The range had coughed up its final smoky and sooty avalanche; but now that Derry was earning they bought a new Rayburn. It was Rosanna's pride and joy, and she was able to expand her cooking skills. No rationing to put the damper on this, as there had been in her mother's day. From the Rayburn they ran three radiators and there was plenty of hot water for washing up, washing and baths. The next thing to buy was a washing-machine. Wendy extolled the virtues of her Rolls twin-tub.

It was good to be so near to extended family, to hope one day to have a family of their own. Meanwhile, they acquired a sturdy pony: all the previous owners asked was for a home where the pony would be loved and ridden, and there was Marcy, who took to the saddle, just as her big sister had done. Marcy often stayed over Saturday nights, and after helping with feeding the fowl and the pony and goat, Rosanna could be persuaded to sit in the chimney corner and to play her banjo and to sing to them. It was just like old times.

1963

It was a severe winter, but as Derry joked, it made them stick close together, especially in bed! Despite the freezing conditions, and the stock to care for, they came through it, and Derry was in robust health. They had been trying for a baby for two years now. The non-arrival was the only thing which marred their happiness.

'We'll have been married ten years in September; we should have a celebration,' he told Rosanna, as they watched Marcy riding in the field. 'We ought to get her a bigger pony, her legs are getting too long for Biddy.'

'Just what Susie said about Merle, when she was that age.' Rosanna realized, with a start, that they didn't often mention Merle nowadays. She added: 'A celebration, yes! Hopefully, we'll have an announcement to make by then.'

He was shading his eyes against the setting sun.

'We may have to accept that it won't happen, darling,' he said quietly.

'I can't do that!' she cried vehemently.

'Time to call it a day,' he called to Marcy, who was cantering towards them.

Those words rang in Rosanna's head. Were they really meant for *her*?

On the day of the party Rosanna wore a flowing, cinnamon-brown dress, contrasting with her sister's tartan mini, for Marcy was intent on wearing the latest fashion. She combed her hair loose, to please Derry.

'You look like a beautiful gypsy,' he murmured, for her ears only. He fastened a sparkling necklace of gemstones round her neck, and she kissed him fervently which surprised and delighted him, and told him she loved him and always would. Then he whispered wickedly:

'Your skirt is transparent if you stand with your back to the sun. *I* like it, though!'

There was a surprise visitor. At first Rosanna couldn't believe her eyes. Derry had driven over to Lynn to help with transporting the family and he opened the car door with a flourish and called out to Rosanna:

'Just look who's here!'

And Merle, with cropped black curls and showing off her shapely legs in a dress which skimmed her knees, ran with arms outstretched, crying in an unfamiliar American accent:

'It's me, little Rosy! I'm home at last, and I may not go back. Grant is suing for divorce, because I had the effrontery to steal his boyfriend!'

She can still make me blush, Rosanna thought, but somehow she rallied, to say:

'Nice to see you again, Merle.'

'You still look so young,' Merle gushed 'That *hippy* look really suits you!'

It was a good party, with a bonfire and fireworks, which made Russ squeal with delight. Derry rescued the potatoes from the embers, and Rosanna split them and served them with plenty of butter. There was homemade gingerbread, sticky and delicious, and a wonderful cake, with DERRY AND ROSY. TEN WONDERFUL YEARS! in icing on the top.

When it got too chilly, and the evening drew in, they went indoors into the living-room, which ran the length of the cottage, put discs on the radiogram and danced, when the rugs were rolled up, on the new parquet floor.

When the others reluctantly made ready to go, Merle said:

'I'd love to stay here overnight, if I may. We've so much to catch up on! I've had too much wine, I'm whoozy. You'll take me back tomorrow some time, won't you, Derry?'

'Whatever you say, madam!' he agreed, not looking at Rosanna.

When the others had gone, Rosanna took off her shoes and padded out into the kitchen in her bare feet.

'Tea – coffee – you two? I think the talking will have to wait 'til morning, Merle, I'm really dying to get to bed.'

'Oh, you won't desert me yet Derry, will you?' Merle asked.

He looked so awkward that Rosanna was suddenly furious.

'Well, I'm going up, suit yourselves,' she said coldly.

As she went upstairs, she heard Merle giggling.

'I'm afraid we've upset her. Pour this awful coffee away, Derry, and open that last bottle of wine. And put another record on – still got *In The Mood*?'

She still wants him, Rosanna told herself, crying angry tears. He's still strongly attracted to her, I could tell – I know him so well. He certainly won't get any celebration loving from me tonight. Why didn't he get up and leave her to it?

After nearly an hour, the music stopped abruptly. She waited tensely, but neither of them ascended the stairs. She couldn't stand it any longer. She pushed back the bedclothes, went downstairs, pushed the living-room door open.

She must be having a nightmare. Two people on a settee, in a passionate embrace, Derry and Merle in the prelude to something much more. She wanted to scream, but that would alert them, make them spring guiltily apart. That other occasion came vividly back to her, when Wendy and Burl had lain like that together.

Then she heard Merle sigh: 'It's been too long, my darling, far too long . . .' and like the other time, she turned and fled.

In the early morning, when she woke after an uneasy sleep to find he hadn't come to bed, she put on the brown dress, packed a bag and pencilled a brief note.

You both have what you want, now. I am going away to forget. Don't try to find me. I won't do anything silly.

Then she picked up her banjo on an impulse and walked away.

Hours later, at dusk, she was trudging along a lonely road, when an old bus stopped.

'You all right?' called a voice. She was lifted aboard and found herself with a band of travellers who didn't ask any questions after that first one; who would look after her in their own way, and take her far away from home.

Epilogue

'I'll walk by the river,' Sim said. 'There's a boat moored up there. I'd like to take a closer look.'

'The skipper's probably legged it to the Ferry pub,' Rosanna said. 'You might as well go there too, for a couple of pork pies and some crisps. Can you get me a carton of orange juice? Do your smoking in the fresh air, there's a good feller. When you light up in the van, it makes me cough.'

'You're a disapproving lady; haven't you ever enjoyed a few puffs?'

She shook her head. 'Never felt the need for funny fags, Sim. It's what it can lead to that worries me.'

'Well, you needn't worry about me.'

'But I do. You ought to go home, see your family.'

'What about you?'

'What about me?'

'Who did you leave behind?'

'My husband, if you really want to know. I've rung my family now and then, just to let them know I'm OK, but I haven't spoken to *him* for five years.'

'Didn't you love him any more?'

'He hurt me badly.'

'Beat you, you mean?' He looked agitated.

'Oh no, he was a gentle, sweet person.' Like you, Sim, she thought. But you're still so young, entitled to make mistakes. Derry was older than me; I believed that he was the strong one in our relationship, but I was wrong. I supported him. I should have known that he and Merle. . . .

Aloud she said: 'I ran away, like someone I once worked with, Nina, did, long ago.'

After a long pause, Sim said: 'I don't understand.'

'Nor do I, Sim. Now, off you go, and be back before dark.'

*

The light was actually fading fast when he returned. She still sat on the stone, but now she was cloaked in a woollen shawl; the moths had been nibbling, but it was soft and warm.

'Here's your pie,' he said. 'I'll let you eat it before you sing for your supper. No full moon tonight, I'm afraid.'

'Meet the boatman?' she asked, taking a bite.

'I did. Guess what, the boat's got the same name as you – *Rosy B.* Well, *Rosy* anyway, I don't know about the *B.*'

He'd never asked her full name, nor had she his. They were lovers: he'd been the only one in her life since Derry, but both were aware that the relationship could not last. He would become restless, it was only natural at his age. He, too, had his dreams. She was honest enough to tell him that she didn't share them. She didn't want to go to India. There was truth between them, she trusted him instinctively. Derry had never admitted that he still had strong feelings for Merle.

He swallowed his pie in three great bites.

'I told the feller that. He said he'd like to meet you. I said he could join us for a sing-song in a while. Was that all right?'

She stood up, peered across the dark water. 'I'm not sure.'

'A gentle kinda guy, like you said,' Sim's voice was soft, tinged with regret. 'I reckon you know each other, Rosy.'

'I reckon we do,' she said.

She was strumming the banjo when he arrived.

'Hello, Derry,' she said. He hadn't changed much. He was thinner, that was all. She recognized the uncertainty in him. 'Well?' she asked.

'It was the last thing I expected, to find you here. I feel quite stunned.' He cleared his throat, glanced at Sim.

'I'll be in the van,' Sim told them. He stepped up, slammed the door.

'Nothing happened that night, you know. We were too drunk. We just fell asleep.' Derry said after a while. 'We couldn't believe it in the morning, when we found you'd gone. We were both so ashamed. Merle couldn't stop crying.'

'You were still entwined in each other's arms when I left,' Rosanna stated baldly. 'Can you really be sure you didn't betray me? I've had plenty of time since to regret my own mistakes. I caught you on the rebound after Merle, inviting you to make love to me, then marrying you before you had a chance to regret it. She thought you'd rush over there, of course, demand that she break off her engagement, that after all the excitement of the chase, you'd be together. You couldn't respond, because of me. Yet I thought I made you happy, Derry.'

'You did, Rosy.'

'I kept on in my job. Oh, I enjoyed my years at Donatti's.'

'You did well. I was proud of you: Mr Donatti's secretary, no less.'

'Only because Bekka left to have babies – four in five years! I couldn't let you know how jealous I was of that. We'd agreed when we married that that wasn't the life for us, hadn't we?'

'But when we moved, when you told me you were having a baby—'

'See! "You", not "we", Derry! We didn't really have time to get used to the idea, did we? You were still number one in my life, weren't you. So, Merle was full of regrets, you say . . .'

'She returned to the States. She got her divorce and married another rich man. She pleaded with you to forgive her, in a long letter addressed to you, which she said I should read. She said you'd always been such a special person to her.'

'She loved you Derry, as I did. It's caused both of us pain, hasn't it.'

'I'm not going away without you, you know. I'm asking you to forgive me, too, Rosy. Because if I hadn't consumed all that wine—'

'Now you're being honest,' she said, turning towards him for the first time.

'Even if you don't want me back, you must be reunited with your family. Can you believe that Marcy is sixteen now, and walking out, as Jan puts it, with Jamie? It's like us, years and years ago.'

'The three of us,' she interjected.

'None of this is their fault, they miss you terribly, think of you every day and wonder where and how you are, as I do, too.'

Sim was revving the engine on the van. It spluttered a few times and then came noisily to life. Then he backed it away, swerved and drove off at speed. They were temporarily dazzled by the lights.

'Sim!' she shouted in a panic.

Derry, who'd scrambled to his feet in an attempt to flag Sim down, now directed his torch at a spot near where the van had been parked.

'What's this?'

'My bag, my things . . .'

'You travel light. Look, there's a paper pinned to it.' He shone the beam on it.

'Let me have it,' she said.

Dear Rosy,

I'm going home, as you told me to, and I hope you are, too. Good luck. I won't forget you. With love from Sim.

'I'll miss him.' She began to weep softly. 'I didn't get a chance to tell him.'

'That you loved him?' Derry asked tentatively.

'Do you resent that?'

'I've no right . . .' He hesitated. 'But he's hardly more than a boy, Rosy.'

'He's gone because of you! He cared for me, you know, he really did.'

'I'm glad. Now, come to the boat with me, you're shivering,' he told her, concerned, adding: 'We'll sail home tomorrow, I promise. I'm not going to ask any more of you than that. I'll carry the bag, and you, your precious banjo.'

'I didn't see a floating moon tonight,' she said almost inaudibly. But my wish will be fulfilled anyway, she thought, in sudden exultation. I'm carrying Sim's baby. He was too young for a responsibility like that. He would have felt trapped. I'll need my family now, especially dear Jan. They're good at keeping secrets, closing ranks. I still love Derry; I realized that the moment I saw him again. He doesn't have to know. The timing is right.

'No floating moon, Rosy B,' he said, 'but I came to you anyway.'